Fiction
by
Filipinos in America

Collected and Edited by

CECILIA MANGUERRA BRAINARD

Published by PALH
(Philippine American Literary House}
P.O. Box 5099
Santa Monica, CA 90409, USA
PALHBOOKS.com

ISBN: 978-1-953716-05-7 (Paperback edition)
ISBN: 978-1-953716-06-4 (Ebook edition)

INTRODUCTION

In the late 1980s I collected and edited the anthology *Fiction by Filipinos in America* when I could not find such a collection of stories in American libraries. This had been an eye-opener to me especially when I knew that Filipinos had been in Louisiana since 1765.

Filipinos in America had done their share of shrimp-drying in the bayous, cutting sugar cane in Hawaii, harvesting lettuce in California's farm fields, gutting salmon in Alaskan Canneries, fighting in World War II-Korea-Vietnam, working in mainstream America as doctors, nurses, engineers, accountants, you-name-it — those Filipinos were living in America, second-, third-, fourth-generation Filipinos pounded the sidewalks of Chicago, Honolulu, Los Angeles, San Francisco, New York; and — I had been utterly surprised to realize that these people were voiceless. So I went to work, finding the writers and their stories, writing to them to make arrangements to use their stories – this was pre-computer age.

I put together a collection that includes classics stories such as Carlos Bulosan's "The Romance of Magno Rubio", Bienvenido N. Santos' "The Scent of Apples" and many more.

Because it was published in the Philippines, it was never easily accessible in the United States, although many of the writers are noted Filipino American writers.

It is a pleasure to present the 2020 US Edition of *Fiction by Filipino in America* in hopes that another audience can enjoy and appreciate the stories. This anthology has a place in Philippine American literature.

In this reissue, I have left the biographies of the authors as they were in the original 1993 edition.

World Literature Today (Al Camus Palomar) praised the book as follows: "(Editor) Cecilia Manguerra Brainard's selection is a delight. Some of the stories are masterly, especially those written by such reliables as Carlos Bulosan, Linda Ty-Casper, N.V.M. Gonzalez, and Alberto S. Florentino. None is less than highly competent, and all are worth reading. Manguerra Brainard has done an excellent job of mixing critical judgement and personal taste."

Starweek of *Philippines Star* (Isaganic R. Cruz) said, "Definitely one of the most outstanding anthologies published, this collection of stories by Filipino writers who work or used to work in the United States is a must-read for all students of Philippine Literature."

~Cecilia Manguerra Brainard, October 2020

CONTENTS

LINDA TY-CASPER

AFTER graduating from the College of Law, University of the Philippines, Linda Ty-Casper took her LL.M degree at Harvard. However, erroneous and biased statements in books at Widener Library converted her into an advocate, through faithfully researched historical fiction, of the Filipino's right to self-definition/determination.

The Peninsulars (1963) *centers on 18th century Manila;* The Three Cornered Sun (1979), *written on a Radcliffe Institute grant, deals with the 1896 Revolution; and* Ten Thousand Seeds (1987), *the start of the Philippine-American War. Contemporary events, including martial law years, appear in* Dread Empire (1980), Hazards of Distance (1981), Fortress in the Plaza (1985), Awaiting Trespass (1985), Wings of Stone (1986), and A Small Party in the Garden (1988).

Her stories, collected in Transparent Sun (1963), The Secret Runner (1974), *and* Common Continent (1991), *originally appeared in such magazines as* Antioch Review, The Asia

1

Magazine, Windsor Review, Hawaii Review, *and* Triquarterly. *One was included in* The Best American Short Stories of 1976 Honor Roll. Philippine Studies, The Christian Science Monitor, City Lights, Asiaweek, Solidarity, *and* Pilipinas *have published her articles.*

She has held grants from the Djerassi Foundation, the Commonwealth of Massachusetts, and the Wheatland Foundation. Her sense of national service derives from her mother, Catalina Velasquez, former textbook author with the Bureau of Public Schools, and her father, Francisco Ty, operations manager for the Philippine National Railways. She and her husband, critic-professor Leonard Casper, have two daughters: Gretchen, professor of the Third World Politics at Texas A&M, and Kristina, anthropology major at Boston College.

A SWARM OF SUN

Aloran, Philippine Islands, 1903.

IT IS A DARK BOAT, coming in from the north just as the year before a hemp boat had come with two Americans, a captain and a lieutenant, to pick recruits for the constabulary. The town gathers quickly, not waiting for the three-man bandillo to announce the strangers, but not moving to the beach either, though the sun, just beginning its long descent, strikes the narrow metal boxes piled astern and flashes light like a ship signaling.

They walk slowly so Padre Cipriano and the town officials of Aloran can precede them to where the year before they had raised a hut to shelter the Virgin during the cholera, and to where, immediately, American soldiers, led by their sanitary inspector and followed by a large cartload of lime, had come to dig, thinking they had buried their dead there. Only the bamboo altar remains inside, and wax from the candles. Burnt wicks are still imbedded in several.

They begin entering the shade, eyes fixed on the boat struggling in the surf, above which the sunlight hangs suspended like a swarm of bees nesting. One or two turn away from the sea to look back at the town hidden among trees. The metal church spires is visible, distorted by sunlight so that it appears like a trunk split by lightning. Chased out of the sun, the children circle just beyond reach while their mothers are distracted by speculations about the boat. They fear another war has broken out.

The war with the Americans came out and went, taking even less time than the revolution against Spain which reached Aloran late because it is not in the way of interisland boats and because there was only one Spaniard there, the lieutenant of the civil guards.

The town fails to count the Spanish widow of the inspector of the fields. A blind woman who has no recent friends in Manila to raise a subscription for her passage to Spain, she waits at her window all day, somehow returning their greetings even when it is only the raising of the hat or a smile. Nor do they ever count Padre Cipriano who is a Recollect friar from Vizcaya. So used to him have they become that when the revolutionary government ordered him driven away with the other friars, they kept watch at the beach to intercept the revolucionarios. They now beg him to stay when he packs secretly to go to Manila, recalling to one another how he sang at the Cathedral the year he came from the Peninsula, newly ordained, fifty, even more years back. He is part of the memory of the youngest and oldest of them, and not expendable.

Of that war, they remember most clearly the town presidente's son running his men through the stand of budding madre de cacao to the American barracks where they were spotted by the boy rising to blow reveille. They buried their own dead that same day, and the Americans theirs: in opposite parts of the convent garden. For the past three Todos los

Santos they have carefully pulled the grass off the American graves and placed candles on the crosses, recalling each one with affection, for somehow the only ones killed in that single encounter were those who had made some effort to know them.

The tide plays with the boat, lifting one end then the other, spinning it towards the shore, then shooting it backward, scraping it against the coral beds until it spills, a tumble of men and oars and long metal boxes the color of gold washings. For a while nothing is seen except four rifles raised just out of the waves, at the sight of which they all rush to the beach just behind Padre Cipriano; Don Alfonso, the presidente; behind Emilio Faustino, the secretary; his brother Pio, the justice of the peace; behind the policeman who wear no guns at their belts.

They watch gravely as the time the American detachment sailed away in a white transport with electric lights blazing. Wielding her parasol like a shield, the American captain's wife had ridden her pony cart to the very edge of the sea, refusing until the end to meet their eyes. Nothing was left by the Americans except a large bonfire of harness, chairs and towels; of cots and tents; condemned and burned to prevent the quartermaster from selling the new articles and presenting the old ones to be recondemned.

Don Alfonso lifts his cane and the policemen rush into the surf to help bring in the boat and the long boxes. They struggle with the sea and the weight of the boxes. It is with great effort that these are deposited side by side on the sand, six of them, away from which the town moves as they are recognized as caskets, lying on the sand like cold fire burning.

The four carrying rifles are Americans. They stand where they emerged from the sea, their drenched uniforms like soft wet shadows. Don Alfonso hurries to welcome them. He has learned English from listening during the American teacher's class, reciting just on the other side of the wall of woven bamboo at the municipio. After he had his own desk moved to where he could casually glance through the gap in the partition, not a word was flashed or written on the board that escaped his eyes.

"Good morning, welcome ..." he says the sounds catching on his breath for lack of practice. He returns slowly from the Americans and the burden of what he has found out traps the words in his mouth. His ceremonial cane is shaking as he says, "They come to get the Americans in the garden of the convent." His words are passed on until they reach those farthest back and return in the form of a single question, "Why?"

"It is not right." Padre Cipriano's voice rises as though responding to a choir. His face is dark above the white flesh of his neck. The hat of woven bamboo is like a fish trap on his head. "No. I will not let them do just anything they please in my garden." But his last words are said softly and without conviction. It is to himself only that he recalls that he had not been asked to bless the bodies; but unable to sleep, he had walked over in the darkness to sprinkle the graves with holy water. The following morning, bothered by the secrecy of his ritual, he had repeated his blessing with the largest candles he could find and with all his sacristans in the attendance, but from the convent window which overlooked the inner garden hedged in tightly by red hibiscus with soft heavy flowers; even then furtively, in case the American sentries in their daily rounds of Aloran came upon his ceremony and interfered.

With a special flourish, his letterings shaded as impressively as gold-lettered invitations, the secretary writes down in his record book what is being said, having already noted the arrival of four American soldiers, nine rowers and six caskets, which are now being lifted by the men of Aloran and carried forward as in a procession.

The road rises along the gay tumult of water rolling down from the mountains. The rushing sound accompanies the men uphill.

The Americans walk with such long strides that they soon overtake the caskets and cross Dawson's creek before the secretary can finish his first page. He is always, at least, halfway behind and has to rely upon the policeman holding his ink bottle for the rest of what is happening. Anyway, it is only after he has read through his account that he understands what he has recorded.

Padre Cipriano catches up with the presidente. "Do you suppose they will merely rebury the soldiers in the garden?" To be able to keep up, he pulls his cassock above his legs, exactly as women lift their skirts above the flood. He is not used to hurrying and his lungs refuse to give up their habitual ease, but he tries to give the semblance of rushing to show he will not be discounted. He is used to being obeyed, of wielding his own and God's authority, yet already he sees his garden upset, the red cutsaritas defining each plot crushed like weeds.

The presidente's wife, who had both corners of the garden planted from her own, is even raising white pitimini to define a cross in the center of each plot. The garden is his country now. No longer does he have any clear and continuing intention of returning to Guipuzcoa with its flat-roofed houses of stone. Only dimly does he remember having led oxen, the yoke softened with sheepskin, through the long parched fields.

"Americans have strange customs," the justice of the peace consoles the town by making them believe that what is happening to Aloran is part of the unyielding pattern of life. Their own experience is that bodies are removed only to be transferred to the church, interred either in the walls or beneath the altar, or thrown out of consecrated ground by the authorities, removed from the sanctidad. "Even the weather changed when they came." Now, everyone knows, it rains hard during the dry season and during the wet, the sun fiercely burns their crops, drawing locusts from the ground to feast on what remains, leaving them only a harvest of dropped wings.

Feeling personally dispossessed, Don Alfonso hurries to catch up with the Americans. Some kind of official communications should have preceded their coming to Aloran. "Not to take us by surprise like this," he wants to explain to the soldiers. The Spaniards would have sent something signed and sealed, brought by a minor but self-important official to make sure no feelings were slighted, to make everyone feel responsible. He knows of course that it is impossible to protest. This is one of the things over which he has no control. The provincial governor is American, the Governor General in Manila is American. Before he was appointed to that highest of positions, Commissioner Taft did not even stop in Aloran to see what kind of government the people there desired. They are too small, a third-class municipality only because there is no lower category. Besides, as the justice of the peace said, the bodies are Americans and their mothers deserve them back. Still, the Spaniards would have given the occasion proper importance, invoked the royal patronage, their duty to the king so they in turn could invoke the saints.

Unable to catch up, he calls to the soldiers to look at one of the outposts the Americans had built in Aloran. The Americans turn but do not stop. Two more outposts are still standing up in the hills, he wants to say.

It had surprised the town that Americans would come to Aloran only to march to and from these outposts, or to watch from the shore when the cable ship passed without anchoring, laying its cable out in the sea. But as soon as it was certain the Americans were staying, his son began to organize against them and to wait for an order from General Martin Delgado of Iloilo who consulted General Aguinaldo of Malolos: Take the outposts in Aloran and rise with us.

Finally, despairing of the message ever coming, his son rounded up his friends and attacked the barracks. Only three lived, his son not among them. He would give anything to have his son back, his hope of heaven even. He struggles with his tears as he crosses the road lined with madre de cacao.

Silently he passes the house where the American teacher lived while he stayed there, about seven months not counting the grand vacation. The children learned several American songs which they now sing at night, their voices reaching the way their hands rose towards the gifts dangled

7

overhead after the processions to the Virgin in May.

The soldiers do not stop to ask about these things, are interested in nothing in Aloran. Tall and wide they occupy the entire road with their marching. If they had ridden the horses that died of surra during the war with the Americans, their legs would not have cleared the ground. The American teacher was smaller, of fine proportions. His eyes missed nothing. He came to the market and tasted their tuyo, tried to trap fish their way, to ride the barotos hewn out of entire logs. He was removed from Aloran for teaching the children the American Declaration of Independence. Apparently, the civil government in Manila felt that it would encourage the people to continue resisting after the war had been declared to be over. It is more than a year and a half since the teacher said he was coming back, time enough to believe otherwise.

Don Alfonso abruptly stops. "Go home," he tells the people walking just behind him. "Go home. It is their dead they take, not ours. Go home." Their presence, almost stepping into his shadows, emphasizes the fact that he is powerless. He feels as if his own son is being taken away and his heart is a hard fist shattering him inside.

Padre Cipriano places a hand upon his arm. "Alfonso, hijo, there are only six caskets. Only six. So, one soldier will be left to us!" Four–five years before, he had condemned the presidente from the pulpit for telling the town to revolt against Spain. Now, he calls him son.

The presidente understands. There are seven American graves. The seventh, the last to be interred is the one who came to open a saloon, buy a plantation or dig gold, anything to get rich with all at once; who sold them talcum powder at quinine rates and informed on the American teacher; finally who told the captain commanding the detachment at Aloran that the music being played in the church was Aquinaldo's march — he had heard it played in Manila where it was banned — so the captain ordered only American music could be played: "The Star Spangled Banner" or "There'll Be a Hot Time in Old Town Tonight." Standing in proper solemnly, the town people uncover their heads when either is heard.

The presidente is appeased. He raises his hat to the Spanish widow though he does not slow down to listen, as usual, to the son, a boy of about ten, playing the piano well enough to accompany a traveling Italian opera troupe should it happen to be stranded in Aloran.

Padre Cipriano relays his discovery to the justice, but bypasses the secretary to whom it would have to be explained at length. The friar is impatient because he already knows what to do so the one left behind would be the soldier who taught the children baseball, who accompanied him on his walks along the shore to wash his dogs, thin rowdy ones, not the white fluffy lapdogs women in Manila pet while they deal their cards: the one closest to the tree.

The civilian is the one farthest from the tree, being the last one buried in the garden convent, dying so slowly, holding on to the American sanitary inspector who immediately afterwards took off and burned his own clothes and washed himself with bichloride solution.

"Go home," the friar tells the children who have come for their afternoon lessons in the convent where these are being held until the return of the American teacher. "Go home." He lifts his hand above their heads so they cannot grab it to kiss. "Enough. Enough. Go." His mind is on several things at once so he wastes no time threatening them with the consequences of disobedience. Furtively, he glances at the church door.

The woman sitting there had come at daybreak with a narrow box that contains a small child whose face has hardened into an image of stone. The mother's seven thin candles have gone out and she has no more to light when he finally decides to notice her, to bless her child for burial. He is infuriated that they would come so early, would wait so timidly and pitifully, making no effort to state their business but expecting him to do everything: to notice them and call and see what they want.

Pretending he still does not see her, the friar enters the

garden. The Americans have stationed themselves under the ilang-ilang tree, through whose leaves the sun strikes their fixed bayonets. Padre Cipriano pulls the rowers away from the tree and positions them at the civilian's grave. "Start digging here. Take the next five."

Deprived of shade, the rowers strike their shovels sullenly. The earth does not resist. It is soft and without stones. The red cutsaritas are easily cut to the roots.

"Alfonso, tell the Americans I will have to celebrate Mass first," Padre Cipriano whispers, figuring out how many candles to light since the soldiers would not be obligated to pay his fees. When the Americans refuse, the friar tells the presidente to invite the soldiers up to his convent. "If they watch below, they might get curious and have the coffins opened."

Calling ahead to his servants to bring out the latest gifts from Manila — Pedro Domecq, fruits in brandy, queen olives, tins of butter and pears, sausages wrapped in tinfoil — Padre Cipriano pulls himself up on the balustrade of stone, ahead of everyone on the stairs. He opens the bottles himself so the cork will not crumble and float like insects in the glass, and licks the spills off his fingers, praying briefly that Padre Simeon would forgive him for serving the throaty Valdepenas being saved to serve with roasted goat that the older friar enjoys during his yearly visit.

The Americans accept and follow directly behind the friar. Their sergeant returns to his pocket the paper he cannot unfold: the wet corners are stuck. Without depositing their rifles below the rack of deer antlers, they enter the convent, stepping between the clutter of broken crucifixes and parts of floats, candelabras and wooden images. Refusing to change into the friar's robes so their uniforms could be dried, they are choosing seats overlooking the garden when one discovers: "Hey, look. Seven crosses and we only have six boxes."

"All the way to nowhere and we're one short." The sergeant pulls out the paper again.

The town officials act like conspirators about to be

caught. Padre Cipriano tells the justice to explain that the one closest to the tree is the civilian.

"But the bottles inside with the names?" The justice is overwhelmed by the fact that he has taken an oath to the American government and the slightest deception entitles him to be exiled to Guam, nearer of course than the Spanish prison outposts in Africa, but no less punitive.

"Silence. Basta ya. From up here, can they tell?" But the friar has absorbed the justice's fears and he goes to the cabinet to bring out the liver tonic.

"Was he an American?" The sergeant accepts the uncorked bottle. For some reason he is reminded of their commanding officer who had hoped to get his name in the newspapers by capturing rebel towns in Nueva Ecija with all their guns blazing, but giving the revolucionarios time to escape, each town welcoming the Americans with a band and a feast. The newspapers played up the receptions.

"I doubt it." Don Alfonso stretches the truth as far as his conscience allows. "He spoke Spanish. He and the Padre played monte after angelus and until curfew. To us, Swiss or English or Germans and Americans all look the same."

"And Spanish," Padre Cipriano adds playfully, looking ahead to the visit of Padre Simeon so he can tell the friar from Aragon how he put one over the Americans. In his dark blue cap, the boina, the other one would immediately challenge him to play pelota against the plain wall of the church though neither of them could see beyond an arm's length anymore. The town would watch to see how soon they would trip on the sotanas they would tuck in their cincture to free their legs.

The sergeant turns to the others who are also lured by the bouquet spreading from the uncorked bottles. "We have six boxes, we get six bodies. Anyway, those volunteers often enlisted under different names ... no way of really returning them to their families."

Their problem solved as easily as it came up, the others take a bottle each and lean back to listen to the town officials explain who the six were. One had traded his shoes for a monkey and a fighting cock. After winning several tupadas in a row he asked to have his cock blessed: the time it was slashed to the bone and ended up in a talunan stew. Another had his medals pinned to his tent, was asleep all day even at the outpost but at night was either blowing his bugle under the spirit tree full of fireflies or trying to convert corn mush into whiskey with a coffee pot and several lengths of pipes. Still another had been saving his pay and card winnings so that upon being mustered out he could buy some bancas and sell the protection of this fleet to coastal towns. "Several thousand islands!" he kept shouting with the intensity of ejaculations.

"How about the one who vaccinated all of Aloran?" Padre Cipriano sits against the wall which he himself had painted to resemble an oak forest. He measures brandy for himself. "I remember him well. Two soldiers with fixed bayonets stood behind him as he scraped flesh, like this, and when the women fainted, they all looked away."

"Didn't they like to use the crows for target practice?" the justice recalls. "When they were not on duty, they were shooting at the sky, ripping up the clouds." It was such a waste of ammunition at a time when his own son would have given up anything to have a small revolver and bullets to fill he chamber. The boy was finally arrested, picked up just before presidente's son led the attack, because he had picked up a bullet left on the beach. Though it had saved his son's life, the justice is bitter because the Americans fired hundreds, thousands of bullets uselessly to puncture holes in the sky.

"I remember very well the Americans arriving in Aloran." The secretary closes his book for a moment. "Their captain ordered the troops to close up on the bamboo bridge, altogether too heavy, massed that way, and Dawson was the first to drop into the creek. He was the happy one, always smiling. No matter how many times you met him within the hour, he always greeted you, 'Good morning.' I miss him."

"Always smiling and trading his hardtack and salmon — Alaska ration he called them — for fruits," the presidente recalls. "And after he had none left, he laid traps for my chickens. I caught him once and he offered to share it with me, if I would have it roasted for him!"

The secretary is tempted to say something else but remembers that he has written only up to the point where the Americans reach the convent garden, so he returns reluctantly to his record book. The trouble is that everyone in Aloran consults his books to see how faithfully he has quoted them. Should one name happen to be written with more flourish than the next, he is accused at once of being partisan.

The burial detail has become so friendly that they laugh when anyone says anything at all. And the town officials are talking all at the same time.

Padre Cipriano's provisions are soon exhausted so the presidente has to send to his house for the leg of ham he has been saving for the fiesta. The justice calls for the blue crabs set aside for his supper. The others send for whatever happens to be in their larder.

Savoring the liver tonic, the sergeant promises to have the guns fired out in the garden, some kind of salute, a return hospitality. Padre Cipriano has never been honored in this way and, touched by the offer which he asks the presidente to verify a second time, he goes into his bedroom to bring out any stray bottle. All he has left is in the liqour estomacal which he serves anyway, reminding himself not to overeat until another supply arrives from Manila.

Finally the visit ends. The soldiers cannot be persuaded to stay for the night since there are other towns and other bodies waiting. They take their leave, bringing along the last bottle. From the stone steps of the convent they fire a volley into the mountains. The smell of gunpowder invokes the flare of fireworks at the end of processions. Then the Americans depart graciously, their rifles slung across their bodies, the bayonets sheathed. Padre Cipriano blesses the caskets as these are carried out of his garden, his arms raised like short branches to the sun.

The secretary rushes to keep up with the proceedings, keeping his flourishes tight but long. As the policeman holds the book for him, the pages flutter and his eyes fall on a line written the past year: Today the graves are planted with flowers from the town presidente's garden. He looks up, remembering what the line stands for: after days of pleading, finally he had helped his sister, the town presidente's wife, to bury her son with the Americans, exchanging him with the one in the middle, so that if the Americans ever ordered the Filipino graves removed, as the Spaniards sometimes did to impress people with the gravity of the offense, her son would remain in the consecrated grounds of the convent. Afterwards, swearing him to secrecy, with her own hands his sister planted the red cutsaritas, decorating all the graves to disguise the exchange.

Flinging aside the book aside as if it has sprouted thorns in his hands, the secretary runs out to overtake the caskets, to have his sister's son returned — which one now? — but they are too far ahead, being rushed to the sea with Padre Cipriano and Don Alfonso in attendance, being borne alongside the tumbling waterfall that rushes even harder as if trying to sweep everyone to sea before the tide goes out.

Stunned by what he has allowed to happen — yet what could he have done had he realized it in time? — by the secret he has betrayed by keeping it too well, the secretary watches the town running fiercely in jubilation, having just then found out how Padre Cipriano had been able to trick the Americans into leaving one of their soldiers in the convent garden.

The town's running scatters the remaining light in the secretary's eyes; tears it into bits of yellow paper: sprung flowers adorning dead children's hair and old dismantled altars.

N.V.M. GONZALEZ

BORN in Romblon, Romblon, on September 8, 1915, N.V.M. Gonzalez is married to Narita M. Gonzalez. They have two sons and two daughters, and are grandparents to three girls and two boys.

His published books of fiction are: The Winds of April *(1941),* Seven Hills Away *(1947),* Children of the Ash-Covered Loam and Other Stories *(1954),* A Season of Grace *(1956),* The Bamboo Dancers *(1957),* Look, Stranger, On This Island Now *(1963),* Selected Stories *(1964), and* Mindoro and Beyond *(1979).* Kalutang: A Filipino in the World, *an autobiography, and* The Father and the Maid, *a collection of essays, appeared in 1990.*

Commenting on his choice of "A warm Hand" for this collection, the author says: "In Elay is probably as viable an image as any of the innocence of the Filipino, given the situation we find him in today."

A WARM HAND

HOLDING ON TO the rigging, Elay leaned over. The dinghy was being readied. The wind tore her hair into wiry strands that fell across her face, heightening her awareness of the dipping and rising of the deck. But for the bite of the noroeste, she would have begun to feel faint and empty in her belly. Now she clutched at the rigging with more courage.

At last the dinghy shoved away, with its first load of passengers — seven boys from Bongabon, Mindoro, on their way to Manila to study. The deck seemed less hostile than before, for the boys had made a boisterous group then; now that they were gone, her mistress Ana could leave the crowded deckhouse for once.

"Oh, Elay! My powder puff!"

It was Ana, indeed. Elay was familiar with that excitement which her mistress wore about her person like a silk kerchief — now on her head to keep her hair on place, now a scarf round her neck. How eager Ana had been to go ashore when the old skipper of the batel said that *Ligaya* was too small a boat to brave the coming storm. She must return to the deckhouse, Elay thought, if she must fetch her mistress' handbag.

With both hands upon the edge of the deckhouse roof, then holding on to the wooden water barrel to the left of the main mast, she staggered back to the deckhouse entrance. As she bent her head low lest with the lurching of the boat her brow should hit the door, she saw her mistress on all fours clambering out of the deckhouse. She let her have the right of way, entering only after Ana was safe upon the open deck.

Elay found the handbag — she was certain that the powder puff would be there — though not without difficulty, inside the canvas satchel that she had meant to take ashore. She came dragging the heavy satchel and in a flurry Ana dug into it for the bag. The deck continued to sway, yet presently Ana was powdering her face; this done, she applied lipstick to her full round mouth.

The wind began to press Elay's blouse against her breasts while she waited on her mistress patiently. She laced Ana's shoes and also bestirred herself to see that Ana's earrings were not askew. For Ana must appear every inch the dressmaker that she was. Let everyone know that she was traveling to Manila — not just to the provincial capital; and, of course, there was the old spinster aunt, too, for company — to set up a shop in the big city. It occurred to Elay that, judging from the care her mistress was taking to look well, it might well be that they were not on board a one-masted Tingloy batel with a cargo of lumber, copra, pigs, and chickens, but were still at home in the dress shop that they were leaving behind in the lumber town of Sumagui.

"How miserable I'd be without you, Elay," Ana giggled, as though somewhere she was meeting a secret lover who for certain would hold her in his arms in one wild passionate caress.

And thinking so of her mistress made Elay more proud of her. She did not mind the dark world into which they were going. Five miles to the south was Pinamalayan town; its lights blinked faintly at her. Then along the rim of the Bay, dense groves of coconuts and underbrush stood, occasional fires marking where the few sharecroppers of the district lived. The batel had anchored at the northernmost end of the cove and apparently 500 yards from the boat was a palm-leaf-covered hut the old skipper of the *Ligaya* had spoken about.

"Don't you see it? That's Obregano's hut." Obregano, the old skipper explained, was a fisherman. The men who sailed up and down the eastern coast of Mindoro knew him well. There was not a seaman who lived in these parts who had not gone to Obregano for food or shelter and to this anchorage behind the northern tip of Pinamalayan Bay for the protection it offered sailing vessels against the unpredictable noroeste.

The old skipper had explained all this to Ana, and Elay

had listened, little knowing that in a short while it would all be there before her. Now in the dark she saw the fisherman's hut readily. A broad shoulder of a hill rose beyond, and farther yet the black sky looked like a silent wall.

Other women joined them on the deck to see the view for themselves. A discussion started; some members of the party did not think it would be proper for them to spend the night in Obregano's hut. Besides the students, there were four middle-aged merchants on this voyage; since Bongabon they had plagued the women with their coarse talk and their yet coarser laughter. Although the deckhouse was the unchallenged domain of the women, the four middle-aged merchants had often slipped in, and once had exchanged lewd jokes among themselves to the embarrassment of their audience. Small wonder, Elay thought, that the prospect of spending the night in a small fisherman's hut with these men for company did not appear attractive to the other women passengers. Her mistress Ana had made up her mind, however. She had a sense of independence that Elay admired.

Already the old aunt had joined them on deck; and Elay said to herself, "Of course, it's for this old auntie's sake, too. She has been terribly seasick."

In the dark she saw the dinghy and silently watched it being sculled back to the batel. It drew nearer and nearer, a dark mass moving eagerly, the bow pointing in her direction. Elay heard Ana's little shrill cries of excitement. Soon two members of the crew were vying for the honor of helping her mistress safely into the dinghy.

Oh, that Ana should allow herself to be thus honored, with the seaman taking such pleasure from it all, and the old aunt, watching, pouting her lips in disapproval! "What shall I do?" Elay asked herself, anticipating that soon she herself would be the object of this chivalrous byplay. And what could the old aunt be saying now to herself? "Ah, women these days are no longer decorous. In no time they will make a virtue of being unchaste."

Elay pouted, too. And then it was her turn. She must

get into that dinghy, and it so pitched and rocked. If only she could manage to have no one help her at all. But she'd fall into the water. Santa Maria, I'm safe ...

They were off. The waves broke against the sides of the dinghy, threatening to capsize it, and continually the black depths glared at her. Her hands trembling, Elay clung tenaciously to the gunwale. Spray bathed the cheeks. A boy began to bail, for after clearing each wave the dinghy took in more water. So earnest was the boy at his chore that Elay thought the boat had sprung a leak and would sink any moment.

The sailors, one at the prow and the other busy with the oar at the stern, engaged themselves in senseless banter. Were they trying to make light of the danger? She said her prayers as the boat swung from side to side, to a rhythm set by the sailor with the oar.

Fortunately, panic did not seize her. It was the old aunt who cried, "Susmariosep!" For with each crash of waves, the dinghy lurched precipitously. "God spare us all!" the old aunt prayed frantically.

Ana was laughing. "Auntie! Why, Auntie, it's nothing! It's nothing at all!" For, really, they were safe. The dinghy had struck sand.

Elay's dread of the water suddenly vanished and she said to herself, "Ah, the old aunt is only making things more difficult for herself." Why, she wouldn't let the sailor with the oar lift her clear off the dinghy and carry her to the beach!

"Age before beauty," the sailor was saying to his companion. The other fellow, not to be outdone, had jumped waist-deep into the water, saying, "No, beauty above all!" Then there was Ana stepping straight, as it were, into the sailor's arms.

"Where are you?" the old aunt was calling from the shore. "Are you safe? Are you all right?"

Elay wanted to say that in so far as she was concerned, she was safe, she was all right. But she couldn't speak for her mistress, of course! But the same seaman who had lifted the old aunt and carried her to the shore in his arms had returned. Now he stood before Elay and caught her two legs and let them rest on his forearm and then held her body up, with the other arm. Now she was clear off the dinghy, and she had to hold on to his neck. Then the sailor made three quick steps toward dry sand and then let her slide easily off his arms, and she said, "I'm all right. Thank you."

Instead of saying something to her, the sailor hurried away, joining the group of students that had gathered on the rise of sand. Ana's cheerful laughter rang in their midst. Then a youth's voice, clear in the wind: "Let's hurry to the fisherman's hut!"

A drizzle began to fall. Elay took a few tentative steps toward the palm leaf hut, but her knees were unsteady. The world seemed to turn and turn, and the glowing light at the fisherman's door swung as from a boat's mast. Elay hurried as best as she could after Ana and her old aunt, both of whom had already reached the hut. It was only on hearing her name that the weak, unsteady feeling in her knees disappeared.

"Elay —" It was her mistress, of course. Ana was standing outside the door, waiting. "My lipstick, Elay!"

An old man stood at the door of the hut. "I am Obregano, at your service," he said in welcome. "This is my home."

He spoke in a sing-song that rather matched his wizened face. Pointing at a little woman puttering about the stovebox at the far end of the one-room hut, he said, "And she? Well, the guardian of my home — in other words, my wife!"

The woman got up and welcomed them, beaming a big smile. "Feel at home. Make yourselves comfortable — everyone."

She helped Elay with the canvas bag, choosing a special corner for it. "It will rain harder yet tonight, but here your bag will be safe," the woman said.

The storm had come. The thatched wall shook, producing a weird skittering sound at each gust of wind. The sough of the palms in back of the hut — which was hardly the size of the deckhouse of the batel, and had the bare sand for floor — sounded like the moan of a lost child. A palm leaf that served to cover an entrance to the left of the stovebox began to dance a mad, rhythmless dance. The fire in the stove leaped intermittently, rising beyond the lid of the kettle that Obregano, the old fisherman, had placed there.

And yet the hut was homelike. It was warm and clean. There was a cheerful look all over the place. Elay caught the old fisherman's smile as his wife cleared the floor of nets and coil after coil of hempen rope so that their guests could have more room. She sensed an affinity with her present surroundings, with the smell of fish nets, with the dancing fire in the stovebox. It was as though she had lived in this hut before. She remembered what Obregano's wife had said to her. The old woman's words were by far the kindest she had heard in a long time.

The students from Bongabon had appropriated a corner for themselves and began to discuss supper. It appeared that a prankster had relieved one of the chicken coops of a fat pullet and a boy asked the fisherman for permission to prepare a stew.

"I've some ginger tea in the kettle," Obregado said. "Something worth drinking in weather like this." He asked his wife for an old enameled tin cup for his guests to drink from.

As the cup was being passed around, Obregano's wife expressed profuse apologies for her not preparing supper. "We have no food," she said, with uncommon frankness. "We have sons, you know, two of them, both working in town. But they come home only on weekends. It is only then that we have rice."

Elay understood that in lieu of wages, the two Obregano boys received rice. Last weekend the boys had failed to return home, however. This fact brought a sad note to Elay's new world of warm fire and familiar smells. She got out some food which they had brought along from the boat — adobo and bread that the old aunt had put in a tin container and tucked into the canvas satchel — and offered her mistress these, going through the motions so absentmindedly that Ana chided her.

"Do offer the old man and his wife some of that, too."

Obregano shook his head. He explained that he would not think of partaking of the food — so hungry his guests must be. They needed all the food themselves, to say nothing about that which his house should offer but which in his naked poverty he could not provide. But at least they would be safe here for the night, Obregano assured them. "The wind is rising, and the rain, too. Listen ..." He pointed at the roof, which seemed to sag.

The drone of the rain set Elay's spirits aright. She began to imagine how sad and worried over her sons the old fisherman's wife must be, and how lonely — but oh, how lovely it would be to live in this God-forsaken spot. She watched the students devour their supper, and she smiled thanks, sharing their thoughtfulness, when they offered most generously some chicken to Ana and, in sheer politeness, to the old spinster aunt also.

Yet more people from the batel arrived, and the four merchants burst into the hut discussing some problem in Bongabon municipal politics. It was as though the foul weather suited their purposes, and Elay listened with genuine interest, with compassion, even, for the small-town politicians who were being reviled and cursed.

It was Obregano who suggested that they all retire. There was hardly room for everyone, and in bringing out a roughly woven palm-leaf mat for Ana and her companions to use, Obregano picked his way in order not to step on a sprawling leg or an outstretched arm. The offer of the mat touched Elay's heart, so much that pondering the goodness of the old fisherman and his wife took her mind away from the riddles which the students at this time were exchanging among themselves. They were funny riddles and there was much laughter. Once she caught them throwing glances in Ana's direction.

Even the sailors who were with them on the dinghy had returned to the hut to stay and were laughing heartily at their own stories. Elay watched Obregano produce a bottle of kerosene for the lantern, and then hang the lantern with string from the center beam of the hut. She felt a new dreamlike joy. Watching the old fisherman's wife extinguish the fire in the stove made Elay's heart throb.

Would the wind and the rain worsen? The walls of the hut shook — like a man in the throes of malarial chills. The sea kept up a wild roar, and the waves, it seemed, continually clawed at the land with strong, greedy fingers.

She wondered whether Obregano and his wife would ever sleep. The couple would be thinking: "Are our guests comfortable enough as they are?" As for herself, Elay resolved, she would stay awake. From the corner where students slept she could hear the whine of a chronic asthma sufferer. One of the merchants snorted periodically, like a horse being annoyed by a fly. A young boy, apparently dreaming, called out in a strange, frightened voice: "No, no! I can't do that! I wouldn't do that!"

She saw Obregano get up and pick his way again among the sleeping bodies to where the lantern hung. The flame was sputtering. Elay watched him adjust the wick of the lantern and give the oil container a gentle shake. Then the figure of the old fisherman began to blur and she could hardly keep her eyes open. A soothing tiredness possessed her. As she yielded easily to sleep, with Ana to her left and the old spinster aunt at the far edge of the mat to her right, the floor seemed to sink and the walls of the hut to vanish, as though the world were one vast dark valley.

When later she awoke she was trembling with fright. She had only a faint notion that she had screamed. What blur there had been in her consciousness before falling asleep was as nothing compared with that which followed her waking, although she was aware of much to-do and the lantern light was gone.

"Who was it?" It was reassuring to hear Obregano's voice.

"The lantern, please!" That was Ana, her voice shrill and wiry.

Elay heard as if in reply the crash of the sea rising in crescendo. The blur lifted a little. "Had I fallen asleep after all? Then it must be past midnight now." Time and place became realities again; and she saw Obregano, with a lighted matchstick in his hand. He was standing in the middle of the hut.

"What happened?"

Elay thought it was she whom Obregano was speaking to. She was on the point of answering, although she had no idea of what to say, when Ana, sitting upon the mat beside her, blurted out: "Someone was here. Please hold up the light."

"Someone was here," Elay repeated to herself and hid her face behind Ana's shoulders. She must not let the four merchants, nor the students either, stare at her so. Caught by the lantern light, the men hardly seven steps away had turned their gazes upon her in various attitudes of amazement.

Everyone seemed eager to say something all at once. One of the students spoke in a quavering voice, declaring that he had not moved where he lay. Another said he had been so sound asleep. "Didn't you hear me snoring?" he asked a companion, slapping him on the back — he had not even heard the shout. One of the merchants hemmed and suggested that perhaps cool minds should look into the case, carefully and without preconceived ideas. To begin with, one must know exactly what happened. He looked in Ana's direction and said: "Now please tell us."

Elay clutched her mistress' arm. Before Ana could speak, Obregano's wife said, "This thing ought not to have happened. If only our two sons were home, they'd avenge the honor of our house." She spoke with a rare eloquence for an angry woman. "No one would then dare think of so base an act. Now, our good guests," she added, addressing her husband, bitterly, "why, they know you be an aged, simple-hearted fisherman – nothing more. The good name of our home, of our family, is no concern of theirs."

"Evil was coming, I knew it!" said the old spinster aunt; and piping out like a bird: "Let us return to the boat! Don't be so bitter, old one," she told Obregano's wife. "We are going back to the boat."

"It was like this," Ana said, not minding her aunt. Elay lowered her head more, lest she should see these man-faces before her, loosely trapped now by the lantern's glow. Indeed, she closed her eyes, as though she were a little child afraid of the dark.

"It was like this," her mistress began again," "I was sleeping, and then my maid, Elay —" she put an arm around Elay's shoulders — "she uttered that wild scream. I am surprised you did not hear it."

In a matter-of-fact tone, one of the merchants countered: "Suppose it was a nightmare?"

But Ana did not listen to him. "Then my maid," she continued, "this girl here — she's hardly twenty, mind you, and an innocent and illiterate girl, if you must all know … She turned around, trembling, and clung to me …"

"Couldn't she possibly have shouted in her sleep?" the merchant insisted.

Obregano had held his peace all this time, but now he spoke: "Let us hear what the girl says."

And so kind were those words! How fatherly of him to have spoken so, in such a gentle and understanding way! Elay's heart went out to him. She felt she could almost run to him and, crying on his shoulders, tell him what no one, not even Ana herself, would ever know.

She turned her head a little to one side and saw that now they were all looking at her. She hugged her mistress tighter, in a childlike embrace, hiding her face as best she could.

"Tell them," Ana said, drawing herself away. "Now, go on — speak!"

But Elay would not leave her side. She clung to her, and began to cry softly.

"Nonsense!" the old aunt chided her.

"Well, she must have had a nightmare, that's all," the merchant said, chuckling. "I'm sure of it."

At this remark Elay cried even more. "I felt a warm hand caressing my-my-my cheeks," she said, sobbing. "A warm hand, I swear," she said again, remembering how it had reached out for her in the dark, searchingly, burning with a need to find some precious treasure which, she was certain of it now, she alone possessed. For how could it be that they should force her to tell them? "Someone," — the word was like a lamp in her heart — "someone wanted me," she said to herself.

She felt Ana's hand stroking her back ungently and then heard her saying, "I brought this on." Then nervously fumbling about the mat: "This is all my fault ... My compact, please..."

But Elay was inconsolable. She was sorry she could be of no help to her mistress now. She hung her head, unable to stop her tears from cleansing those cheeks that a warm hand had loved.

JUAN C. DIONISIO

"A SUMMER in an Alaskan Salmon Cannery" first appeared in the Philippine Magazine *(1931), one of three Manila magazines which published the dozen or so short stories about the life of the Pinoy immigrants of the 1920s and '30s by J.C. Dionisio, then a student at the University of Washington.*

Born in May 1910 in a barrio of Aklan Province in the Visayas, Dionisio went to America in 1926 to further his education. He supported himself through high school and college by working as a "school boy" in college fraternities and in the Alaskan salmon canneries during summer vacations. In 1944, while living in Stockton, California, with his wife and four children, he was summoned by President Manuel L. Quezon of the Philippine Commonwealth Government-in-Exile. Quezon wanted to know more about the plight concerns of the Pinoys on the West Coast, which were the subject of Dionisio's many articles in the Pinoy *Press. After their bedside meeting in the hospital room in Miami Beach, Florida, where the President, gravely ill with tuberculosis, was confined, Quezon told Dionisio, "Well, you are now in the government."*

Thus started his government career which spanned 31 years: first as Western Representative of the Resident Commissioner in San

Francisco, then as Vice-Consul of the New Republic (1946), then as Consul, Consul General, Minister, and finally Ambassador.

He was Consul-General in Honolulu, Singapore, and Kuala Lumpur; and concurrently Ambassador to both Iran and Pakistan for nine years until he retired in 1975.

In 1977, he published and edited a fortnightly paper, Hawaii Filipino News, which he had to give up for medical reasons in 1985. He lives in Honolulu, and is finishing a novel on the Filipino immigrants of the 1920's.

A SUMMER IN AN ALASKAN CANNERY

I

"BIG MISTAKE" nervously paced the mess-house floor. Around him were gathered the men — towels and toothbrushes still in hand. There was tense apprehension in the air. It was 5:20 o'clock, and in ten minutes the bull cook would beat the gong. Breakfast.

We all blessed that gong when it sounded at noon and at six o'clock in the morning. For its devilish sound pierced your ears no matter how deep under the covers you buried your head. And when you have stood for 18 hours in the cold, slimy fish house, you'd wish to God you were out alone on a lonely island where there were no bosses nor gongs to break your sweet dreamless sleep.

But we were not gathered there that morning to protest against the gong. It was bad enough, but we knew it was necessary. After all, they had to wake us up: we were not paid to sleep. We were gathered there because the previous day we had lodged a complaint against the Chinese cook. We let it be known that as human beings we could not stand working from six in the morning to twelve at night and be given hard rice and salted salmon for breakfast. We simply could not eat the stuff.

We demanded coffee — and no salted salmon.

The cook was apparently in sympathy with us. We could understand his position well enough, but by some queer twist of human nature we blamed our lot on him. He was a Chinese and the contractor was his countryman. When Big Mistake as undelegated leader of the gang apprised him of our demand, he said absently, "I no know. You ashee boshee."

Our Filipino foreman was a middle-aged person who had been handling cannery crews for some fifteen years. He had an unusually flat nose, and his eyes closed and opened incessantly while he talked. He had a hard mouth and his face was slightly pockmarked. He seemed amiable enough, but he sided too much with the Chinese. We didn't think that was right.

Anyway, when Big Mistake approached him one morning, Louie — that was his name — anticipated him, bellowing threateningly: "I know what you want, Big Mistake. You want to complain about the chow. What do you think this is — a restaurant? A chop suey house?

Why'd you come to Alaska — for vacation? Hunh!"

That night the conspiracy was hatched. We greenhorns were scared but were spurred on by the hardened oldtimers. "The only way we can get our rights around this dump —" Big Mistake murmured to us as we huddled in our bunks. "— is to tell them where to get off. Vacation — hunh!"

If the bull cook sensed something wrong that morning, he did not show it. To be sure, he looked astonished as he saw the whole crew of one hundred twenty men seated at their tables at 5:28. "Wassa malla?" he said. "Allo come down oierly today."

Ah Shi, the cook, in badly soiled denim overalls, leaned out the kitchen window and shouted, "Kan Kang loh!" The bull cook banged the iron bar. We grabbed our chopsticks and proceeded to eat.

Conversation was unusually dull, but the idle chatter and the noise of the chopsticks belied the tension among us. Then suddenly a voice shrilled: "Hee-ee-eep!" Simultaneously the basins containing the rice were flopped upside down on the tables, the chopsticks described arches in the air, and salted salmon and dried cabbage littered the floor.

Pandemonium reigned. A party raided the kitchen, and half of the crew was munching cupcakes, apple pies, and jelly rolls. Ah Shi ran to the cottage which served as our foreman's quarters, shouting desperately, "Louie-ah! Louie-ah!" But Louie had already gone to the cannery.

The Chinese had barricaded themselves in their quarters. Ah Shi ran there, pounding frantically on the door. It opened a little and a hand pulled him in; but before he was entirely inside, a piece of pie, perfectly aimed, landed on his back. The volume of laughter increased. We were having a grand time.

When we came home at noon, there was a sign on the bulletin board. It read: "Anyone caught dumping food on the tables or on the floor will be shipped back to Seattle." We looked at each other, amused. We knew that was a scare. They wouldn't dare send anyone back. It was the peak of the season and they were short of men.

We noticed also an improvement in our menu. More meat was mixed with the dried cabbage. We had fried fish salmon. Big Mistake beamed triumphantly. "Didn't I tell you?" he said.

"Uh, huh!" I exulted. "So they won't give us salted salmon anymore!"

Pete, our "retort boy," who had a genius for reticence, gulped down his soup. "They can't, he said simply, marveling at my innocence. "We threw the stuff in the creek!

II

Joe was a gambler. He was also rumored to be a gangster. He was a "tough egg." The men were not wont to befriend him. They said they felt "clammy" when he was near. His eyes slanted just a little, giving him the appearance of a half-breed Chinese. But he had no Chinese blood in him.

It was whispered that Joe had scars of bullet and knife wounds on his body. It was also whispered that he had killed a rival in love in his hometown in the Islands, and that he had come to the U.S. to escape punishment. I didn't know whether the rumors were true, but I did know he was once an inmate of San Quentin Prison in California. He told me so himself. Of the circumstances he didn't tell me.

Joe had a mercurial temperament. Easily provoked, he struck in a flash. But he was not a bully. He did not pick quarrels unless he was abused. Also, he had a redeeming sense of humor. He delighted in telling jokes — sometimes dirty, sometimes perfectly innocuous.

One afternoon — this was yet early in the season and the work was only a few hours a day — Joe was playing blackjack with the bunch. "Bulutong" Mac was the banker. (There was nothing unusual about Mac, except that despite his homely appearance, he was the only man in the bunch who attracted the attention of Harriet, a winsome young Minnehaha.) Anyway, Joe had the highest bet — twenty-five dollars. He had a couple of jacks in his hand. Mac had a seven up. Mac thought for a moment; then deftly, swiftly, he drew a card. A five. In a flash Joe's right hand shot out, in its grasp gleamed a menacing eight-inch automatic knife.

Mac rolled to the floor, jumped up, and ran. Joe followed him a few paces, turned around, and darted up to his room. We were all so stunned by the suddenness of it that we stood there, our mouths agape.

Presently, Joe came down, a .45 caliber gun in his hand. He was shaking with rage. But Mac was nowhere to be found. Joe ran outside. Shots rang out. We crowded in the doorway, fearful that the worst had happened. And we saw. There on the walk stood Joe — in his hand a smoking revolver, and twenty paces away lay an empty salmon can riddled with bullets!

Late that night Big Boy and I were watching the "hook fish" gang unloading the fish from the scows when Shorty

Aliston came running up to us, gesturing wildly. "Come on," he panted. "Mac's fighting Indian! Mac's fighting Indian … hun … hun … Indian!"

We scrambled after him. Big Boy muttered under his breath, "The damn fool! He should have known this is Saturday night. He should have kept away from that crazy girl. The boss has warned him."

"There they are!" pointed Shorty. And there they were, but they were three. Two were Filipinos. The girl apparently had taken to her heels at the first sign of hostilities.

Joe and Mac were giving the brave a bad beating. But he was fighting. Suddenly a right uppercut from Joe caught the native on the jaw. He reeled, sagged, and fell to the boardwalk. Walking over to Mac, Joe grabbed him by the shoulders and without warning shot a similar uppercut to his chin which knocked him completely out. "You lousy skunk!" he swore at Mac as he dragged him home. "You'd get into a fight over a lousy girl like that!"

And from that night on Joe and Mac were real friends. They slept in the same hotel room in Seattle and tramped together in California. I have not heard of them since.

III

Among the collegiate element in the crew was a handsome young man named Licerio. For the sake of expediency we called him, incongruously enough, Lizzy.

Lizzy belonged to an influential family in the Islands. His father held an important political post in his province. But Lizzy, like Hardy's reddleman, relinquished his better position in life for want of an interest in it. His father wanted him to be a lawyer, but Lizzy wanted to be "sailor on a tramp steamer." Then, discovered one day in a compromising situation with a young lady acquaintance whom he did not love, he "hotfooted it to America to escape the impending doom of inevitable marriage."

In America he developed a condescending democratic attitude towards his fellows. Fundamentally he was an aristocrat — as the term is understood in the Philippines. He was easily identified with elevated-nose contingent. He had, however, a charm all his own. His careful speech, erect bearing, affable manners, and a certain subtle suavity suggested good breeding.

Lizzy regarded the natives (Alaskan Indians) as far below him. He didn't have anything to do with them. He worked in the warehouse with the girls. His job was to pile up the "coolers" or metal trays as soon as the girls emptied them of their salmon contents. He stood in one corner and waited for them to be emptied. He didn't even condescend to speak with the girls, and scoffed at their flirtations.

Then one day we saw him carrying some kindling for Esther. An act of chivalry, we thought ... but we were wrong. It was love — at least he said so. The knowing ones said it was sheer midsummer madness.

The affair continued all summer. Nobody paid any particular attention. Summer romances like that flared up, then evaporated. Nothing unusual in the canneries. Nothing unusual to the native girls who were unknowing advocates of free love. But Lizzy was getting serious. Bad. One evening while we were preparing to go back to Seattle he came up to me and said, "I think I'm going to marry Esther."

"You're what!" I was so surprised I nearly choked on the piece of apple I was eating.

"Well," he said, with a naiveté that was devastating, "what's wrong with that? She's used to elemental living, and I won't have to slave to keep her. Besides, we love each other. There she is now; I'm going to speak to her." And he ran out.

That night when he came home, he dropped on his bunk, grunting heavily. I stuck my head out of the covers and inquired, "Well, did she say yes?"

Lizzy didn't look up. "You know," he said, "there are lots of things in this world which you can't take for granted. Take Esther. When I told her I wanted to marry her, she looked at me kind of surprised and said, 'Now you're getting serious. Don't, because I won't like you if you do ... Let's just be like we are now. After all, we're happy while it lasts. You go your way and I'll go mine. Then we'll remember each other — live in sweet memories.' That's all. And she kissed me and ran away. And after all we've done —"

"Never mind that," I interpreted. "You'll forget her when you get back down below."

"Forget her? Believe me or not, you'll never see me in Alaska again."

And I never did.

BIENVENIDO N. SANTOS

BORN IN TONDO, Manila, of Pampango parents from Lubao, Beinvenido N. Santos was a government pensionado to the United States in 1941. During the war years he studied at the University of Illinois, Columbia, and Harvard, and served with the Philippine Government-in-Exile in Washington, D.C. In 1946 he returned to the Philippines, taught school, and became a university administrator. In 1959 he was a Rockefeller Foundation fellow at the Writers Workshop in the University of Iowa, where he later taught as a Fulbright Exchange professor. He is the recipient of numerous awards including a Guggenheim Foundation fellowship and a Republic Cultural Heritage Award in Literature. In 1981, his alma mater, the University of the Philippines, and Bicol University in Legazpi City gave him honorary degrees in letters and the humanities. He was Distinguished Writer in Residence at Wichita State University from 1973 to 1982, and was awarded an honorary degree in humane letters upon his retirement.

He resides in Greeley, Colorado, but spends several months each year in the Philippines. In late 1986 to 1987, he was Visiting Writer and Artist in Residence at De La Salle University in Manila.

SCENT OF APPLES

WHEN I ARRIVED in Kalamazoo it was October and the war was still on. Gold and silver stars hung on pennants above silent windows of white and brick-red cottages. In a backyard an old man burned leaves and twigs while a grey-haired woman sat on the porch, her red hands quiet on her lap, watching the smoke rising above the elms, both of them thinking of the same thought perhaps, about a tall, grinning boy with blue eyes and flying hair, who went out to war: where could he be now this month when leaves were turning into gold and the fragrance of gathered apples was in the wind?

It was a cold night when I left my room at the hotel for a usual speaking engagement. I walked but a little way. A heavy wind coming up from Lake Michigan was icy in the face. It felt like winter straying early in the northern woodlands. Under the lampposts the leaves shone like bronze. And they rolled on the pavements like the ghost feet of a thousand autumns long dead, long before the boys left for faraway lands without great icy winds and promise of winter early in the air, lands without apple trees, *the singing and the gold!*

It was the same night I met Celestino Fabia, "just a Filipino farmer," as he called himself, who had a farm about 30 miles east of Kalamazoo.

"You came all the way on a night like this to hear me talk?" I asked.

"I've seen no Filipino for so many years now," he answered quickly. "So when I saw your name in the papers where it says you come from the Islands and that you're going to talk, I come right away."

Earlier that night I had addressed a college crowd, mostly women. It appeared that they wanted me to talk about my country; they wanted me to tell them things about it because my country had become a lost country. Everywhere in the land the enemy stalked. Over it a great silence hung; and their boys were there, unheard from, or they were on their way to some little known islands on the Pacific, young boys all, hardly men, thinking of harvest moons and the smell of forest fire.

It was not hard talking about our own people. I knew them well and I loved them. And they seemed so far away during those terrible years that I must have spoken of them with a little fervor, a little nostalgia.

In the open forum that followed, the audience wanted to know whether there was much difference between our women and the American women. I tried to answer the question as best as I could, saying, among other things, that I did not know much about American women, except that they looked friendly, but differences or similarities in inner qualities such as naturally belonged to the heart or to the mind, I could only speak about with vagueness.

While I was trying to explain away the fact that it was not easy to make comparisons, a man rose from the rear of the hall, wanting to say something. In the distance, he looked slight and old and very brown. Even before he spoke, I knew that he was, like me, a Filipino.

"I'm a Filipino," he began, loud and clear, in a voice that seemed used to wide open spaces, "I'm just a Filipino farmer out in the country." He waved his hand towards the door. "I left the Philippines more than twenty years ago and have never been back. Never will perhaps. I want to find out, sir, are Filipino women the same like they were twenty years ago?"

As he sat down, the hall filled with voices, hushed and intrigued. I weighed my answer carefully. I did not want to tell a lie, yet I did not want to say anything that would seem platitudinous, insincere. But more important than these considerations, it seemed to me that moment as I looked towards my countryman, I must give him an answer that would not make him so unhappy. Surely, all these years, he must have held on to certain ideals, certain beliefs, even illusions peculiar

37

to the exile.

"First," I said as the voices gradually died down and every eye seemed focused upon me, "First, tell me what our women were like twenty years ago."

The man stood up to answer. "Yes," he said, "you're too young ... Twenty years ago our women were nice, they were modest, they wore their hair long, they dressed proper and went for no monkey business. They were natural, they went to church regular, and were faithful." He had spoken slowly, and now in what seemed like an afterthought, added, "It's the men who ain't."

Now I knew what I was going to say.

"Well," I began, "it will interest you to know that our women have changed — but definitely! The change, however, has been on the outside only. Inside, here," pointing to the heart, "they are the same as they were twenty years ago. God — fearing, faithful, modest, and *nice*."

The man was visibly moved. "I'm very happy sir," he said, in the manner of one who, having stakes on the land, had found no cause to regret one's sentimental investment.

After this, everything that was said and done in that hall that night seemed like an anti-climax; and later, as we walked outside, he gave me his name and told of his farm thirty miles east of the city.

We had stopped at the main entrance to the hotel lobby. We had not talked very much on the way. As a matter of fact, we were never alone. Kindly American friends talked to us, asked us questions, said goodnight. So now I asked him whether he cared to step into the lobby with me and talk.

"No, thank you," he said, "you are tired. And I don't want to stay out too late."

"Yes, you live very far."

"I got a car," he said, "besides ..."

Now he smiled, he truly smiled. All night I had been watching his face and wondered when he was going to smile.

"Will you do me a favor, please?" he continued smiling almost sweetly. "I want you to have dinner with my family out in the country. I'd call for you tomorrow afternoon, then drive you back. Will that be all right?"

"Of course," I said. "I'd love to meet your family." I was leaving Kalamazoo for Muncie, Indiana, in two days. There was plenty of time.

"You will make my wife very happy," he said.

"You flatter me."

"Honest. She'll be very happy. Ruth is a country girl and hasn't met many Filipinos. I mean Filipinos younger than I, cleaner looking. We're just poor farmer folk, you know, and we don't get to town very often. Roger, that's my boy, he goes to school in town. A bus takes him early in the morning and he's back in the afternoon. He's a nice boy."

"I bet he is," I agreed. "I've seen the children of some of the boys by their American wives and the boys are tall, taller than the father, and very good-looking."

"Roger, he'd be tall. You'll like him."

Then he said goodbye and I waved to him as he disappeared in the darkness.

The next day he came, at about three in the afternoon. There was a mild, ineffectual sun shining; and it was not too cold. He was wearing an old brown tweed jacket and worsted trousers to match. His shoes were polished, and although the green of his tie seemed faded, a colored shirt hardly accentuated it. He looked younger than he appeared the night before now that he was clean shaven and seemed ready to go to a party. He was grinning as we met.

"Oh, Ruth can't believe it. She can't believe it," he kept repeating as he led me to his car — a nondescript thing in faded black that had known better days and many hands. "I says to her, I'm bringing you a first class Filipino. But Roger, that's my boy, he believed me immediately. What's he like, daddy? he asks. Oh, you will see, I says, he's first class. Like you, daddy? No, no, I laugh at him, your daddy ain't first class. Aw, but you are, daddy, he says. So you can see what a nice boy he is, so innocent. Then Ruth starts griping about the house, but the house is a mess, she says. True, it's a mess, it's always a mess, but you don't mind, do you? We're poor folks, you know."

The trip seemed interminable. We passed through narrow lanes and disappeared into thickets, and came out on barren land overgrown with weeds in places. All around were dead leaves and dry earth. In the distance were apple trees.

"Aren't those apple trees?" I asked wanting to be sure.

"Yes, those are apple trees," he replied. "Do you like apples? I got lots of 'em. I got an apple orchard, I'll show you."

"Those trees are beautiful on the hills," I said.

"Autumn's a lovely season. The trees are getting ready to die, and they show their colors, proud-like."

"No such thing in our country, I said.

That remark seemed unkind, I realized later. It touched him off on a long deserted tangent, but ever there perhaps. How many times did the lonely mind take unpleasant detours away from the familiar winding lanes towards home for fear of this, the remembered hurt, the long lost youth, the grim shadows of the years; how many times, indeed, only the exile knows.

It was a rugged road we were traveling and the car made so much noise that I could not hear everything he said, but I understood him. He was telling his story for the first time in many years. He was remembering his own youth. He was thinking of home. In these odd moments there seemed no cause for fear, no cause at all, no pain. That would come later. In the night perhaps. Or lonely on the farm under the apple trees.

In this old Visayan town, the streets are narrow and dirty and strewn with coral shells. You have been there? You could not have missed our house, it was the biggest in town, one of the oldest, ours was a big family. The house stood right on the edge of the street. A door opened heavily and you enter a dark hall leading to the stairs. There is the smell of chickens roosting on the low-topped walls, there is the familiar sound they make and you grope your way up a massive staircase, the bannister smooth upon the trembling hand. Such nights, they are no better than the days, windows are closed against the sun; they close heavily.

Mother sits in her corner looking very white and sick. This was her world, her domain. In all these years I cannot remember the sound of her voice. Father was different. He moved about. He shouted. He ranted. He lived in the past and talked of honor as though it were the only thing.

I was born in that house. I grew up there into a pampered brat. I was mean. One day I broke their hearts. I saw Mother cry wordlessly as Father heaped his curses upon me and drove me out of the house, the gate closing heavily after me. And my brothers and sisters took up my father's hate for me and multiplied it numberless times in their own broken hearts. I was no good.

But sometimes, you know, I miss that house, the roosting chickens on the low-topped walls. I miss my brothers and sisters. Mother sitting in her chair, looking like a pale ghost in a corner of the room. I would remember the great live posts, massive tree trunks from the forests. Leafy plants grew on the sides, buds pointing downwards, wilted and died before they become flowers. As they fell on the floor, Father bent to pick them and throw them into the coral streets. His hands were strong. I have kissed those hands … many times, many times.

Finally we rounded a deep curve and suddenly came upon a shanty, all but ready to crumble in a heap on the ground. I thought of the cottages of the poor colored folk in the south, the hovels of the poor everywhere in the land. This one stood all by itself as though by common consent all the folk that used to live here had decided to stay away, despising it, ashamed of it. Even the lovely season could not color it with beauty.

A dog barked loudly as we approached. A fat blonde woman stood at the door with a little boy by her side. Roger seemed newly scrubbed. He hardly took his eyes off me. Ruth had a clean apron around her shapeless waist. Now as she shook my hand in sincere delight I noticed shamefacedly (that I should notice) how rough her hands, how coarse and red with labor, how ugly! She was no longer young and her smile was pathetic.

As we stepped inside and the door closed behind us, immediately I was aware of the familiar scent of apples. The room was bare except for a few ancient pieces of second-hand furniture. In the middle of the room stood a stove to keep the family warm in winter. The walls were bare. Over the dining table hung a lamp yet unlighted.

Ruth got busy with the drinks. She kept coming in and out of a rear room that must have been the kitchen and soon the table was heavy with food, fried chicken legs and rice, and green peas and corn on the ear. Even as we ate, Ruth kept standing and going to the kitchen for more food. Roger ate like a little gentleman.

"Isn't he nice-looking?" his father asked.

"You are a handsome boy, Roger," I said.

The boy smiled at me. "You look like Daddy," he said.

Afterwards I noticed an old picture leaning on the top of a dresser and stood to pick it up. It was yellow and soiled with many fingerings. The faded figure of a woman in Philippine dress could yet be distinguished although the face had become a blur.

"Your ..." I began.

"I don't know who she is," Fabia hastened to say. "I picked that picture many years ago in a room on La Salle Street in Chicago. I have often wondered who she is."

"The face wasn't a blur in the beginning?"

"Oh, no. It was a young face and good."

Ruth came with a plate full of apples.

"Ah," I cried, picking out a ripe one, "I've been thinking where all the scent of apples came from. The room is full of it."

"I'll show you," said Fabia.

He showed me a backroom, not very big. It was half-full of apples.

"Every day," he explained, "I take some of them to town to sell to the groceries. Prices have been low. I've been losing on the trips."

"These apples will spoil," I said.

"We'll feed them to the pigs."

Then he showed me around the farm. It was twilight now and the apple trees stood bare against a glowing western sky. In apple blossom time it must be lovely here I thought. But what about wintertime?

One day, according to Fabia, a few years ago, before Roger was born, he had an attack of acute appendicitis. It was deep winter. The snow lay heavy everywhere. Ruth was pregnant and none too well herself. At first she did not know what to do. She bundled him in warm clothing and put him on a cot near the stove. She shoveled the snow from their front door and practically carried the suffering man on her shoulders, dragging him through the newly made path towards the road where they waited for the U.S. Mail car to pass. Meanwhile snowflakes poured all over them and she kept rubbing the man's arms and legs as she herself nearly froze to death.

"Go back to the house, Ruth," her husband cried, "you'll freeze to death!"

But she clung to him wordlessly. Even as she massaged his arms and legs, her tears rolled down her cheeks. "I won't leave you, I won't leave you," she repeated.

Finally the U.S. Mail car arrived. The mailman, who knew them well, helped them board the car, and without stopping on his usual route, took the sick man and his wife direct to the nearest hospital.

Ruth stayed in the hospital with Fabia. She slept in a corridor outside the patients' ward and in the daytime helped in scrubbing the floor and washing the dishes and cleaning the men's things. They didn't have enough money and Ruth was willing to work like a slave.

"Ruth's a nice girl," said Fabia, "like our own Filipino women."

Before nightfall, he took me back to the hotel. Ruth and Roger stood at the door holding hands and smiling at me. From inside the room of the shanty, a low light flickered. I had a last glimpse of the apple trees in the orchard under the darkened sky as Fabia backed up the car. And soon we were on our way back to town. The dog had started barking. We could hear it for some time, until finally, we could not hear it anymore, and all was darkness around us, except where the head lamps revealed a stretch of road leading somewhere.

Fabia did not talk this time. I didn't seem to have anything to say myself. But when finally we came to the hotel and I got down, Fabia said, "Well, I guess I won't be seeing you again."

It was dimly lighted in front of the hotel and I could hardly see Fabia's face. Without getting off the car, he moved to where I had sat, and I saw him extend his hand. I gripped it.

"Tell Ruth and Roger," I said, "I love them."

He dropped my hand quickly. "They'll be waiting for me now," he said.

"Look," I said, not knowing why I said it, "one of these days, very soon, I hope, "I hope, I'll be going home. I could go to your town."

"No," he said softly, sounding very much defeated but brave, "Thanks a lot. But, you see, nobody would remember me now."

Then he started the car, and as it moved away, he waved his hand.

"Goodbye," I said, waving back into the darkness. And suddenly the night was cold like winter straying early in these northern woodlands.

I hurried inside. There was a train the next morning that left for Muncie, Indiana, at a quarter after eight.

CECILIA MANGUERRA BRAINARD

CECILIA Manguerra Brainard was born in Cebu, Philippines, the youngest of four children, to Engineer Mariano Manguerra and Concepcion Cuenco Manguerra. She attended St. Theresa's College, Cebu and Manila; and Maryknoll College in Quezon City. In 1969, Cecilia migrated to the U.S. to do graduate work at U.C.L.A. Honolulu was her port of entry; she first stepped on American soil on a Wednesday, March 16.

This was how she became a writer. After her father died when she was nine, she started a diary in which she would sometimes update him on her life. Cecilia published her first short story in high school, but she never dreamed of becoming a fiction writer until a college friend showed her her published story. It was in a major Philippine magazine — very impressive. Cecilia read the story and silently said to herself, "I can do better than this."

At some point in Cecilia's life she found herself with some free time, and she remembered "I can do better ..." She started writing.

Cecilia's stories and essays have been widely published in the U.S. and the Philippines. She has written three books: Woman with Horns and Other Stories *(1988),* Philippine Woman in America *(a collection of essays (1991), and* Song of Yvonne *(first novel, 1991) — all New Day publications. She has been fortunate in receiving several awards including a California Arts Council fellowship in fiction, a City of Los Angeles Cultural Affairs grant, a Brody Arts Fund Award, and a special Recognition Award from the Los Angeles City Board of Educators.*

Her husband is Lauren R. Brainard, a former Peace Corps Volunteer to Leyte, and now a lawyer. They have three sons, Chris, Alex, and Drew. Cecilia also teaches creative writing at UCLA-Extension. She has served in the board and as an officer of PEN USA West, Midnight Special Cultural Center, PAAWWW (Pacific Asian American Women Writers West) and the Arts & Letters at the Cal State University, LA.

In her writings she likes to explore the history of the Filipino, in the Philippines and in America. The following novel excerpt looks at a traumatic period of Philippine history, World War II. It reveals, she thinks, of the strength of the Filipino despite adversity—his sense of humor, his mysticism, his tenacity.

DOC'S CRUCIFIXION

(An excerpt from the novel *Song of Yvonne* also known as *When the Rainbow Goddess Wept*)

Philippines, 1943

PAPA USED his professional voice when he told Doc Mendez it was not a good time to be crucified. "Wait until the war is over. The Americans will soon be here. We just received a report that General Kenney's planes destroyed some Japanese destroyers between Rabaul Harbor and New Guinea. Air and sea lanes in the Southwest Pacific belong to the Allies," Papa said.

"It's God's will, Nando, and I might as well get it done

while there's a lull," replied Doc.

"The Japanese are getting more aggressive, Doc, and there's no telling when the men will need you. Besides, you might damage your hands from the nails."

"Nando, after what happened to my family I went to hell. All of you thought I had lost my mind, and I suppose I appeared to have lost my senses, but I was in hell, Nando. Personally, I would rather have died, but God didn't will it that way. I was alive but burning in hell, and I prayed for salvation. He showed me what to do, Nando, how to pull myself out of that hell. I prayed about this; I have no choice. If the nails go through the metacarpal area in just the right away, there should be no damage."

Papa sighed, remembering Doc as he had been in Mindanao after the massacre of his family. "Doc, if you insist on getting crucified, don't get yourself nailed. You're a doctor and the wounded need you. You can't do much if you're maimed yourself."

Doc considered Papa's words, then went to church and prayed. Finally, he agreed to have himself tied to the cross. He immediately began making arrangements for his crucifixion. I accompanied him to Elpidio, the town's carpenter, whom we found fuming and kicking a wooden coffin.

"What's the matter, friend?" Doc asked.

"It's a long story, Doc, but someone just cancelled an order for a coffin."

"How did that happen, friend?" Doc asked. "Dead people don't return coffins."

"It's this way, Doc," Elpidio explained. "The seamstress Marta's husband ate too many crabs last night and had diarrhea and stomach cramps. Thinking he was dying, Marta called me to measure him so I could make a coffin — the cheapest, she said. I said it would cost four hundred pesos, and right there, in front of her dying husband, she said, 'That's too much. How about two hundred pesos? 'Well, Doc, I may be poor, but I've got dignity. I wasn't about to haggle with that poor man listening, so I said yes —"

"— A dying person's sense of hearing is the last to go,"
I added, remembering what Nida once said about her mother.

"That's right, girlie," Elpidio said, and continued,
"Then as I was leaving, I suggested she call the faith healer. No
offense meant, Doc, but around here, people prefer Mang
Viray."

"It's all right, it's all right," Doc said, waving his hands
in the air. "What did he do?" asked Doc, interested in learning
something new.

"I wasn't there. I was busy making the fucking coffin.
But what I heard is he drew out all his poison."

Doc perked up. "Did it work?"

"Did it work, you ask me? I'm telling you, Marta's
husband got well. Healthier than he'd been in a long time.
Marta came running over to cancel her order for a coffin.
'Excuse me,' I told her, 'but the coffin's done.' Would you
believe it, she refused to pay? Marta's tougher than flint; she
kept whining. 'This is clearly God's will. Would you argue
against God's will?' On and on she went until I got fed up
listening to her." He kicked the side of the coffin.

"Well, friend," Doc said, "don't worry about it, because
I've got a job for you. I need a life-size cross of wood. I'll have
myself crucified this Good Friday."

"Susmaryosep!" exclaimed the carpenter. "I've never
seen a real crucifixion. I've just heard about these fanatics in
Luzon who have themselves hanged every year. Two hundred
pesos, Doc, gold or guerilla notes, none of that fucking
Japanese Mickey Mouse money."

"All right, friend."

I was feeding the chickens when the Virgins — Meding
and Petra Santiago — second cousins of Gil Alvarez, the ones
who had seen the enchanted black giant relieving himself,
stopped by our house one morning. Meding, the older one,
called out, "Yvonne, is Doctor Mendez in?" They must have
just come from church because they smelled of incense and

had their black veils around her shoulders.

After kissing their hands to show respect, I led them to Doc, who was boiling guava leaves for medicine.

"Meding, Petra, how are you? What can I do for you?" Doc beamed as he wiped his hands on a piece of cloth.

Charmed, the Virgins smiled demurely. "Getting old, Doctor, but praise God and the saints, we're doing well," Meding replied. The dry skin on her face crinkled like old leather. She glanced at her sister; they stared at each other for a moment, then I caught the younger one give a slight nod. Meding took a deep breath and continued as if delivering a memorized speech: "Doctor Mendez, we heard about your plans, and we know it's an imposition, but my sister and I have come to request that you walk down Gumamela instead of De Leon. We'd like to see you carrying the cross, Doctor Mendez. Please."

The sisters were remnants of the Santiago family and people related that they had once owned the entire town of Taytayan plus surrounding areas. Mama said their name brought to mind Spanish land grants and sugar cane haciendas. Actually, the sisters were not as rich as they once had been because their father had squandered most of the Santiago fortune on women and liquor. But the sisters still lived comfortably in the oldest house on the other side of town.

They were in their sixties and deeply religious like their mother who died when they were mere children. Never married, the sisters were called "the Virgins," for obvious reasons. Meding, the older one, had a solitary suitor when she was twenty, but when their good-for-nothing father died one dawn in his mistress' house, Meding broke off with the man and vowed to take care of the sickly Petra. Aside from contracting typhus, which made her lose most of her hair, Petra also had asthma and eczema. The townsfolk swore she never attracted a single man in her life.

Even with the war going on and with Cristobal (Gil Alvarez's son) living with them, they continued their regimented life, getting up at five every day, praying, bathing, and making their beds; later Petra attended to the garden while Meding supervised their servant. After breakfast and with Cristobal usually at her heels, they hailed a horse-drawn carriage, did their marketing, and then stopped by San Antonio church to light a candle. Petra would pay one of the women to dance a prayer to the Child Jesus, while Meding (a devotee to our Lady of Carmel) said the rosary in front of the statue of our Lady.

They spent their afternoons washing rags, cutting bandages, and sorting out produce for the guerrilleros. Late in the afternoon, they had their merienda on the verandah with a view of Petra's squashes, tomatoes, cucumbers, string beans, and the single row of calla lilies, the only luxury she allowed herself this wartime. Usually visitors stopped by because the sisters were friendly. The sisters would offer them cassava cakes and inquire about war developments or local gossip. When the sun set and the sawing of the crickets echoed throughout the yard, they had supper. Later they put Cristobal Alvarez to bed, tucking him in like a six-year-old, instead of the eleven-year-old he was. Meding said additional prayers to our Lady of Carmel while Petra ironed clean rags for the hospital. At eleven they said their evening prayers retired.

As she now eyed Doc, Petra coughed, ran her hand through her skimpy hair, and echoed her sister's appeal. "Please, Doctor Mendez, we'd like you to carry the cross by our house."

Embarrassed, Doc said, "Excuse me, Meding and Petra, but that is terribly out of the way. I'll be going the opposite way."

The two sisters fanned themselves in an agitated manner. "Doctor, we know it's a detour, but we are two old ladies who cannot possibly stand on De Leon Avenue under this summer sun to see you. If you walk down Gumamela Avenue, we can at least see you from our balcony."

Doc considered the one-kilometer detour.

Meding fluttered her right hand over her chest. "I'm an old woman, Doctor Mendez, with a weak heart."

Doc sighed and threw his hands up in the air. "All right."

That was one thing with Doc Mendez, he was always willing to accommodate other people. I admired this generosity, but at the same time, I felt that Doc went too much out of his way to help others. That was what had happened when his family was massacred; he had been out helping a pregnant woman. But, I suppose, even if Doc had stayed at home, there was no telling if he could have fought off the Japanese. Chances are, he would have been hacked up like the rest of them. So, altogether, his kindness towards others saved him. As people say, "Fate pretty much determines things."

Summer and lent went together, and you knew it was summer by the way the breeze turned warm, so warm it took your breath away.

Even though it was wartime, it was a colorful kind of hot, with mounds of fruit of riotous colors displayed on rickety wooden stalls in the outdoor market. It was a rainbow sort of hot that not even the war could destroy — flowers displaying petals of magenta, yellow, tangerine, and chartreuse. It was the sort of hot that made ladies expose luscious brown shoulders and knees as they sighed, "Susmaryosep" — Jesus-Maria-Joseph; and they shimmered under the rippling sun.

When Holy Thursday came around, the entire town knew about Doc's plans. A community spirit gripped the people and even the stingy seamstress, Marta (the one who had returned the coffin to Elpidio the carpenter) surprised us all when she donated costumes for the participants of this real Passion play. She sewed a brown sack robe for Doc, and another brown robe for Max who played Simon. There were two Roman soldiers who would help with the crucifixion. The residents of Gumamela Avenue decorated their street with sampaguita flowers, woven palm leaves and freshly cut banana trees with enormous bunches of bananas. Even the shy Good Shepherd Sisters dragged benches against the high wall surrounding their convent to catch a glimpse of Doc as he walked by carrying his cross.

For a while, war was forgotten, and a fiesta spirit overtook Taytayan. Even my parents, who had been convinced a crucifixion was a fanatical idea, wavered and I overheard Mama say, "He blames himself for what happened to his family, and he wants forgiveness."

Papa nodded in agreement. "I guess, Angeling, we all have sins that we could use forgiveness for."

Good Friday, I woke up at dawn, excited over Doc's crucifixion. I had never witnessed such a spectacle. I looked at the silver crucifix above the doorway and tried to imagine Doc looking like Christ. When light filtered the room, I hurried to the kitchen where I found Doc having his breakfast. "Yvonne, I had the loveliest dream," he announced. "It was about Jesusa and the children."

"Did your wife say something, Doc? Laydan said dreams talk to us," I said.

"Well, Yvonne, I don't remember all the details, but I do recall the flavor of the dream. There she stood with the children, and they were smiling and waving at me. If this dream talked to me, it would have been something good, Yvonne."

We continued chatting until we heard the noise of people outside. Townsfolk were congregating around our house and along Gumamela Avenue to see Doc carry his cross. His cross was outside; everything was ready, and after donning the brown sackcloth, he excitedly picked up his cross and propped it on his right shoulder. With Max beside him and the rest of us trailing behind, Doc begun dragging his cross.

It was a warm day and preparation dripped down Doc's face. At first he kidded, "What kind of wood is this? It would have been nice if this were made of balsa." Max and Nida took turns wiping his face, and twice I broke him off from the procession to ask for a glass of juice or water for Doc from the people who generously obliged.

At the end of Gumamela Avenue, the Virgins, with Cristobal shrinking behind them, stood on their balcony, grinning and waving at Doc and the crowd. Doc nodded a greeting, then he made a U-turn to return to De Leon Avenue. It was at this point when his breathing grew shallow. He stumbled once, but Max took the cross from Doc to allow him to catch his breath. After a few seconds, they marched on, past the Good Shepherds Sisters who peeked over their high wall.

By the time we reached Mount Buntis, Doc was grimacing in pain. Salty sweat rolled into his eyes, blinding him at times. I had never seen Doc look so tired and I was getting worried. When he fell at the summit, Nida wanted to call the whole thing off, but the people booed and several threw pebbles at Doc.

"Hey, I risked my life walking through enemy territory just to see him. If he wants to be crucified, let him be crucified. It's his promised to God anyhow."

"He's right," Doc whispered, "it is my promise. Let's continue. I'm okay."

"Doc, you don't look good," Max said.

"I'll be fine, Max."

He lay on the wooden cross and Max tied his hands and feet to the cross. When Max and two other men propped up the cross, Doc groaned, but he nodded his head to indicate that everything was all right. We stood staring at him bound to that enormous wooden cross. It was a rather remarkable sight, with the hot summer sky above him. I thought to myself that surely whatever Doc owed God, whatever sins he had committed, whatever it was that he needed salvation for, was now being paid for. Doc was magnificent on that cross.

He was up there for a full seven minutes before Mama noticed that he had stopped breathing. "Look at him, look at him, he's not moving," Mama shouted. Because she was rather high-strung, the men didn't take her seriously. But when Doc remained still even as a bee buzzed in front of his nose, I said, "Mama's right." Papa studied Doc and ordered the men to bring the cross down quickly. Mang Viray, the faith healer, hurriedly checked Doc's pulse. He furrowed his brows as he ran his fingers over Doc's wrist, temple, and neck. Then he confirmed my mother's observation. "He's dead," he said simply.

The people gasped in disbelief at Mang Viray's words, making me confident that the faith healer had made a mistake. Mama made the sign of the cross while Nida pulled at the rope around Doc's hands. The people were pushing, shoving but I kept my ground near Doc. I observed Doc's chest to see it if rose and fell, but it did not move at all. As people milled about not knowing what to do, I ran to Doc and pounded on his chest. That was one thing with dead people, they did not move. If Doc's chest would only move — if it would only go up and down —

"Yvonne, stop it!" Mama said. "Nando, Nando, do something."

Papa pulled me away. "It's no use," he said, as he held me close to him. I could smell my Papa's sweat, feel his warmth. "We'll take him home," he called out to the men.

My arms were wrapped around my father. I discovered that if my eyes were closed, I could blot out the world around me. It was all a silly mistake; Doc was fine. He was just tired from the walk. It was all because of the silly Virgins, asking him to make that detour.

Papa picked me up and started carrying me home. I felt tired, and I could hear father's voice echo in my head as he told people to clear the path for Doc's body.

Later he put me down, and hand in hand we walked ahead of the men carrying Doc's body on their shoulders.

"He's all right, isn't he?" I insisted.

"Child, Doc's gone."

"Where?" I looked back at Doc's body with his arms dangling like pendulums. The hot summer air felt oppressive.

"He's dead, child," Papa repeated.

"But there's no blood." That was the other thing with dead people; they usually had blood on them. There was no blood; surely he was still alive.

"It is good that he fulfilled his promise," Papa continued in a soft voice. "A man is only worth his word."

Farther down the road, Elpidio the carpenter — with the extra coffin — practicallly danced around us while dropping broad hints about his available coffin. Unable to hold himself back, he finally approached my father and said he'd sell the extra coffin to us for a hundred pesos, a steal, he insisted. It was too much, even for my patient father, and he snapped, "We'll discuss it later on."

The idea of this man trying to get rid of the ill-starred coffin made me feel like giggling. There he was, a grownup, behaving that way. It was rather funny, and I could feel myself on the verge of a giggling fit. Holding myself back, I remarked, "Pa, he's embarrassing himself."

"He's poor, child. Poverty makes people do all sorts of demeaning things." Papa's voice had softened; he had already forgiven the ridiculous carpenter.

Later I could barely look at Doc lying in his cot, totally limp and lifeless. I saw Doc crazed; I saw him pull himself together and use his talents to ease other people's purgatory. He was a good man, and something inside of me felt like it was cracking. Doc was gone, I told myself over and over to comprehend this reality. Another one dead. We were all dying one by one. We were gnats that lived for a moment, then fluttered down dead to the brown earth. Still, he did fulfill his promise to God, and what was that Papa said? — A man is only as good as his word. Doc's word was always good.

The women wept unashamedly as they removed his brown sackcloth. Mama kept repeating he shouldn't have done it, that it was a foolish thing to do, that she had been against the idea in the first place. Nida, who had special affection for Doc, was too overcome with sorrow to speak.

"We had better wash him before he turns stiff," Mama said.

Stiff — I had forgotten that a person turned rigid after death. Once Laydan told me of how mountain people handled their dead. They tied their dead to a chair near the entrance of their house. There the person stayed for three, four days. Meanwhile, the corpse slowly bloated up, and sometimes quite suddenly, the fattened thighs would force the legs apart so it seemed the corpse moved. Then body fluids oozed out of the openings — eyes, nose, mouth, ears — at which time people plugged up these openings with cloth. And meanwhile, the stench increased. All this happened to the dead man strapped to the chair by the doorway; he was a kind of spirit guard so nothing evil slipped into the home. Then eventually, when the body was no longer recognizable, the people buried the corpse. Later, much later, they dug him up, cleaned his bones, and placed these in an enormous jar.

Was Doc really turning stiff? I chased away the mental image of his bloating corpse. I studied his body; he appeared as though he were merely sleeping. The women had composed themselves, and they had a basin of water, a wash cloth, and some soap, and they began cleaning Doc. I was pondering the melancholia of the moment, when the women suddenly screamed, dropping the basin with a clatter. I looked at Doc's naked body and saw that he was developing an enormous erection. As they stared at Doc's organ that had miraculously stirred to life, the women continued screaming, but they recovered and quickly threw a sheet over him before the men arrived. Doc heaved a deep sigh, than sat up and calmly said, I'm so hungry. Could I have some bitter melon and rice?"

Doc was alive! Suddenly the air turned light and clean, and sparkling sunshine streamed into the room. My soul within me expanded.

While shoveling the food into his mouth, Doc described what had happened. It was like a dream, he said. He was carrying his cross up a steep hill. The cross was heavy and, growing tired, he wished he could get to the top where he wanted to be. Sweating profusely, with constricted chest, he climbed on. Near the peak, he found a stream blocking his path. He was deciding whether he'd wade across, when a woman called him from across the stream. It was his wife, with their three children skipping around her. They appeared lovely with golden auras, like angels without wings. Doc started to cross the stream, but his wife shook her head. "Go back, it's not time yet." It was at that moment when Doc sat up.

I observed Doc eating with a tremendous appetite. He was perspiring from his frenzy to satisfy his hunger. I dished out more food, and he smiled at me. Yes, Doc was alive! And I grinned back at him.

Even as Nida's belly grew, no one discussed her condition. She had gotten rid of her pallid look and her nausea; now she had a lovely flush on her cheeks and a rounded belly. Everyone knew she carried life in her, everyone, that is, except her husband Max. Max had slowed down; the war had been unkind to the aging boxer. Once he had been a young warrior, but now he was too old for the fighting, the discomfort, the nerve-wracking uncertainty, the pain and illnesses surrounding him. He himself had contracted malaria, and even though Doc gave him quinine, Max never really recovered and was prone to shivering and sweating. Once a hefty man, he had become a gaunt. Once strong with an easy laugh, he had become morose and talked often of his mortality. It was not that Max was afraid to die, because death he said was a brief matter. It is easier to die than to live, he often said. What concerned Max was that one day he would die and leave nothing of himself behind.

"There is a cycle in nature," he pointed out once. "Look at the trees, see how they drop seed that grow into other trees; look at the animals and observe how they reproduce. They continue to live, but I, when I die, I will be gone forever." He was referring to the fact that he and Nida had never had children. Now with Nida being the way she was, things became rather awkward, and so we all kept quiet, leaving it up to Nida to tell Max, or to Nature, for surely one day soon, the size of her stomach would reveal it all.

One night after Doc's crucifixion, Nida gathered enough nerve to talk to Max. "Max," she blurted out during supper with everybody listening, "I'm pregnant."

Max blinked his eyes, like a startled turtle. His nose that leaned to his cheek flared.

Nida continued, "It's not yours, Max. The father's not anyone you know. All I can say is that I'm this way because I had to do what I had to do."

The silence in the dining room was broken only by the sawing of the crickets outside.

Doc, who had acquired a special status after his resurrection, came to Nida's rescue. He cleared his throat and with a scholarly voice said, "It's a fine child, Max. Nida has fine pink aura surrounding her. A fine child."

"I wanted to get rid of it. I already made arrangements with the midwife, but I couldn't do it, Max. When it moved inside of me, I knew it had its own life. It moved, Max, inside of me, and I couldn't kill it." Nida placed both hands on her protruding stomach. Her lower jaw jutted out with determination.

Max remained quiet. He was staring at Nida with an expression that was difficult to decipher. I wasn't sure if he was going to hit her, or if he was going to weep. Very slowly he got up and walked toward Nida. He put his arms around her, grit his teeth and begun crying.

"I'll dish out more rice," Mama said, as she hurriedly left the dining table.

"Well, now, I have some work to do," Papa said, also leaving the table. "Go get the map, Yvonne."

Everyone trickled away leaving Max and Nida alone. In the next room, our ears were cocked, but all we heard was Max's sobbing.

The next day, before the men returned to the mountains, I saw Max and Nida under the enchanted jackfruit tree. Max had his right ear against Nida's stomach, while Nida stroked his head. Max was happy. I had to shake my head in wonder at how life poked fun at Max. He went to America to be a famous boxer, and he drove a cab and never found fame. He returned to the Philippines to marry the sweet passive Filipina of his dreams, but he fell in love with Nida, a woman with a past. Max and Nida were childless, and now life presented them with a Japanese soldier's bastard. But they accepted what life offered them, welcomed it, with mind-boggling joy. Max kissed Nida and lingered beside her for as long as he could before he finally left.

MANUEL A. VIRAY

MANUEL A. Viray is the author of Shawl from Kashmir *(collection of short stories); and three books of poetry,* After This Exile, Morning Song, *and* The Automatic Glass Door.

Epistolary Criticism, *edited by the American literary critic, L.M. Grow, is a collection of literary critiques as culled from Viray's letters to Bienvenido N. Santos and Dr. Grow himself.*

He was born on April 13, 1917, and received his Ph.B. From the University of the Philippines in 1936.

He is a retired Philippine Foreign Service official who served in Philippine embassies abroad: Washington, D.C.; Djakarta, Indonesia; Bonne-Bag Godesberg, Germany. His last post was Philippine Ambassador to Cambodia, where he stayed until its capital, Phnom Penh, fell to the Khmer Rouge.

He resides in Norfolk, Virginia, where he is now working on a book of essays.

LAPSE

Nazario Munzon

HE STOOD at the bustling corner of Perdigon and Eden, the back of this thin undershirt drenched with sweat, after the early twenty-minute walk through the scarred, sometimes unidentifiable streets of the tragic city. Deliberately, lest his appointment and equanimity be disrupted by another glimpse of Magdalena, he refused to turn around to see the Dew-Drop Inn, with its cheap facade and challenging feel. Both streets had already assumed their heedless vitality; both had turned alive with groups of arriving GIs with their eager looks; girls with tired eyes shambling inside the bar; music scratchy, jerky, blaring. He peered at the long line of advancing jeepneys. Most of them were full of passengers. He was eager to get on.

It was only after some time had lapsed that Nazario Munzon realized that men are confined in a world of their own diminution and failures.

There had been some opposition to his plans for the day. But it was done and over with.

He was going down the crumbling stone steps, a little confusion in his blood since the day previous he had told his child and his sister-in-law about the job. He saw his hands trembling; he felt again his blood slowly returning to his lips. He had paled as he argued with his mother-in-law. Yet as he went down the steps, he felt all his senses functioning smoothly, ordering the simultaneous shock of the world of morning impressions — the warm sunlight on his hairy arms and sunken cheeks; the surprising but faint breeze cooling his smarting eyes and the tiny beads of perspiration — the impact blunting his visibility. Watching his eight-year-old Ana playing gleefully with a neighbor's child in the shabby yard, he could see himself in her place on one end of the raveled, weather-fretted seesaw, rising and declining with every tilt of the inclined plane with the girl on the opposite side, merging and mingling with the sad and shaking landscape before him: the cruel sunlight revealing the shambles of a wall of the house across the street, the filthy yard with the starved grass, the swaying fence, and the white painted cross shadowed by the kitchen which marked the emergency grave of the once vivacious girl who had been hit by a shrapnel from the Japanese artillery on the south side of the river.

Sunlight did not seem as equivocal as it had been two months ago, although it shone every day with maddening clarity and could not keep secret the lingering evidence of military operations in this particular area of their own desolation.

In children or perhaps in the womb, or further back, in dreams of love and lust, he thought, begin our responsibilities. He had put Ana during the Occupation in the first grade at St. Catherine's but on the very first day she had come home walking — alone — crossing the Rotunda and the busy avenue, clogged with rattling enemy tanks, heavily booted Japanese soldiers, whirring rigs. She had protested: she was not going back to school since even the Sisters had been compelled to teach Nippongo.

But this morning they had thin gruel. Smoked fish. Salt. He could still see the askant eyes of the kid, the sharp outline of her cheeks, her thin neck with the blue veins showing, the prominent clavicle.

But in his family, no one protested. Not Ana; not Magdalena, his sister-in-law; only his mother-in-law.

He could still hear the rocking of her chair, now softer and more regular, sounding as it had subsided with her final assent and unspoken reconciliation with the unpredictable turn of things.

He was going to get a job. At last. After three and a half weeks. Hadn't Major Dent assured him about it? Hadn't Flora?

He leaped over the runnel of water flowing sluggishly

with its slime, micturation, rolled paper, pieces of stick. Down the length of their street, white in the glaring light, he could see again the three girls, whom he had seen on the day they first arrived in the City. They were outlined against the warehouse, their dresses as tattered as their emotions, drawing water through a manhole from some broken pipe of the city's water supply.

"I'll have to pass by Guipit for our drinking water this afternoon," he thought.

Then he was on the edge of the national highway, after having swung around a shirtless, loquacious hooligan trying to attract pedestrians to bet on beto-beto. In his hands there were three twenty-peso Victory notes.

Crossing the highway's island, he saw again the dark empty lot, pockmarked with holes. Weeks ago, the GIs had camped there with their sweating, half-naked bodies, long Toms, and bazookas, consistently, impatiently shelling Intramuros.

It seemed strange to him that what had happened passed like some fitful dream, without any emotional quality at all. And he remembered that one could not, contrary to what the writers claimed, possibly label as nightmare his experience or that of others, who had fled and returned with every remorseless tide of the war. Men readily call their tight, collective experience a nightmare, since the term is a part of common lexicon. Perhaps, reality is only a nightmare since it is impossible to rationalize about a swift progression of mortal events with all its implications of danger and the hot breath of death.

Everyone had said they would all be safe in that sleepy, small-town at the foot of the mountains. In the last war, one had averred, the Americans never came here. No, one, however, could have foretold that the Japanese in this war would make a last desperate stand in the mountains.

For, clearly, the Americans had known of the Simbun line. One morning in early February, a helicopter had appeared over town. Minutes later, artillery shelled the church and the presidencia. The firing went on fiercely at regular intervals for two more days and nights.

He had fled with his family to the hills north of the town, not even daring to go back for the half-cavan of rice they had left behind in the air-raid shelter.

The morning after that, they had trekked toward Sibul, arriving at the dam on Monday. Wednesday morning, inevitably, helplessly drawn by the clamor and argument of other evacuees, they decided to hitch a ride on one of the lumbering army trucks shuttling between Sibul and Manila, transporting food and ammunition.

Only his mother-in-law and Ana were able to get a ride. The driver had seen him helping his mother-in-law and Ana's pale and seared look. He and his sister-in-law had been left behind. As he recalled it, Ana had bravely said, "I'll be all right, Papa, don't worry."

"Take care of your Lola." His voice had been lost in swirling dust as the truck suddenly lurched forward.

There were dozen others with them as they straggled on the lonely highway in the blazing heat. It was past noon before they were able to get a ride. Under a noonday sun, he and his sister-in-law huddled with the others in the shaking truck. It brought them as far as Extremadura. From Extremadura they had walked on to Poniente Boulevard. His shoulders ached from the weight of the buri bags filled with their clothes, bundles of blankets, jars of salted horsemeat and fish. They had overtaken two boys — pushing a cart loaded with burnt timber and rusty corrugated iron roofing — who had been kind enough to let them place their bags atop the roofing.

"We are going as far as San Salvador," one of the boys had said.

"The Japanese passed through here, didn't they?"

Yes, they had. Many people were herded and killed there during the retreat, the other one explained, as he braked with two hands the speed of the pushcart on the sloping road.

Zar remembered that then he saw on the left side of

the road a crumpled Japanese tank. And a few yards away, barely perceptible in the thick clump of talahib, lay the body of a Japanese soldier, his legs and arms now black stumps, his face unrecognizable in the anonymity of death and burning.

"Zar," his sister-in-law had said, "my stomach. It's about to turn." She, too, had seen the dead one.

After San Salvador, they had wearily dragged themselves to the blown-up bridge of Reposo. The riverbed was dry. It was the beginning of the hot season. They were able to convince two American MPs in a shiny compact jeep to drive them to their place. It was just two blocks after that bend of the road.

On the first night the city, his mother-in-law moaned constantly. Long paralyzed — her right leg it was — she felt her failing eyes bothering her. There were plenty of night insects: mosquitoes, beetles. They had been able to salvage only few things. They had slept on the floor, under a dark-green mosquito net full of holes and smelling of their long journey. It had been with a brief realization of the senseless suffering, common disabled times, that he suddenly felt one is never able to foresee the true nature of the future. What they had left behind in the evacuation center had been their best possessions. He saw the disorder in the house.

"Let's put the house in order." And Ana had said, "Yes, Papa." Magdalena, his sister-in-law, also said, "Yes," and immediately started dusting the furniture and counting the plates and pans they had left behind in the wobbly cabinet. He sounded as if his wife, Maria, was still around. He could not help himself. Maria was not here. She had died in '43 of gastroenteritis.

Magdalena was a few inches shorter than Maria, but she was fairer. Her gentleness had stemmed, he thought, more from an inherent awareness of good and evil, than from the long years of training she spent in Hong Kong, where she had attended an exclusive religious school for girls. She still spoke with a perceptible British accent. At one time or another, he had caught himself admiring the contour of her shapely neck

65

and shoulders as when she washed their clothes in the shallow river of the evacuation town or play of the sunlight on her dark hair and cheeks as she wheedled Ana into eating part of her own rations for the day. While Magdalena cajoled Ana into eating her own share, he had seen the greedy look of his mother-in-law on the steaming rice and the pieces of carabao meat floating on the soup mixed with radish and pechay leaves.

He had stridden up the street, thinking he would save money if he walked up to Perdigon and Eden. From there I can get a jeepney for the South Harbor. If I get the job, it will not be so bad.

He had walked past many streets, most of them full of craters, many a dead building, then the line of liquor stores, restaurants, and bars.

How many times in the past three, four weeks had he trudged these same streets, broken, shelled, nameless, dusty, desolate, looking for a job after that fiasco in the Ministry of Agriculture? His former chief who claimed he had not worked for the Occupation government had received him coldly, and curtly said: "You collaborated. You cannot get your job back. Why come here?"

He had been too angry to reply. He had gone out silently, a fierce anger in his breast, like some heavy lump of stone; only when he had reached the Ministry gate was he able to reassemble his thoughts and scourged feelings to think of a suitable reply. He should have said: "Hell, *you* collaborated, too. You sold rice and machinery to the enemy. Not in your name of course. But in your wife's name.

He deliberately turned his back to the door of the Dew-Drop Inn. It was the next bar from the corner. Like the other bars and restaurants spawned by Liberation on the entire length of Perdigon and Eden, it was smokey, crowded, a little dark, but full of reckless and heady movement. Its strident music merged with others: its ornate mirror reflected the heedless talk, the shrieking laughter, the shuffling movements of young American soldiers and stolid Blacks. He dared not peer inside. He did want to see Flora again. If I do, I'll ask her again about her son. I'll press her for details. I'll ask where he is buried, he thought.

He had met Flora in his last year in college. She was working in a nightclub. This was two years before his marriage to Maria. He had gone to Albay. When he came back, married to Maria, Flora had called him up over the telephone. She had already delivered. "But you didn't tell me," he said. "I didn't know where you were." Then, anxiously, "How is he?"

"He looks like you. Your splitting image."

Zar had told her about Maria. She said she understood. I only called you up, she said. In the end, although she said she did not want anything, Zar had written his father for a loan, given it to Flora, "until you find something."

He had seen Flora three days ago. He had tramped the alleys and streets. Then he had espied her amid the bustle of the noisy street.

He thought he had seen his kid brother Jimmy enter the door and had followed the figure to the bar. He had been mistaken. When he stepped across the door, he heard someone cry out his name — in gladness and welcome. It was Flora. She turned around her stool, shapely legs crossed, a cigarette — most probably Philip Morris —I n her hand. A bulky Major, seated on the stool beside hers, had his pale blue eyes turned towards him, too. She had run forward, embraced him tightly, softly saying, Zar, Zar. You had to admire her quick thinking. When she had disentangled her warm arms, the faintest trace of a mist in her dark eyes, she had told the Major, This is Zar Munzon. My half-brother. We've not seen each other since '41. Here. Zar, let's get a table," and the Major appeared content, although his eyes betrayed his wish for further revelation. He had excused himself so that he could, as he laughingly said, go to the "King's Room. Too much beer."

"Oke doke," Flora had said, pulling him down towards an empty table, adroitly slithering through jostling soldiers, the thick cigarette smoke, the babble of talk.

"That's Major Dent."

"*He's* Major Dent," Zar said, smiling, correcting her

language, and she had smiled. "Zar. Zar. Always the precise, the language-conscious Zar."

Abruptly, he said, "How did it happen?"

Flora knew him in more ways than one: his moods, his line of thinking. He, too, knew Flora. Impulsive, but never mercurial. Fiery in bed, gentle with people she deeply loved.

What happened to us should not have happened, he thought, waiting for her answer, and unconsciously comparing the shape of her shoulders and hips to Maria, his dead wife, and of Magdalena, with her delicate features, small but firm breasts, and small hips.

"I could not keep track of them. We almost died of hunger. The morning the tanks lined up at the University, I found out that he had gone with the other boys to the supply depot. A sniper saw him. He got it in the neck."

"I don't blame you for looking like that," Flora continued. It seemed funny that her lips moved as if compelled by her own peculiar brand of loneliness and kindness. "We have never been able to help ourselves, have we?"

Major Dent came back and seated himself beside Flora.

The next moment, as he briefly recounted what happened to her and the boy, she breathlessly interspersed her recital in English with the vernacular.

"Was this the same Flor Mortal I used to know years ago?" Zar asked himself silently. The clear forehead; the curly brownish hair; sensuous lower lip; the long, dark eyelashes; and the large mole on the right cheek -- all were still there. But two deep lines dragged themselves from each side of her nose, slanted down both sides of her full lips. Her eyes still smiled. But perhaps the smile was forced. One had to make a living nowadays.

A drunken sailor toppled at the next table.

In deference to the Major who was quaffing his beer with a certain kind of deliberate patience, sometimes he looked at him and smiled.

"And your family?"

Zar said they were all alive. "You know, of course, that

Mary died, gastroenteritis in '43. There are four of us now. My mother-in-law."

"I know," said Flora, laughing suddenly as if the memory would trap her now. "The high and mighty. The religious Teresa Vda. De Morales."

Zar nodded. "My sister-in-law, Magdalena."

"The convent girl."

"And me."

"And Ana? How is she?"

"Thin. Hungry like the rest of us."

"But you have your job back," there was an edge of anxiety in her voice, the same characteristic gesture of concern she showed when he first knew her.

"No. Couldn't get it back. Collaborators are not needed in the government, didn't you know? I've been tramping the streets for almost two months now."

"But that's fine. The Major here was telling me just a few minutes ago if I could find a personnel assistant for him. He is with Base R. Out at the South Harbor. Major —"

Zar looked at the Major more closely. He was the beefy type. Red hair, reddish face, thick eyebrows, but with a look which to Zar, appeared to stare above and beyond his head, as if he were thinking of something. America, perhaps, Guadalcanal, Australia.

"You still need a personal assistant, Major Dent?" Flora said.

"Why, yes," the Major was jerked out of his reverie, a smile appearing automatically on his face. He looked at Zar. "You have administrative experience, of course."

"Ten years, Major." Without his knowing it, Zar's reply had become more effective because of its modest pitch. And he felt that he would get the job.

"You'll do." The Major turned around his glass. "See me tomorrow at ten. I'll wait for you. Fill up the forms. You know. Matter of routine. You can start right away."

"Gee ..." but before Zar could continue his sudden lapse into the American idiom. Flora quickly inquired the

Major how much the job would bring.

"I'd say, three-fifty, four." He looked at Flora fondly and fondled her hand.

"Thanks a lot, Major."

"See you at ten, then, tomorrow."

"Check," Zar said, feeling elation rising up as if from nowhere and warming his turgid blood. "Well," he extended his hand, "Goodbye."

"Why don't you drop in at the house one of these days?" Flora said.

Zar had a hard time stifling an impulse to look at Major Dent, especially at the leather belt wound tight around the bulging girth. He was not certain whether Flora was living with the Major. He banished both thought and impulse. Maybe the Major was just a casual costumer. He supposed, however, that with the Major's intelligence, he had already caught a drift of their conversation. He; Flora; the dead boy.

"Thanks for the drinks," he said.

"Drop by some time here, Zar," Flora said.

"I will." It was easy to make promises. War and the Occupation had taught him to slide over superficial; complications, unless they directly threatened the regular pulsing of the heart, were not as fatal as one imagined them to be. In any case, the debris of the war had orphaned men and emotions, and while death appeared everywhere, at least operations had now shifted to Okinawa and Japan. The clutch of danger had relaxed.

He hurried home, rushed up the stone steps, clasped Ana, and seeing Magdalena, who had just come out of the kitchen, said, "At last. I am going to have a job."

"But how it happen? How come?

Before he knew it, he had blurted out the whole truth in tumbling syllables.

The moment his mother-in-law heard of the name Flora, a grimness appeared on her thin lips. But there was no backing out now.

"Don't take the job. I won't have it. I would rather

starve." The old woman was angry.

"But it's a good chance. After all, there's no money in the house."

"She only tried to help."

"That's right, Mother, she was only trying to help Zar," Magdalena interrupted.

"Not from a slut. Hers is tainted money."

"She's not anything of the kind," Zar cried. "Besides, she was not the one who offered me the job. It was the Major. Major Dent."

"No," his mother-in-law snapped, the veins on her forehead, blue, rising, pulsing. "No. No."

"But, after all, Mother, it could have been any other person — a friend of Zar — who would have told him about the job. It's not Zar's fault if Flora unwittingly became the instrument of his good fortune."

His mother-in-law's sternness was now tightly locked with her fierce, moral code and flaming anger.

He strode into the kitchen. He opened the tap with a kind of habitual reflex. There was no water. He grabbed a can of water on the sink and savagely poured it over his throbbing head and flushed face. He looked out of the window, the drops of water streaming from his hair down his neck. He gripped the sill.

"Papa." Ana was suddenly beside him. "You wasted the water for the sinigang."

"I know. It's warm. I wanted to cool my face."

"I'll go down and draw water from the broken pipe."

"All right." He patted her head again gently.

He went to the window. The sun shimmered before his dazed eyes. Ricocheting over the other roof-tops, the rays brought out the dazzling blue of the skies.

Then he went back into the living room and patiently and slowly explained how impossible it was to go on living as they did, how impossible it seemed to get a job. Here was a chance. "You know that I can't get my job back at the Ministry." He kept his anger to himself with a stern will.

"When things get stabilized, I'll get that Ministry job back, I promise."

"He's right, Mother," Magdalena said. "I'll buy you steak. We'll not be eating salted fish all the time. Look at your grandchild. She'll get sick if I don't get a job."

Zar did not wait for his mother-in-law's reply. He left the hall again.

He went into the room, pretended to look at the beddings. He went into the next room and picked out from the shelf the book on office management. Warily, he looked at his mother-in-law from the corner of his eye. He could see the slow rocking chair, to which she had been exiled because of her paralyzed leg. Her anger, her impatience had receded. He saw her slit eyes following Ana as the child came up the stairs carrying the pail of water.

Teresa Vda. de Morales

If only my husband were alive today. In her helplessness and reconciliation, she kept knitting steadily. She dropped a stitch as her spectacles with the faded frame slid over her nose. On her lap the bedspread lay, its butterfly pattern delicately and effectively limned against her dark skirt. Her bad leg had twitched when Zar had mentioned Flora.

What can the old do? The house in Legazpi had been sold years ago. She could still see her children romping in the yard, the sun lighting the perfect cone of the volcano, the wind restless against the trellis and the waving leaves of the plants. Now all of them dead save Magdalena. She could still see her husband coming home from the warehouse with his riding crop and tousled hair in the wind. He, too, was dead. She had not seen his grave for two decades. The inscriptions of memory remain. Mary, with the dimpled cheek, in the North Cemetery. Raymundo, the quick, mercurial one, drowned at sea, resting forever in the alien soil – Hong Kong. Pecto, who had been with the United States Navy – buried beside her father. Theirs have been short exiles. Magdalena's and mine are long ones. She used to go to church every morning. The stations. The weekly confessions. Father Calderon at the moss-covered Dominican church; Father Destry at the church on the hill. Then her leg numbed, paralyzed.

One can lift, use one's hands, but one cannot rise anymore. Not with a paralyzed leg. We are all infirm. There is a lack in us that we would like to forget the rest of our sleeping and waking hours, but which we can never remedy nor evade. What does one do during a war? Reluctantly, she remembered Zar carrying her gently, carefully across the shallow river into the hills and his voice saying, "Come on, Mother. We've got to make the other side." There was that long, lurching ride on the truck, with Ana beside her, docile, quiet. She remembered, too, how much more patient Zar had become since Maria's death. Sometimes he slyly sacrificed his own food. Now he would give her his own juicy piece of steak. Now he would give it to Ana. I suppose that the disorder and the cruelty in the world cannot be helped. There are certain things a man is supposed to do. And he does it out of generosity and kindness. This diminution, this disorder, this cruelty Zar did not help bring about. They are not of his own making. Where would Magdalena and I be if it had not been for him? Not in Albay. All our relations by now are dead. We cannot help ourselves. She dropped her needles and reached for her rosary. I wonder if Zar would marry Magdalena. It would be good for the child. A crafty smile came to her wrinkled face. She started praying as the crass sounds from the street below drifted upwards and reminded her time was lapsing relentlessly out of her hands.

Her right leg twitched again. Her failing eyes would soon close. Perhaps, she thought, it is just as well. Most men are never able to impose any kind of surcease on regret, any kind of order on instability of the world, nor can they undo what seems to be a blemish in their mortal hearts, a flaw in their will.

Magdalena Morales

She had not slept because of the sudden outburst the day before. She thought her own world would collapse with her mother's anger. But Zar had handled the situation tactfully. He had left the conversation dangling where it was. Like him, she was sure that her Mother had been defeated. But it was in her nature that she accepted her defeat, no matter how disastrous, in silence. Zar, on the other hand, acted in a similar way. He knew he had won, but he never flaunted his victory. He had hurriedly dressed up early in the morning and said he was going to get drinking water from his cousin who stayed at Guipit. There was an artesian well there, Dal remembered. It was Zar who kept her family together. She and her mother. The time of her adolescence was past.

The house needed cleaning and scrubbing. The dust and cobwebs on the ceiling. But there was no maid. There was a straggling semblance of order in the house. There was a scarred table in the dining room; the four chairs, two with rotten bottoms, were a little shaky; the creaking rocking chair; the sewing machine; the sofa where Ana often sprawled, rereading a dog-eared Aesop. How many fables there are in the world, I'll never know. One can only wish that, in the glitter of castles, the sleeping Princess would wake up at once. But outside, the sunlight is clear and sharp; the street despoiled. Time shifts constantly. Funny, but at this time she could see herself an awkward girl in that school in Hong Kong. Sisters praying, the cursive handwriting on the blackboards, the lifting fog, the hungry Chinese coolies, the slow ships docking at the harbor, the afternoons of cracking between her young teeth salted melon seeds, the luscious autumn cakes, a trek through the hills of her own country with Ana, her niece. Father coming in one of the ships they used to own.

Sometimes, she thought, Ana looked more like her than her sister, her dead sister Maria. It's a pity that the child is lonely. Perhaps if Maria were alive, but Dal knew it was useless protesting. The Sisters had taught her and the others well.

Patience. Faith. Charity, but, above all, patience. These virtues do not shore up when your emotions get awry, Sister. When you look at your brother-in-law, you can hardly analyze how you feel. You know you are farthest from his heart and you concentrate your attention, even in a number of trivial ways, on your ailing mother and his child, trying as much as possible to ease his pain, to help him ride over a panic, to smoothen a violent scene which catches him in its vortex.

That February night, she could see the scene again; they had crouched under the house. Near the air-raid shelter. Cowering under the first salvo, as though the gesture would insure their safety, she had felt the tight grip of Ana's fears. The shelling became regular. It arched over them with its piercing whistle, its blop, blop, at the end, resounding, it seemed to her, on the town square, blowing it to fragments. The arc had shortened. There had been a tearing noise, culminating as she learned later, on the concrete house on the street where they were.

"Ma, Ana, Dal, let's get going," Zar had suddenly cried. "The next shot may fall on us."

She had grabbed Ana, in some kind of panic, responding to the urgency in Zar's voice. She slid over the bamboo gate. "Did you get the bag?" Zar had asked, following her, her mother in his arms. That meant the jewels and the money belts. "Let's go in the direction of the artillery. Damn these Americans. Don't they know the town is full of civilians?"

Out in the narrow and dusty street, the momentary flash of weak starlight and tracer bullets showed a surging crowd going in the same direction he said they would take, and muttering almost the same identical things. Hurriedly he had whispered to her to keep near him. There are brigands, even among our people, rapists. Keep near me, he had said. There was no time to think of anything else. Not pillows, blankets, mats, clothes, food.

"Let's wait for the artillery to subside," he said. "Tomorrow, let's go to Sibul. In the daylight it is easier to walk.

To hitch a ride." In the dark, one recognized one's friends by the inflection of their voices.

"Moy said the Japanese had retreated to the Mountains."

Slowly they had wended their way back to the house in the dark. Zar's elbow had brushed against her breasts, and she felt ecstatic waves pass over her whole being. The sheets and blankets were missing.

"Our best Ilocano blankets. New. New," she had cried.

"Be thankful you're alive," snapped her mother.

"But thieves. Robbers. Our own kind."

"Never mind, Dal. There's a war going on, remember? And in the dark Zar gripped Ana, smoothing her hair briefly.

I should have darned his sock, Dal thought. He might make the mistake of crossing his leg in front of the Major. It might cost him his job.

Zar had stood for a while on the threshold before stooping down. She had to tiptoe in order to get another glimpse of his back.

"Zar, you might get hungry. I'll wrap a sandwich for you."

He had turned around, his eyes lit up by eagerness, his smile clear in the morning light. "It's all right, Dal. I'll manage."

You leave, Dal felt, responding to the urgency of your needs and those of your own flesh and blood. That's the way it goes. Yet, it is rare that one does things for friends, acquaintances.

She avoided her mother's querulous expression. "I hope he gets the job."

We slip, sometimes, Zar did. But even that, perhaps, is justifiable, forgivable. It is not given to every man to be without flaw or blemish. As her thoughts lingered on Zar, she could not stop the numbing of her thoughts -- the night flight and the shelling that February came back again -- in the sudden heaving of her breasts and the trembling of her knees.

Nazario Munzon

He squeezed himself between two burly men as the crowded jeepney moved forward, his feeling diminished by the thought that, perhaps in these agitated times, somehow the lapse of his diminution, the distress arising not so much from tight circumstances as from a transient lapse in his judgment, would be remedied.

CARLOS BULOSAN

CARLOS Bulosan was born on November 24, 1913 in the town of Binalonan, Pangasinan, to a peasant family of five brothers and two sisters. After several years of secondary schooling, he left for the U.S. To join his older brother Aurelio. Bulosan arrived in Seattle on July 22, 1930. He became a migrant worker and union activist, and blossomed as a writer during his hospital confinement. Bulosan wrote short stories, essays, editorials, letters, poems, plays, and his autobiographical novel, America Is in the Heart. *He died in Seattle on September 13, 1956.*

Bulosan's good friend, P.C. Morantte (author of Remembering Carlos Bulosan *and* God Is in the Heart), *provides a side of Bulosan that is little known. In his 1944 article published in* Bataan Magazine *Morantte writes:*

"... Though he's only five-foot one, frail bodied, lame and coffee brown, he's an impressive character ...

"When Bulosan gets serious, which comes at periodic intervals as a fitting punctuation to his bouncing impishness, his voice changes and his eyes become fiery. His brow turns into a railroad track and the corner of his mouth forms acute angles ...

"His lighter moments are always a mosaic of fun. What for?

How come? This line is an index to the good mood he is in. And then he would proceed to wipe off his face an imaginary string of perspiration, a peculiar mannerism expressive of his constant search for fun ...

"To Bulosan his father is a gold mine, and out of his stories about him he has already realized a dozen pairs of made-to-order shoes, half a dozen expensive suits, plus a house in swank Beverly Hills, California, which is populated by a lone black cat whom he calls My Soul. He maintains an office in the Wall Street section of Los Angeles, with three telephones and no secretary. He used to have a bunch of secretaries, mostly blondes: but on one occasion a Los Angeles cop came up to his office and tried to arrest the puny guy on charges of maintaining a harem ...

The trouble with Bulosan is that he has no sense of immortality, and that's why he has a hedonistic attitude toward life and is fond of splurging, throwing his money for the fun he gets out of life. That's why he has no serious pretensions, and you can't accuse him of being conceited, though he plays himself up without a ceiling. He just tells you stories and anecdotes that entertain. They are always inflated, but they carry imaginative truths like Alice in Wonderland. *Only his characters are modern, like you and me and Bulosan himself. His humor is extravagant, and there's where his charm lies."*

THE ROMANCE OF MAGNO RUBIO

MAGNO RUBIO, Filipino boy. Four-foot six inches tall. Dark as a coconut. Head on body like a turtle. Magno Rubio. Picking peas on a California hillside for twenty-five cents an hour. Filipino boy. In love with a girl he had never seen. A girl twice his size sideward and upward, Claro said ...

I was listening to their heated discussion.

"I love her," he said.

"But how could you?" Claro asked. "She's twice your size sideward and upward."

"Has size got anything to do with love?"

"That's what I've heard from my uncle."

"Your uncle could be wrong."

"My uncle was never wrong, God bless his soul."

"Was he an educated man?"

"Not in the book sense."

"I don't know," he said, screwing up his fish-eyes. Then he saw me. "You went to college, Nick?"

"Yes."

"How many years?"

"Enough to understand a few things, Magno."

"Now tell me," he said. "Has size got anything to do with love? I mean real love, an honest love?"

"I don't think so."

He brightened up. He turned to Claro. "That's what I thought," he concluded.

"But," Claro protested, "he hasn't seen the girl he's supposed to be in love with!"

He looked at me hopefully.

"The object of love may be an idea, a dream, a reality," I explained. "The love is there. And it grows — depending, of course, on the ability of the lover to crystallize the beloved."

He opened his black mouth, showing rotten teeth. He jumped to his feet like a monkey. "That's it!" he cried. "I don't understand all your words, Nick. But I get it that it's possible for me to love a girl I've never seen!"

"That's exactly what I mean, Magno."

"Nick, you've saved my life!"

"It's all wrong," Claro said, grabbing the long neck of his jug of red wine on the table. His throat gargled. His stomach rumbled. "Words, words, words! They don't mean a thing. My uncle couldn't be wrong: he was a gentleman!"

They were sitting directly opposite each other. They were pushing the jug of wine back and forth across the bare dining table in the smoky kitchen of our bunkhouse. It was early spring and the sun outside was glittering on the dew-laden hills, where the royal crowns of edelweiss, the long blue petals of lupines and multicolored poppies were shaking slightly in the wind. It was morning and we had to work. Some members of our crew were sleeping in their straw beds, some playing cards in a corner of the bunkhouse, some playing musical instruments on the porch. We were pursuing the daily routine of their lives when we had no work. But the three of us were thinking of Magno Rubio's romance with a girl in the mountains of Arkansas. A girl he had been corresponding with but never seen.

"Will you help me, Nick?" he asked me suddenly.

"Sure, Magno."

He looked at Claro with displeasure. "Please go away," he told him.

"This illiterate peasant tells me to go away," Claro said contemptuously. "This ignoramus tells a man who has gone to the second grade to go away! Listen, peon —"

"Here's a dollar," he said, disregarding the insult. "Now go away. Drink the wine in your room. I was crazy to pay for it anyway."

"Look, Igorot —"

"Here's two dollars. Be a gentleman like your uncle."

Claro looked tentatively at the money. He picked up the crisp bills on the table. He grabbed the jug of wine to his room.

"What is it, Magno?" I asked.

"I like you to write a letter for me, Nick."

"Where to?"

"My girl in Arkansas."

"I thought you've been writing to her."

"In a way."

"I can't express your feelings, Magno."

"Sure you can. I'll dictate in our dialect and you translate it into English." He looked in the direction of Claro's room, where a bed was squeaking like a dozen little pigs. He turned to me and frowned. "You see, he has been writing my letters. But he's very expensive. Very, Nick."

"You paid him?"

"And how!"

"How much per letter?"

"No, no, no!" he protested. "It's very complicated. At first there was only a gallon of wine. Later he thought of making some money. I don't know where he had stolen the idea, but it must have been the movies. He demanded a flat rate of five dollars per letter."

"That's reasonable, Magno. After all, he spent some money when he went to the second grade."

"But it's not that, Nick! You see, I wrote to my girl every day. I earn only two dollars fifty cents a day. Still, I had to write her. I love her. You understand, Nick?"

"I nodded my head. I said, "Five dollars per letter. That's more than I earn a day as a bookkeeper for our crew."

"That's not the end of it, Nick." He leaned toward me, his fish-eyes shining like mud. "Realizing that I truly love the girl, that I can't live in the world without her, he demanded one cent per word!"

"One cent per word? It's robbery!"

"Yes! And do you know what, Nick? He wrote long letters that I couldn't understand. And he used big words. How would I know if he wasn't writing for himself?"

"It's hard to say."

"However, I'm not worried about that part of the deal," he said, showing his protruding rotten teeth. He bit at a twisted chunk of chewing tobacco, rolled it from cheek to cheek and said, "I've confidence in myself. But some men use their education to enslave others. I thought education is meant to guide the uneducated. Did some educated man lie about this thing called education, Nick?"

"I don't think so, Magno. Education is what you said: for the educated to guide the uneducated. And it's more than that. Education is a periscope through which a common ground of understanding should be found among men."

He coughed up the slimy wad of tobacco in his mouth, licked the brown shreds of saliva dripping down his thick lips with the tip of his serrated tongue. He banged the splintery table with a fist and said, "The thief! He acts like an exploiter, always squeezing the last drop of my blood! You know what he did to enslave me for a lifetime if you didn't come along, Nick?"

I looked at his coconut head. I looked at his turtle neck. "No," I said.

"Later he charged me ten cents per word!"

"What?"

"You heard me right, Nick! I paid him twenty dollars per letter! Sometimes more! There!"

I studied his monkey face. I said, "It's unbelievable, Magno."

He bit another chunk of tobacco, swallowed his saliva and bared his ugly teeth. He said, "I didn't mind paying him that much money. But the words were too long and deep for me. Again and again I say: how would I know if he hadn't been writing himself? Do you think he's that low, Nick?"

"Some men are capable of anything, Magno. Some men could crawl on their bellies on human filth to earn a dollar."

"I didn't know that, Nick." He was disappointed. "I thought we were all born honest."

"We were born honest, Magno. But along the way some of us lost our honesty."

"I didn't lose my honesty."

"Keep it, Magno. Honesty is the best policy."

"That's what I've heard. Still ..."

"You heard right, Magno."

"I will, Nick." He brushed off a scab on his flat nose. "But I'm free now because I have you. Will you write for me from now on, Nick?"

"Sure, Magno."

"What would you like to have? You don't drink like Claro. You don't go after girls like our foreman. You don't gamble like the hoodlums on the poolroom in town. You don't smoke like the whores at the Elite Hotel. You don't chew tobacco like —"

I stopped him. I said, "Don't start anything, Magno. I'll do it because I like to help you. Maybe I'll need your help someday."

"That's what I like about you, Nick. You use your college education in the right direction."

"By the way. Magno," I said, "how do you know your girl in Arkansas is tall and big on the beam?"

"She wrote to me about the matter."

"You mean Claro told you that's what she wrote?"

"Exactly."

"Did she send you a picture of herself?"

He fumbled in his pockets and produced an old wallet. He extracted a snapshot from a bunch of bills and magazine clippings.

"This is it, Nick."

I looked at the snapshot. It was faded due to too much handling. It was impossible to determine the girl's age and shape and height.

"How tall is she according to Claro?"

"Five-foot eleven inches," he said. "But I don't mind. I really don't. I like tall girls."

"Everybody does, Magno," I told him. Who is short like you, I almost added. Instead I asked him, "And how heavy is she, according to Claro?"

"One hundred ninety-five pounds on bare feet," he said. "But I don't care about that either. I like heavy girls. I really do."

"Everybody does, Magno," I said. Who is a featherweight like you, I almost added. Instead I told him, "It doesn't really matter how tall she is and how much she weighs if you love her."

His flat nose flared up. "I love her, Nick," he said.

"I know you do."

"Will you write a letter now?"

"Sure, Magno."

He ran to his room. He came back with a pencil and a pad of notepaper. Plus a big dictionary, I didn't know why. He put his hands behind his back, walked around the table a few times, stopped in front of me and screwed up his monkey face.

Then he began to dictate in our dialect.

Magno Rubio. Four-foot six inches tall. Dark as a coconut. Head small on a body like turtle. Filipino boy. In love with a girl five-foot eleven inches tall. One hundred and ninety-five pounds of flesh and bones on bare feet. A girl twice his size sideward and upward, Claro said ...

"How did you know Clarabelle?" I asked him.

"I found her in a magazine," he said.

"How?"

"You know, one of those magazines that advertise the names and addresses of girls for one dollar."

"A Lonely Hearts magazine."

"I guess so."

"But you can't read, Magno?"

"Claro read it for me."

"And he found the name for you?"

"He did."

"And of course you gave him the dollar."

He nodded his turtle head. He inserted a finger in his hairy nostril to extricate a slab of dried mucus. He made a face when he pulled it out, looked at it a minute, flung it aside and wiped his hand on his trousers.

"How long have you been writing to her?" I asked him.

"Three months. Do you remember the time when we were picking tomatoes and I didn't want to work? That was the time when I found Clarabelle."

"I remember, Magno."

"For a long time I had nobody to work for, Nick," he explained. "But when I found Clarabelle ..." He grunted because he had swallowed the wad of tobacco in his cheek, bringing tears to his dull eyes. "You know what I mean, Nick."

"I do."

"Well, that's why I've been working every day since.

85

And I don't regret it either."

"That's the spirit, Magno."

He put his chin between his hands. I looked at him and wondered what was transpiring in his bird brain. But I recalled about three months before, he used to stay in the bunkhouse all day. I saw him looking with a dreamy eyes at the pages of the dime magazines. I knew he couldn't read, but the magazines were illustrated with photographs of nude and semi-nude girls. I was tempted to teach him the alphabet, which I did for a few days, but he lacked concentration. And his memory was bad because his mind was taken up by the enticing photographs. So he made excuses that he was either ill or too busy to study.

But he was not ill. Of course, he was ill with love. The foreman scolded him once for staying out of work, but he complained that he was suffering from arthritis. The foreman left it at that because, if Magno Rubio had the illness that he claimed, it would be dangerous for him to work in the cold weather. It was winter then, and the tomatoes were almost frozen. But the crop was saved by our industry and endurance.

And he was not busy, either. He had nothing to do in the bunkhouse, because we had a cook who cooked our food and cleaned the place. Magno Rubio seldom washed his clothes, if he ever did. He had the same rags on him all the time, even when he was in bed. It was insufferable to sit beside him at the dining table. He smelled of mud, sweat and filth, and more, he smelled like a skunk. He had forgotten that some human beings had a sensitive sense of smell, and unlike him, he who had been a peon and a companion of pigs and goats all his life.

But now he had Clarabelle. He was in love for the first time in his life. And also for the first time in his life the filthy rags clinging on his back was discovered. I recalled that when he burned them in the back yard, I dashed out of the house to the foothill for fresh air. But even then my stomach betrayed me, and made me curse the ugliness of some human beings. However, it was all over, Magno Rubio was a human being again. And he was in love.

It was in the middle of spring and we were picking peas on the hillside near our bunkhouse. Magno Rubio and I were working side by side, astride neighboring rows that began from the slope of the hills and ended atop a stony plateau, where goats and sheep were set loose by farmers to eat the destructive loco weeds. We worked up and down the hills, crawling on our knees like brown beetles.

I threw a handful of pea pods into my can and looked at him. "What are your plans for Clarabelle? "I asked.

"I want to marry her, Nick," he said.

"Would you like to say that in your next letter?"

"That's what I've been planning to tell you."

"Well, you should propose to her. How much money have you already spent on her?"

He counted on his fingers, his thick lips moving the while. "A little over two hundred dollars, Nick!"

"That's plenty of money, Magno."

"It's worth it."

"If you think so."

"I spent every cent I earned for her. I also borrowed some money from the foreman with interest."

I studied his flaring nose. It was caked with dirt and mucus.

"But it's worth it, Nick."

"Of course, Magno. Would you like me to write a letter of proposal of marriage tonight?"

"Yes, Nick. The sooner the better."

"Suppose she'll change her mind when she arrives in California?"

There was a flicker of momentary doubt in his monkey face. "I don't think Clarabelle will do that. She's a good girl."

"I hope you are right."

"I've confidence in her."

So I wrote the letter of proposal. She answered

immediately saying that she was accepting his proposal, but unfortunately, she had to stay home for a while because of her sick mother. However, she urged him to send her the ticket money and some extra for expense, in abeyance, since she expected the old woman to get well.

The money was sent. Several days passed. Two weeks passed. Three weeks, and a letter arrived from Clarabelle. I read and gave the translation to Magno Rubio. Clarabelle said, in resume, that her mother died from a lingering disease and she had to spend the money on her funeral. And not only that, she wrote sobbingly: now she had to take care of her little brothers and sisters, all under ten. But, she added, her heart was with him: she was looking forward to the day when she would be free from her family obligations.

"Poor girl," Magno Rubio commented sadly.

And that was all he said, nothing more. So we kept on writing to her. Sometimes we sent her money when she asked for it, sometimes we sent clothes for her brothers and sisters. Magno Rubio never complained. Not a word of protest. The plight of the girl in Arkansas made him more industrious and frugal. He even cut down his expenses of chewing tobacco, which made him look like a Moro juramentado about to go berserk among Christians so he could go to heaven an honored heathen. And of course he was back to his rags.

He worked and worked. He worked like a carabao but lived like a dog. Then the pea season was over. We had to rest for a week, before we started planting celery and carrots. Then the lettuce season came. We thinned and irrigated the seedlings. So the months passed, the seasons came and went. And a year passed by uneventfully, sadly, for Magno Rubio.

A stream of letters flowed from Arkansas to California. Clarabelle was still supporting her little brothers and sisters. And poor Magno Rubio, he didn't suspect anything wrong. He was still looking forward to her coming to California.

"Will you wait?" This was her constant plea in every letter.

"I'll wait," Magno Rubio said to himself.

And he waited. It was now two years and a half since he first contacted her through Claro. Then the third year passed, and he still waited. What sustains a man to have such patience? What quality of soul does he possess to have so much faith in something he has never seen?

I don't know. But Magno Rubio had the patience and the faith. Where most men would have given up long ago, he kept on beyond belief and all reason.

"I'll wait," he said every day.

Magno Rubio. Filipino boy. Four-foot six inches tall. Dark like a coconut. Head small on a body like a turtle. Picking tomatoes on a California hillside for twenty-five cents an hour. In love with a girl he had never seen. A girl five-foot eleven inches tall. One hundred ninety-five pounds of flesh and bones on bare feet. Filipino boy. In love with a girl twice his size sideward and upward, Claro said ...

"What are you giving Clarabelle for Christmas, Magno?" I asked him.

He grinned like a goat. He was carrying a big bundle under one arm. "I'm giving her a radio," he said. "A combination radio-phonograph. It cost me nearly two hundred dollars."

"That's good, Magno."

"Let's send it right away, Nick."

We did. And we waited in vain for her letter. Then Christmas day came.

We were all in the bunkhouse. The foreman and two others were playing poker in a corner of the kitchen. Claro was drinking wine at the dining table. Magno Rubio was oiling his hair near a window, where he had propped up a broken mirror. He was grinning like a monkey. He was in love.

"So Clarabelle will know I'm clean tonight," he explained.

"It doesn't make any difference to her," I said. "She's

too far away to appreciate your cleanliness."

He stopped combing his oily hair and turned to me. "We'll tell her about it in the next letter, Nick."

"Sure, Magno."

"You see, Nick, I'm clean in my soul, thinking of her."

I stopped playing solitaire. I studied his monkey face, and somehow felt that a pure soul was hidden by his flat nose and fish-eyes. I glanced over at Claro. He was getting drunk. Saliva was dripping down the corners of his twisted mouth. His eyes were popping red, like frozen tomatoes.

"Don't you have a girl, Nick?" Magno Rubio suddenly asked me.

I turned my face away from Claro and looked at Magno. "No," I said.

"You should have. You are a college man."

"Education has nothing to do with love."

"You really don't have a girl anywhere in the wide world?"

I shook my head vigorously.

"If I were you I would write to all the pretty girls. There must be a girl somewhere for you, Nick."

"I don't think so, Magno."

"How come pretty girls fall for an uneducated guy like me, huh?"

"You tell me, Magno."

"Now take Clarabelle. Why didn't she fall for you, Nick?

"You found her first."

"If you found her first and I horned in, would she still fall for me?"

"I guess so, Magno."

He laughed like a horse. Claro banged on the table with both fists and leaped to his feet.

"Listen, you peon!" He pointed a finger at Magno. "What are you laughing about?"

"He's happy, Claro," I said. "He has a girl, that's why he's happy."

"I got Clarabelle," Magno said.

"Clarabelle, my eye!" Claro screamed.

"What do you mean by that foolishness?" Magno asked. He put the comb in his shirt pocket and advanced toward Claro. "Will you clarify your statement?"

"You mean to tell me that a girl like Clarabelle loves a donkey like you?"

"What's wrong with me?"

"What's wrong with me?" Claro imitated him. "Don't you know, peasant?"

Magno advanced closer to his adversary. I stopped playing solitaire.

"Don't you know that you look like a monkey?" Claro continued his tirade. His voice was becoming hysterical, his eyes redder, and his mouth was foaming. "Don't you know that besides being a peasant you are also illiterate? Girls like Clarabelle don't fall for your kind, illiterate peasant!"

"You are also a peasant."

"An educated peasant! There, monkey-faced dog peasant!"

"What's the difference?"

"What's the difference?" Claro imitated him again.

"I don't care what you say. Clarabelle loves me."

"Prove it, dog eater!"

Calmly Magno produced his old wallet. He threw a lock of hair on the table. "Here's the absolute proof. She sent it to me. It's from her own head."

"You think you are the only man with a lock of hair from Clarabelle?" Claro also produced a lock of hair and flung it on the table. "There, monkey! That's the real proof. And it's not from her head, either!"

Magno Rubio was astonished. He leaned over the two locks of hair, examining one then the other. Then the two of them were leaning over the table, examining the two locks of hair in all their minutiae, as though they were looking down the magnificent lens of a microscope. And they were growing suspicious of each other, their heads bent close together, their eyes popping like over-ripe guavas. But, finally, Magno Rubio calmed down. He didn't want any violence. His soul was clean and beautiful.

"Your lock of hair doesn't prove anything," he told Claro. Carefully he put Clarabelle's faded snapshot on the table. "But this proves something definite," he added.

Claro sneered. He flung a snapshot beside Magno's face down and said, "Proof, my ass! This is the irrefutable proof! Look for yourself, pig!"

Magno Rubio reached for the snapshot. Claro snatched it away. I had a quick glance at it. I hoped Magno wouldn't see it, because it was the picture of a pretty girl, quite young and proportionately shaped. But he was aroused.

"Let me see!" he demanded.

"Go to hell!" Claro shouted.

The coconut head sunk into the turtle body. The fish-eyes shone. The flat black nose flared. The ugly mouth snarled. Then the gorilla legs leaped. Then they were rolling on the floor. Then Magno Rubio was on top of Claro, beating his face into a pulp with his whirlwind fists.

I jumped to my feet. I grabbed Magno Rubio's hands. But he was strong. He was like a mad dog. I looked toward the poker players.

"You guys!" I called. "Help me!"

They looked in our direction for a minute, then continued their game. I changed my tactics on the mad dog. I squeezed his neck and kept on squeezing until he released Claro. He gasped for air, while Claro scrambled to his feet and dashed outside. I went back to my game of solitaire.

Magno Rubio walked straight to a wall. He began beating it with his fists, weeping at the same time. He kept beating the wall until his fists began to bleed. Then he sank exhausted in a corner of the kitchen, while Claro shouted obscenities from the porch.

Magno Rubio. Filipino boy. Four-foot six inches tall. Dark as a coconut. Head small like a turtle. Magno Rubio. Cutting celery for twenty-five cents an hour. In love with a girl in the mountains of Arkansas. Filipino boy. In love with a girl he had never seen. A girl twice his size sideward and upward, Claro said ...

"Have you heard from Clarabelle, Magno?" I asked him one day.

"No."

"We should write to her."

He looked at me. His serrated tongue darted out of the black pit of his mouth. Then he yawned, and the orifice at the root of his tongue revealed its yellowish membrane.

"It's no use, Nick." he said finally. "Claro fouled up everything."

"I don't think so," I consoled him. "Besides, he's gone."

"He's a louse."

"How do know?"

"He's been writing to her."

"Well, the best man wins, Magno. And you are the best man."

"Do you think so?"

"Don't you?"

He sighed. "We'll write her tonight."

"Are you sure you didn't get a letter from her since –?"

He did not let me finish. "I have, Nick," he confessed. "Ten letters in all. I didn't want to show them to you. The letters are in my room."

"Why didn't you let me know?"

"I thought Clarabelle —"

"Of course you were wrong, Magno," I finished it for him.

"Well you read them tonight, Nick? And write a letter for me?"

"Sure, Magno."

We were packing lettuce in the shade. It was May again

and the crop was good. It was now three years and four months since he had first written to her. I read all of Clarabelle's letters in translation to him. They were arranged chronologically; he had stacked them in an empty cigar box as they arrived. Clarabelle's plea of love become more fervent in every letter, for it seemed that her responsibilities were diminishing. Magno Rubio nodded his head. A genuine smile decorated his black face. When we came to the last letter, I couldn't believe its message. But it was true. Clarabelle was coming to California. She was already on the way.

"When did you get this letter?" I asked him.

"This morning."

"Clarabelle is on the way."

His dull fish-eye shone for the first time. "Did she say she's coming to marry me?"

"That's what she says, Magno. Did you save enough money for this emergency?"

"I've fifty dollars."

"But I thought —"

"You'll have to get out of the state to get married, you know."

"Can't we get married in town?"

"You can't marry here, Magno," I explained. "You can't marry in the whole state of California. You must go to New Mexico or Washington. These are the nearest states where you can get married. And you'll need at least two hundred dollars for the whole affair."

"I didn't know it would cost that much to get married."

"It's only the beginning, Magno."

"You mean there are other expenses?"

"Well, later."

Dreams of glory misted his eyes. "I know what you mean, Nick."

"I know you do."

"I'll borrow some more from the foreman."

"You are mortgaging your whole future," I told him.

"It's worth it, Nick." Dreams of glory crossed his face

again. "When is she arriving?"

"Saturday around noon, the letter says. Today is Thursday. You've barely two days to prepare. You are supposed to meet her at the bus station."

"Will you come with me, Nick?"

"Sure, Magno."

He licked his thick lips and turned away from me. "Will you lend me a hundred, Nick?"

"I'm very sorry, Magno."

"I understand. I'll go to the foreman ..."

"I'm sure he'll help you."

"Do you think she wrote to Claro?"

"I don't know."

"I will kill him."

We were loading the crates of lettuce on the waiting trucks when a telegram came for Magno Rubio. It was from Clarabelle. She was arriving in town sooner than she had expected, at five o'clock Friday afternoon. And it was already Friday noon. He had only four hours to prepare, and we had five more trucks to load. He was stunned for a moment. Then he started throwing the loaded crates into the trucks, working like two men. I followed him, hoping we would finish the job before the momentous hour arrived.

We did. We rushed to the bunkhouse and took a quick shower, changed our clothes, borrowed the pickup from the foreman and drove into town.

Clarabelle was waiting in the bus station. I knew her right away. I had seen the snapshot in Claro's wallet. He didn't recognize her. He was expecting a girl five-foot eleven inches tall, one hundred ninety-five pounds of flesh and bones on bare feet. I pulled his arm. I propelled him toward her.

"Clarabelle?" I greeted her.

"Yes," she said. "Are you Claro?"

Magno Rubio winced.

"No," I said.

"I wonder why he didn't meet me. Are you his brother?"

"Claro is gone," I told her. "Claro has no brother. My name is Nick."

"Glad to meet you, Nick. Where did he go?"

"Alaska."

"Why did he go there of all places?"

"He's working in the fish canneries."

"He didn't tell me about it. Will he be long?"

"He left suddenly, Clarabelle. He'll probably be gone for several months. Maybe longer. I can't tell."

She looked like a prospector who had reached the promised hill in vain. The hill was there all right, but the gold—

"What a way to treat a lady," she complained.

I grabbed Magno's arm. "This is Magno Rubio, Clarabelle."

Her blue eyes flickered. The promised hill of gold reappeared. The rose mouth unfolded sweetly. The dying prospector murmured a prayer: the vein of gold was not a mirage after all.

"Yes, yes!" She grabbed his hand. "How are you Magno?"

He blushed. He muttered something. She turned to me for help.

"May I speak to him for a minute?" she asked me.

I nodded my head. They went to a corner. I walked to the restaurant and ordered a cup of coffee. Then I saw him motioning to me. I left my cup and went to him.

"She's trying to tell me something, Nick," he said. "But I can't understand her. Will you help me?

I followed him in silence. "What is it, Clarabelle?" I asked her.

"It's difficult for me to make him understand," she explained. "This is what I like you to tell him: I must check into a hotel before we talk things over. He understands the marriage part of our conversation. But I need some rest. Explain it to him, Nick."

I explained it to him in our dialect.

"Tell him," Clarabelle added, "that I need some

expense money."

I told him.

"And tell him that I sold our engagement ring. Tell him that I need another ring."

"He can't do it today, Clarabelle," I said. "The banks are closed now."

She looked at the big clock on the wall. "Tomorrow will be okay."

I told him. He gave her fifty dollars.

"Now that everything is arranged properly," Clarabelle said, "let's look for a hotel."

He carried her small suitcase. We walked a block and found a hotel. I followed her to the desk, while he sat in a chair near the door. She signed her name on the registry and turned to me.

"Too bad you are not interested," she said in a low tone of voice. "I like you, Nick."

I shook my head.

"I suppose not," she said. "Will you come with him tomorrow?"

"I will, Clarabelle."

She threw a kiss at Magno and walked to the waiting elevator. We went out of the lobby. He was the happiest man on earth. He hopped and jumped like a little boy. He was in love.

The next day he borrowed two hundred fifty dollars from the foreman. Then we went to town again. He bought a diamond ring for one hundred dollars. I phoned Clarabelle, and she met us at the door of her hotel. He gave her the ring, and she put it on her finger. Then she kissed him. On the tip of his small flat nose.

"We'll get married tomorrow, Magno," she said.

He understood. He nodded his head.'

"Have you got a car, Magno?" Her voice was like a song.

He shook his head.

"It doesn't matter," she said. "How about my expense

money, Magno?"

He opened his wallet and gave her two hundred dollars. Clarabelle kissed him again. On the tip of his small flat nose. She looked at me for a moment, trying to say something with her blue eyes. One gesture — and life was broken forever. One word — and it could have been mended.

"You understand, Nick," she told me at last.

"Yes."

"Thanks."

"You should at least be alone with him."

"I know."

"I'll see you both tomorrow," she said.

We left her. We rode back to our bunkhouse. Magno Rubio couldn't sleep even when midnight came. I heard him prowling restlessly in his room. He knocked at my door when daylight struck the windows.

"This is the day, Nick!" he greeted me. He was carrying a small suitcase.

"Where are going to get married?" I asked him.

"New Mexico. It's the nearest place."

"You have enough money?"

"I borrowed some more from the foreman. I'm the luckiest man in the world!"

I followed him to the pickup. We drove into town. We parked outside Clarabelle's hotel and both went into the lobby. We went to the clerk, and asked for Clarabelle.

"She just checked out," the clerk informed me. "Her husband came for her."

"Her husband?"

The clerk looked at me with eyes that said more than the whole words in the dictionary. Magno Rubio was beginning to understand. He pulled at my arm. We went outside in silence.

We were walking down the street when we saw Clarabelle in a car pulling out from the curb. She was sitting beside a man with brown hair and thin mustache. She was laughing. He was laughing, too.

Magno Rubio watched the car pull away. He was speechless for a moment. Then he understood everything. He brushed his eyes with a finger and took my arm.

"I guess we'll start picking tomatoes next week, Nick," he said.

"Yeah," I said.

"Well, what are we waiting for? Let's hurry back to the bunkhouse. Those guys will eat all the chicken!"

Why does everybody make it difficult for an honest man like Magno Rubio to live in the world?

Magno Rubio. Filipino boy. Four-foot six inches tall. Dark as coconut. Head small on a body like a turtle. Magno Rubio. Picking tomatoes on a California hillside for twenty-five cents an hour. Filipino boy. In love with a girl one hundred and ninety-five pounds of flesh and bones on a bare feet. A girl twice his size sideward and upward, Claro said ...

LIGAYA VICTORIO FRUTO

BORN AND raised in the Philippines, Ligaya Victorio Fruto was trained as a teacher at the Philippine Normal School. While still in her teens, she began teaching and at the same time wrote stories which were published in leading national publications. Because she taught in Baguio, her early stories were mostly about the people of the mountain region.

Ligaya later worked for the pre-war Tribune, *forerunner of the* Manila Times. *Of her contemporaries, Ligaya is one of the few who have not deviated from writing as her main profession. She has covered the field of journalism and creative writing in the Philippines and her adopted country, the U.S., in a range so wide it would be hard to contest. She has written two books,* Yesterday and Other Stories *and* One Rainbow for the Duration, *proceeds from which have gone to charity in her motherland.*

She was married early but was widowed during the Japanese Occupation of the Philippines. She worked for the Philippine Foreign Service; it was in Honolulu that she met and married Larry Fruto, a Filipino, who, as a very young man, went to Hawaii on his own and finished his engineering education there. Her only son by her first marriage, Ramon V. Reyes, lives in the U.S. with his wife and children. Although she has lived in Honolulu for many years, Ligaya visits the Philippines at intervals.

THE FAN

Honolulu, 1950:

DO YOU REMEMBER my Nana Juanita? She died last Saturday. We had to fly to Hilo on the Big Island for her funeral. She did not live in Hilo City, actually. Her home was in a village nestled deep in the sugar plantation where her husband works.

I stayed for almost a month with my Nana Juanita the year I came to America to do graduate work in Washington. That was the year before my marriage.

I was born in Manila, if you recall, and I have never lived in the country. That month on the Big Island was one of the most unusual months of my life, lonely yet so full of so many things I could not understand then that I was never bored.

In the first place, it gave me a chance to know my aunt. We had lived in the same house when I was a little girl and I thought my Tita Juanita — that was I called her then — the prettiest and daintiest creature I had ever seen. She was very fair, like the sampaguita flower that she always wore in garlands around her neck, and had the prettiest, gentlest smile on her pale pink lips and soft brown eyes. My grandfather doted on her, and the only time I saw him caress any living thing was when he laid a light finger on the curve of her cheek.

Then there was her marriage, probably the first traumatic experience in my brief and sheltered life. I have never been able to forget the scene that preceded it. I was not even in my teens yet, but the portrait is as vivid now as though the emotions and the bitterness that charged it were painted in only yesterday.

I had been practicing on the piano and was busy with my scales when my mother's gentle hand was laid over mine to cut off the sound. When I looked up, I saw that she was not even looking at me, and that her hand was laid on mine almost without volition. Her eyes were turned towards a group of people who had not been in the room when I sat at the piano, and as I swiveled round in some curiosity, I felt this charge of emotion like an electric shock emanating from that group.

There was this man, tall and very good-looking, with a face and hands so brown that my Tita Juanita's small hand floated like a bit of fine creamy fabric on mahogany when she laid it on one of those hands. She stood beside him, a small, delicately built woman, her face pale and her eyes steady, like a figurine in pinkish marble. She was dressed in a light pink outfit which, in the fashion of the day, covered most of her figure and allowed only her silken slippers to show. As usual, sampaguita garlands rested against the fairness of her neck and the slight curve of her breast, and the little blossoms shivered with the beating of her heart.

Before them sat my grandfather, his ordinary pale face so suffused with color I was afraid he would have a stroke. He was part Spanish, you know, and was educated in Madrid. From where I sat I thought I could see the blood throb on the veins of his cheek.

Both of his hands gripped his camagong cane, and so tightly did he hold the silver eagle head of this cane that you would think he would plant the thin pointed end into the hardwood floor. He always wore a white linen suit with a high closed collar and buttons of mother-of-pearl.

For a while his mouth was a tight straight line under his white moustache. His eyes were so cold they made me shiver, and except for the rapid pulsing on the throat that showed above his collar, one would believe he was made of stone.

Then he began to talk, first in Spanish, then in Tagalog,

the native dialect, and his voice was so controlled I could barely hear him.

Suddenly, his control deserted him and he thundered, "No! No! Not with my consent! Not with my blessing!"

I stared at him, aghast, then at his hands so tightly gripping his cane. If he relaxed that control, I thought, he'd strike at something. Or someone.

Shaking with an emotion I could not understand, I quietly got off the piano stool and stole out of the room. Looking back, I think I was not really running away from my grandfather's anger. I had to leave because I could no longer bear to look on so much pain mirrored three times.

As I ran to my room, I heard my grandmother sobbing in hers, and I heard my mother's voice raised soothingly in remonstrance. But from Tita Juanita and the man whom I know as my Tio Tomas, there was not a sound.

I had taken a swift glance at the faces of these last two, and on the brown face of the man there was the stony look of calm defiance, while my Tita's countenance was so pale and so devoid of expression it might have been that of a lovely corpse.

My Tio Tomas and my Tita Juanita went away that night to be married. In the years that followed, I never heard of their names mentioned in my grandfather's hearing. He did not disinherit this daughter whom he had loved above all others, for he was not that kind of man. But for him, the night that she went away to be with the man she loved in a foreign land was the day in which she died.

Twelve years later, I got this scholarship for graduate studies in Washington and I had to pass through Hawaii. By then my grandfather had been dead a couple of years, and my Tita Juanita could correspond with her family again. My mother had written her that I was passing through Hawaii on my way to the Mainland, and we received a warmly affectionate letter from my Tita Juanita asking me to time my departure so I could spend a vacation with her. She explained, and with reason, that the Hawaii stopover would help prepare me for my life on the Mainland among Americans.

I felt some dismay when I first saw her home. I could not help but contrast it with the beautiful large city house where we both had lived, with its lovely carved antique furniture and grand piano, the intricate grillwork that had come from Spain and heavy paneled walls and doors. There was a fountain in the formal garden where my little aunt used to read or embroider, and to which she would go to read the letters that Tio Tomas had written her. I never did learn how they had met, for she seemed as cloistered as a nun.

My Tita Juanita's plantation home was made of stained wood a faded kind of red, just a few wooden steps above the ground, with a small living room and three even smaller bedrooms. There was a tiny kitchen with a nook for eating.

It was when I looked at how this home was turned out that my dismay vanished, to be replaced by a kind of wonder. My little aunt had furnished this unpromising structure with a taste nurtured in one of the loveliest homes in Manila and in the best convent school. There was a feeling of rightness about everything, a simplicity that was truly impressive. And both inside and outside the house were plants and flowers that were so beautiful they seemed unnatural to a city girl like me. Surely, I thought, the colors of the flowers could not be so brilliant if they were not painted on, and the leaves must have been polished one by one to achieve that bright glow.

My Tita's face was not as I remembered it. Of course she was older, but it was not age that made the difference. She had achieved a beauty that was a strange mixture of a deep happiness and a deep pain. I do not really know how to explain this. It could be because she did not laugh as often as I remembered, and the twinkle in her eyes had softened to tenderness. There was a look in those eyes sometimes, when she looked at my Tio Tomas, which, surprisingly made me want to cry. Those same eyes would take on an expression that I could only describe as haunted when she lifted her eyes from her flowers and her shrubs to glance at the barricades of sugar cane that hemmed in the little house.

"Tomas and I will probably get a house soon," she said

to me one day.

"A house in town, I mean," she hurriedly explained. "On the rare times I go into town, I would walk about until I saw a 'For Sale' sign. I would stop outside, trying to imagine what the house looked like inside, and in my mind I would furnish it and plan drapes for it. I would smile at myself when I realized what I was doing, and move on. I never seem to find the time to make inquiries about the house or to meet the owners or the agents.

"But soon, perhaps, Tomas and I can really look for a house and live in town. Soon perhaps."

I wanted to ask her why she never went inside a town house. I wondered if this was because she was afraid that once she found herself inside of one, she might never wish to leave it. It could also be because she never asked my uncle for very much and making him change his way of living was more than she would demand of his love for her. She must have longed to be near the shops again, the concert hall and movie theaters, and to be with people congenial enough to ease her back into a semblance of the life she had given up for love of a man. I would listen to her as she softly hummed some of the melodies she had known as a girl and guessed at the memories with which she lived.

I could not ask her these probing questions. I did not really know her. Although we had lived in the same house for more than ten years, there was a gap between a child and a girl in the first bloom of her womanhood which is hard to bridge, especially if there had been a long absence separating them. My aunt was beautiful and very kind, but there was not much trace of the gaiety I had known and always associated with her.

Sometimes in the evening before my Uncle Tomas came home from work, my Tita Nita and I would walk slowly along the plantation roads and she would talk of trivial things or ask questions about our family in Manila. She never once made the slip of asking about her father, of how he died or the kind of man he had become before his death. And although I was a mere child when she had left Manila, I could not bring myself to recall to her the way she had left and the family anguish that followed her departure. Now I can say that her father seemed to have died with the daughter who had died in his heart when she chose to leave him. But in those lonely walks along the plantation roads I could not even mention the name of that sad, formidable old man who was always so kind to me and whom we both loved.

And now, in the remembering, I can see my little aunt walking beside me with her eyes to the ground, never looking to right or left at the yellow-green cane stalks that rose or tilted or sprawled along the narrow roads. I wonder now if this avoidance was not unlike that of a prisoner's who was determined not to see the prison bars before and about him, as if by not looking at them made it easier to believe that they were not there.

On that long first visit, of course, I had no such thoughts. I was so intent on getting to know this strange woman in whose veins flowed the same type of blood that was in mine.

One day, when I had been with my aunt more than a couple of weeks, I left her tending her flowers and wandered by myself among the canes. I do not recall now why I had done this. It could be because many things puzzled me and I could ask my aunt no questions.

I had a feeling of being smothered, not so much by seemingly endless stretches of sugar cane stalks that walled me in but by the thoughts clashing in my mind. I even reveled in the sense of imprisonment that the tall cane gave me and I had a wild desire to step off the path and plunge into the thicket of smooth stalks and lazily swaying tops. I had my hands on two of the tall, slender bars of green and had bent them slightly to allow me to step into the thicket beyond when I felt a rough hand laid gently on my arm. I did not at first know it for my aunt's hand, probably because in that moment what I was seeing in my mind was a white hand, soft as silk, floating lightly on the strong mahogany of my uncle's own.

"Where are you going? What are you thinking?" my

aunt whispered.

I shook my head, not knowing what to say. For indeed I did not know what I was doing or thinking. I evaded her questions with a query, "Do you know that if you hide in this cane at night no one can find you until morning?"

My aunt made no reply, and we stood in tableau for a moment, my hands on the cane, my aunt's hand on my arm, her eyes on the ground. Then she turned and with her hand in mine led me to the house. Inside she did not go to the kitchen as I had expected but took me to a bedroom that she used for storing things she did not use daily.

She settled me on a worn but still graceful sofa and went to a beautifully carved chest standing alone near a corner. She lifted the small flowering plant that rested on an embroidered doily at the top of the chest and turned to me.

"Your mother sent this to me soon after I left Manila," she said. "It took me more than two months to get here. I have not opened it since that first time — this will be the second time.

"You might like to see the contents. They're very old-fashioned by now. Even your mother would have outworn or given away the items similar to these and you probably would have no recollection of them. Consider this, therefore, a history lesson," she added with a smile.

She opened the intricately carved and inlaid top and a fragrance compounded of the scent of fresh aromatic herbs and expensive perfume and rain-washed flowers seemed to fill the little room. My aunt lifted a long skirt of heavy pink silk shot with silver threads and showed it to me. "This is the skirt I wore at your mother's wedding," she said, and she traced with a finger a band of silver embroidery that undulated just below the knee and above the gracefully flaring, stiffly lined lower portion of the skirt.

"We called this the serpentina," she said, "and you can see why. That embroidered silver band winds like a serpent around the skirt and is a tease, binding the garment closer to the figure and after giving the shape to it drops a heavy fall of material to wrap the limbs in voluminous folds. Your mother's wedding gown — have you seen it? — was of the same design but in white silk brocade with seed pearls embroidered on the serpentine band."

Slowly, almost reverently she lifted skirt after skirt out of the chest, unfolding each to reveal the matching butterfly-sleeved camisa or blouse and scarf of stiff rengge — a material woven of silk and pineapple fiber, I think, now no longer in existence. Sometimes an outfit would include a fancy little apron or tapis of lace and net, embroidered with beads and multi-colored gems.

I was speechless with delight. Here was wealth undreamed of, garments that should grace a museum, made of materials that neither love nor money can buy now, and fashioned with a skill that is gone.

Fragrance enveloped each outfit and as my aunt caressed the lovely materials or looked lingeringly at a specially beautiful or unusual piece of embroidery or beadwork, I tried to guess at what she was thinking and imagined how she must have looked in the now priceless finery.

At the bottom of the trunk was what I thought the most beautiful outfit of all. This was a set of wide-sleeved blouse or camisa with matching panuelo or scarf and a skirt that flared gracefully from a small waist to a wide hem that converged into a small train. It was made of pineapple linen so heavily and exquisitely embroidered by hand that hardly two inches of plain material could be glimpsed here and there. I gasped with delight over this outfit that we called Maria Clara, named after the legendary maiden beloved by the national hero of the Philippines, Jose Rizal. Even I could recognize that particular style for it never disappeared from our fashion scene. Even today the most fashionable society brides get married in outfits similar to this that my aunt cradled in her arms. As her work-toughened fingers outlined the raised embroidered flowers that floated like fairy blooms on the wide hem, I got off the sofa and placed both my hands on hers.

"This was what I was supposed to wear for my

wedding," she said, her eyes on the flowers, her fingers caressing them. "Now I can only wear it for my burial."

I cried out, and she quickly looked up at me and smiled. But she said nothing. From beneath the folds of heavy skirt she lifted a box of inlaid mahogany and slid the cover off.

This time my cry was pure joy. For inside was a fan, the like of which I had never seen before nor expect to see again.

It was bigger than most fans, about a foot in length. The handle and the frame were of ivory carved and aged so delicately it looked like fragile lace. Each ivory stick had the detailed carving of a dove, with an eye that I discovered later was of pink diamond. Heavy silk embroidered with gold roses was laid on the ivory frame and inside each rose was a diamond dewdrop. A scent of sampaguita — or jasmine — rose in ghostly fragrance as my aunt waved the fan delicately once or twice then held it to her breast. I could see the diamonds on the roses quivering as in a faint breeze with the beating of her heart.

"Papa gave this to me on my sixteenth birthday," she said. That was the only time in my long visit that I heard her mention her father by name. I was then only a schoolgirl, ignorant of many of the things that filled living, but suddenly I understood the depth of the love and of life which she gave up to come to Hawaii to be with the man she married.

When she finally handed the fan to me to examine, my eyes were filled with tears and a teardrop fell, luckily on the ivory handle. To stain that lovely thing with my innocent teardrop would have been a desecration.

If my aunt saw the teardrop she did not mention it. Perhaps she did not see it, for she was looking at her clasped hands, no doubt lost in memories. When she raised her eyes to mine, they had the limpid look of brown gems, and when she smiled I felt like dementedly shouting, "Please cry! Please cry so I can cry with you!"

But we both kept silent and after that long look between us I bent my eyes again on the fan, pretending to examine it.

"That fan was over a hundred years old when it came to me," she said. "It will probably last for another century."

On the silk on one side of the fan was written in a bold but fading script: "A mi querida hija, Nita. Con amor, Papa."

When I returned the fan to my aunt, her fingers went over the script but she did not look at the inscription. Her beautiful eyes had a blind look — the blind look of one who has rejected sight.

I was certain we were seeing the same mental images — of a young Nita flirting with that fan, hiding her blushes behind it, her eyes lowered just above the silken curve so that her lashes touched the gold border. For a magical moment the reality of this beautiful but drably clad woman was lost in the vision of a delicate phantom flashing her fan so that the diamonds twinkled as she moved gracefully in the stately steps of the rigodon, her slender body covered almost entirely by the heavy silks and satins that like beautiful bodies folded in death lay on the rough floor of the little plantation house.

As though waking up from a dream, my aunt hastily lifted each outfit off the floor and carefully placed it in the chest. As each colorful bit of richness disappeared into the fragrant imprisonment of the heavy chest, my heart fancifully, said goodbye not just to silks and laces and silver and gold but to a way of life and youth now truly dead. And somehow I felt that my goodbyes were not being said by me alone. I wondered how so small a figure could hold so many tears and not lose a single one.

When I left the plantation home I promised my aunt I would come again, perhaps on my way home to Manila after my studies. But I married a Mainland doctor after my doctorate and I could not keep the promise. Until now.

A month before my wedding, I wrote my Tita Nita to ask her to come to San Francisco "to represent the family" as my mother could not attend. She replied with a most affectionate letter and told me she had not left the Big Island since she came to live there and would not know how to behave in the world outside. I knew she meant this for a humorous refusal, not only because she did not want to be with strangers but because she could not represent the family. For she had renounced all claims to family ties when she defied her father to marry the man she loved.

She sent me a diamond brooch — I have shown it to you, haven't I? — an exquisite piece with emerald leaves framing a rose composed entirely of diamonds. She never explained if this was an heirloom or something she had bought with her savings. I suspected it was part of her inheritance but I could not ask her. And when I mentioned it to my mother she wouldn't explain it either. It remains the most precious jewel I possess.

When I wrote her again four years after my marriage that we were moving to Hawaii to live because my husband thought the climate would be good for me and the baby, she sent me a rapturous welcome. In the letter she did not mention that she was then very ill.

We were just getting settled in our Honolulu home when a telegram came from my Uncle Tomas. That telegram blotted for a moment the glorious sunshine that flooded our lanai, and when I showed it to my husband he came to enfold me in his arms so I could hide my face against his heart.

We closed the house and with the baby flew to Hilo. My Tio Tomas met us and after kissing me on both cheeks and shaking my husband's hand and touching the baby's cheek, took us in his car to the church where my aunt's body lay.

I had grown very fond of my Tio Tomas and seeing him so calm and so sad almost unnerved me. He was one of those men who never seemed to change, always in their prime, neither young nor old, just strong. His face seemed more than ever like something carved in bronze, handsome, even forbidding. A very private face.

I have never made the mistake of thinking a stern man an unfeeling one, and when I see a forbidding face I wonder what hurts it is hiding.

When my uncle stood by my aunt's coffin and with a

smile of great tenderness stroked the pale cheek with a gentle hand I shamelessly burst into tears. He absently placed an arm around my shoulders but his gaze never wavered from that thin but still very beautiful face, the eyelashes curling delicately to hide forever the secret in the eyes that even in life were not easy to read.

I dared not guess at my uncle's feelings — I had sorrows enough of my own. But even in my grief I could not help but wonder at his thoughts in that long moment of love and loss which I outwardly shared with him. He did not bend to kiss her in what could be a needless display of farewell, but the love that flowed from his heart could have given life back to hers if such things were possible.

Then as before I found it easy to understand how my aunt could have given up the life that meant family and joy to her for her sugar cane prison camp. If there were two people who had reduced life to its simple and most profound meaning, they were my Tita Nita and Tio Tomas. They had wrung the sweetness out of the cane and discarded that which was of no use to them.

After the funeral, my uncle came to me with the heavy inlaid chest where I had discovered so many delights so many years before.

"Nita wanted you to have this and all it contains," he said. "You are the only daughter she ever had. And she asked me to tell you that she hoped you will understand why the pineapple linen Maria Clara is missing. She said she told you about that."

He did not look at me while I sobbed and covered my face with my hands. He opened the trunk and took out the narrow box that lay on top of the heap of dazzling beauties. "She loved this," he said, his hand tenderly caressing the smooth mahogany. "She said this is the heirloom you will most treasure and is giving it to you with all her love."

My hands trembled as I took the narrow box from him and my eyes were full of tears and my mind so cluttered with memories I did not even know when my uncle left me alone.

I slid the cover off and the perfume of sampaguita rose like a wraith as I took out the fan. Slowly I opened it and my delight in it on that long-ago day was a memory that stabbed my heart with a pain so sharp I thought it would stop.

I looked at this exquisite reminder of an existence and an age long gone and recognized it for what it was — not a gem of an heirloom made of perishable silk, aged and lacy ivory, gold and diamonds, but the ageless souvenir of a life boxed in fragrance, imprisoned in beauty that rose above the trivial and impermanent because of a love that was beyond measure and thus could not be encompassed in the height and breadth and depth of one pitiful lifetime.

JEAN VENGUA GIER

JEAN Vengua Gier was born in San Francisco, and raised in Santa Cruz, California. She is a second-generation Filipino American. This is her first published short story. Jean's poetry has been published in various magazines, including Quarry West, Poetry Flash, Berkeley Poets Cooperative, *and the anthology* Homeless Not Helpless. *Her work in improvisatory and collaborative poetry has been recorded on audio-cassette for* We, *an anthology of experimental poetry. She is especially interested in exploring and crossing, through language, the boundaries of culture and region.*

Jean has been a coordinator of the Louden Nelson Community Center Reading Series for four years. She is also a member of BAPAW, the (San Francisco) Bay Area Pilipino-American Writers group.
Aside from her writing interests, Jean is a visual artist. She works part-time for a dance company.

DANCERS

CAULIFLOWER, cauliflower, spinach — chard. Sprouts. Artichokes, artichokes ... artichokes. Topless Brand. Pure Gold. Zmudowski Beach. The slough's giant snail tracks shimmering through the valley. I lean against the inside of the car window, watching as we whoosh past the combed fields, where workers loosen sweat-soaked bandannas from around their faces, pull off gloves and caps, and walk stiffly to pickup trucks and battered buses.

We are driving to Salinas. It's 1964. Me in the back seat with my mother, Auntie Vicky in the front seat, Uncle Johnny at the wheel. The radio is playing a triple header R&B, no commercials. "Oh, I HEARD it through the grapevine, not much LONGer will you be mine, uh OH, I HEARD it."

On time as usual, the Coast Starlight advances on tracks parallel to Hwy. I, finally outrunning us. We'll meet it again at the First St. intersection, and have to wait as the passenger cars rattle through, one after another.

When we arrive it's near dark. The windows in the dining cars are lit up all warm and cozy, framing the people inside, who are seated at dinner, talking and laughing like they don't have a care.

On First Street, winos stagger in front of the bars and Chinese restaurants. Rolling down the window a little, I smell chow yok and axle grease. All the smells of a hot, summer day drilling the air, colliding with the tang of cooling tar and asphalt.

My stomach feels tied up in knots after waiting all day for this: the drive to the dance hall. I've spent the whole day with my hair in curlers, stereo turned up, practicing my steps. I don't think about why I'm doing this, or why I have to experience these small agonies of self-consciousness, vanity, fear, and excitement. I'm thirteen, and I've gone to these dances nearly every weekend for two years. I don't know the words for it yet, but what I want is to move through this landscape with audacity and grace, and I'm ready for anything.

In 1964, I lived in two worlds: Santa Cruz, a California town of mostly white, Anglo-Saxon Protestants, where I was one of only two or three Filipinos in the district, where my movement was constraint by the limits of the local bus line, the school calendar, and my mother's work hours at the cannery; then there was the world of the dances: populated by Filipino cannery and farm workers and their extended families, a world that moved outwards, expanding as far as Stockton, Delano, L.A., or contracted to the closer towns of Salinas or Watsonville, depending on where the next lodge dance or meeting was held.

Santa Cruz in the 1960's was a resort town on Monterey Bay, a little island of perpetual summer. The County was bordered on the north and south by miles of farmland. The Filipino and Mexican kids that worked in these fields appeared in Santa Cruz schools sporadically, if at all. As I got older, I realized the edge I had on them, simply because my father had a job in the Civil Service.

My mother was determined that I become "cultured." Thanks to her job at the cannery and my Dad's job with the merchant marines, we were able to live in a clean, if somewhat boring, middle-class neighborhood. I was able to take piano, dance, and art lessons.

At that time, most of my few friends were Okies, but I had one friend who was different.

Laura spoke with a lisp. She had long brown hair, and a pale complexion. There were fine bluish veins at her temples and wrists. We were friends for one year in junior high. Just before we started high school, she started to do that shuffle that some friends do when they begin to find you tiresome; she started hanging out with other girls, shortening the periods she spent with me, finally disappearing altogether. I was spending too much time talking about boys, dancing, and music — talking about these things as if they were survival skills. I was spending less time on books and movies, our once-shared passion.

Her parents were French. Every other year they traveled to the Old Country so they could retain their citizenship. They owned a restaurant called *Le Provencal*. The school was just a couple of blocks away, so we'd walk to the restaurant every day at lunchtime. There were no customers at noon — they served dinner only, so her father would be in the kitchen cooking a roux, or chopping onions for soup. Laura would take me down to the musty wine cellar and show off old bottles, then we'd go upstairs and have onion soup with grated Swiss cheese and croutons.

Even at twelve her tastes were refined. I remember wanting to go with her to see *The L-shaped Room*, hoping to catch a few sizzling scenes, but Laura consulted her parents first, then steered me to see *To Kill a Mockingbird*, a movie I was surprised to find I enjoyed, but which filled me with vague anxieties.

By the time I was thirteen, I'd had seven years of ballet classes, and several years dancing with a Filipino folklore group in Watsonville, so I felt comfortable with the way I moved, although at that age, I wouldn't be caught dead folk dancing. I watched dance shows on TV every weekend, and was starting to get the moves down.

I tried to teach Laura the jerk. I couldn't understand why she couldn't get it. She'd watch me, then move her body like a puppet, each section a stiff piece of wood.

"You gotta put some oomph into it," I'd say, whipping my hips back and forth. She couldn't snap her hips. She couldn't let her knees go slack at the right moment. I'd point out teenagers on American Bandstand, dancing like their very lives depended on it.

"Look! Just move like that!" There were mostly white kids on the show, a few black couples, all neatly dressed. There was something about the way they moved ... a certain tension that flowed through their limbs and bodies, a tension which they threw off with abandon. I could feel it, but I couldn't explain it. Laura's delicate hands flapped helplessly, like broken propellers. Her fingers were stiff, but her wrists hung limp. It was hopeless.

I had another friend, or more of an acquaintance, named Marci. No one at school messed with this girl. That was one good thing about hanging out with her. She liked to brag about beating up girls from schools she had attended before coming to Santa Cruz, although I'd never actually seen her in a fight. It was common knowledge that if you messed with Marci, you messed with her family. Her hair was a dull blonde color, bangs cut straight across her forehead. She was pale, too, white as homogenized milk, and even skinnier than Laura, but she had a bull-dog walk that compensated for her thin frame.

She had a strange brother, who always met her after school and walked her home. I could never understand why a girl like her needed an escort. He always wore an old cloth jacket, baggy wool pants, and shoes that looked like they came out of the Goodwill bin. There were stories about him stealing unopened milk bottles off front porches. But what was really distinctive about him was that he smoked a pipe, one of those curvy-looking things with a round, polished bowl at the end. I'd see him walking down King St. at six a.m., dressed in his hobo clothes, tamping a small wad of tobacco into his pipe.

One day, in the school yard, I was sitting on the grass near Marci. She lay on her back, staring up at the sky, unlit cigarette hanging out of her mouth, like she might actually smoke it right there in front of the schoolyard monitor. Giggling, I leaned over to tell her something, and a small drop of saliva spilled from my mouth onto her chin. Her eyes opened wide. She suddenly yelled — "FUCK!" — swung herself upright, and slugged me in the jaw with her fist.

Marci and her brother were two of the six offsprings of the Maynard family, one of the three most notorious families on the westside of town. These families had certain traits in common: they were all dirt-poor, and the kids were

118

good at fighting. Smart-assed and temperamental, they had also developed what might be called "character" at an early age, and they made school a lot less boring than it might've been.

I invited Marci to one of the dances. The first one was in Watsonville, at the Veteran's Hall. I felt sure she'd understand the concept of the social box, something Laura would never understand, nor forgive. Ten chairs were placed in front of the stage while the band was on break. Ten teenage girls or young women were chosen to come up front. They sat there arranging their knees, tugging at their skirts. One at a time, they each had a turn to stand up as the band played *"Maria Elena,"* and the men came, flashing bills to a man behind a microphone: FIVE DOLLARS! ... TEN DOLLARS!" he'd announce, "from Brother Frank Penitencia of the Rizal Lodge ..." Sometimes it was twenty-five dollars or fifty dollars. Each girl stayed on her feet as long as the money was coming, fifteen minutes, thirty minutes at the most. There were tall guys, short guys, most of them old Filipino farmworkers spiffed up for the evening. They'd left their harsh jobs behind for the weekend, and now they were respected leaders of the local lodge. Some were married, their wives sitting heavily on the folding chairs, nursing beers, fanning themselves with paper napkins. Occasionally, one of the older women would get up and dance with a girl, waving a twenty dollar bill, smiling self-consciously, but confident that she was maintaining her standing in the community.

The social box usually took place late in the evening; by that time, my feet were already aching in my pointy-toed shoes. Afterwards, I'd get a half the take, maybe one hundred dollars if I was lucky.

Marci's eyes lit up when I explained it. This was easy money.

"Just don't tell my mom about this," she said. It wasn't that she was embarrassed about participating, she explained. She didn't want her mother to know she was making money on the side.

But she never got very far with her social box career.

Her mother showed up at the second dance, just as she was getting ready to sit in one of the social box chairs.

Mrs. Maynard was a well-endowed woman of medium height, wearing stiletto heels, black matador pants, and sleeveless cotton-print blouse. She was accompanied by two men. One was blonde, his wavy hair greased back into a modified ducktail. The other man was older, with short, dark hair, and pencil-line mustache. He wore a red and white plaid shirt tucked into his jeans, and black cowboy boots. You could tell by the way they were dressed that they had just come out of a bar, or they were headed for a bar. A cowboy bar.

Marci's mother walked in confidently, like she owned the place. She didn't have the same bull-dog walk as Marci, but you could tell where her daughter got her aggressive stance.

The two men, however, seemed uncertain. They glanced nervously at all the Filipinos: the teenaged boys hanging out by the front and back doors, the men and women sitting comfortably, sipping from cups of Coke and whiskey, the older white and Mexican women sitting with their Filipino husbands.

I watched as Marci's mother leaned down and talked to her daughter. Marci sat slouched on her chair, arms folded over her chest. She shrugged at a question directed at her, and stared fixedly past her mother at some imagined point in the hall. Her mother glared at her.

Marci stood up and walked over to me. "Well, shit," she said. "I gotta go somewhere." She looked at me and shrugged again.

She never went to another dance with me. In fact, like Laura, she soon disappeared. I called her up one day. We bragged about ourselves for awhile, then she capped the conversation by announcing: "Well, I lost my virginity." I couldn't say the same thing for myself.

"Know what else?" she said. "I was back in Bakersfield last week, and beat the shit out of this chick, Ramona. Fuckin' showed *her*. Pushed her into a garbage can. She's not gonna mess with me anymore!"

It was too bad Marci stopped going to the dances; she missed the most exciting event we'd had in a long time, Sonny Bautista's shooting. The local newspaper ran a story on it:

YOUTH IN CRITICAL CONDITION AFTER DANCEHALL SHOOTING

I remember it was a series of firecracker pops, screams and the embarrassment of having my mother drag me into a hallway for protection as I saw the gunman exit from the dancehall. Sonny was slumped on the floor beside the hard wooden bench on which he'd been sitting, crimson welling out from beneath his tie in big blotches.

Afterwards, we all sat around the hall listening to his moans as he was lifted onto a stretcher. We watched a detective walk around with a notepad, asking questions. I noticed he was wearing a curly brown toupee.

I didn't really know Sonny, but I knew the gunman's brother, Chino, a small, wiry young man in his twenties, who sported a pencil-line mustache, and heavily greased hair. At this point, no one had identified the gunman as his brother, even though everyone knew them both. He sat next to me, chain-smoking nonchalantly discussing the event. He always behaved towards me as if he were an older brother, bragging a bit about himself, giving me advice, sometimes dancing with me.

That evening, he proudly discussed the trajectory of bullets and the make of pistols, particularly his own, and after the police left, he even unfolded a small switchblade, which he said he kept for protection. He'd been drinking a little; I could smell the stuff on his breath. I was bored and disappointed. I had planned to make a lot of money in the social box that night.

Sometime during the course of the evening, Chino disappeared from the dancehall. After that, I only heard about the shooting through the grapevine. A week later, the newspaper came out with more stories:

YOUTH DIES IN GANG-RELATED SHOOTING

And a few weeks later:

FILIPINO YOUTH CHARGED WITH MURDER IN DANCEHALL SHOOTING

It turned out there had been an argument, a serious insult, and a debt to be paid.

Chino actually visited us a couple times after his brother had been sent to jail. My mother blanched each time he showed up, but she welcomed him anyway, afraid to cause any bad feeling between them, or give him reason to get angry. She now associated him forever with that violent act, and she was sure his presence in the house was bad luck. We all sat around the living room, sipping iced tea and eating donuts, carefully avoiding any talk of murder.

The shotgun, and the hitchhike. The jerk, the swim and the monkey. That was my repertoire, not including the boogaloo because only guys did that, and no one could do it as good as James Brown anyway, so why try?

But it wasn't enough. I was at that terrifying age, thirteen. I didn't hang with a particular crowd, and that was enough to make me a misfit in school. It was better to be part of the wrong crowd, than have no crowd. Besides, I was the wrong color, and the few friends I had were goofy, or downright dangerous.

The Filipino dances were a different world, operative only on Fridays or weekends, with a different class system, a different sound, a different smell. It was pure working class, and no matter what pretensions my mother may have had about my cultural education — at the dance, we were all equal.

The talk at the dances was of lodge doings, the Delano grape pickers' strike, the old days of working the canneries in Alaska or sacking potatoes in Oregon and above all, **gossip**: the glue of the Filipino community. The air in the dancehall was thick with it — who was cheating on whom, who was up for treasurer next term, who was good, who was bad, who cooked the best adobo. There was always laughter, and stories that changed with every telling, all in the staccato speech of Tagalog, Cebuano, Ilocano, or Waray, mixed with florid tones of Spanish, and the occasional twang of Central Valley Okies.

Scientists and authors of sex manuals say that memories linked to certain scents last the longest. I smell cigarette smoke and the sweet-sour fumes of whiskey-Cokes, and my head fills with the clamor of dancehalls. There was also that warm, greasy smell of deep-fried pastries, as I sold my mother's homemade lumpia rolls stuffed with vegetables and shrimp, and coconut balls drizzled with burnt-sugar glaze. Often, I stood behind the counter for several hours, making change, pouring hot coffee from the dented urns we brought, and longing for various adolescent boys across the hall.

Here it wasn't shameful to dance with an old man — many of them had honorary "Uncle" status, "Manong." The women were "Aunties." I was taught to think of close family as extensions of the family. For lack of a more conventional partner, old men danced with young girls, women danced with women.

Dancing with a Manong, however, could be complicated. It meant learning a whole new set of steps: There was a sort of generic two-step that could get you through the fox-trot and the waltz, then there was the cha-cha, the samba, and a modified be-bop, a kind of swingy rock n' roll.

One old man still danced the continental, a complicated off-shoot of the foxtrot he'd probably picked from old Fred Astaire movies, or perhaps he learned it at the taxi dances of the 1930's. Imagine him as a young paliquero, still dapper in an ice-cream suit at the Manila Ballroom, his week's wages blown on a roll of dance tickets and a bottle of bootleg.

He was at least four inches shorter than I, and as we danced, his bald pate would bob below my chin as he trotted, skipped, swayed, and swiveled around me. I felt like I was standing still.

The one dance to avoid was the tango. Several of the old guys were crazy for the tango. Most of the younger girls disappeared when the band struck up "Valencia" or some other hot Latin number. If I wasn't careful, one of the men would step up, dressed in his ancient mackintosh suit with its wide lapels and even wider shoulder padding, and fling me onto the dance floor.

Then it was all over. I'd hear the other girls snickering as I struggled with the plunge, the twirl, and the flamingo dip.

One man in particular, after twirling his partner around, would let go her hands, then begin dancing solo, snapping his fingers like a flamenco dancer, improvising while his partner stood by, feeling foolish. In his mind, he was under a spotlight in some L.A. Ballroom, 1937, everyone's eyes riveted on his dancing feet, his fine suit.

I stopped inviting my school friends to the dances. How could they understand?

"Wha —? Dance with old guys? What for?"

"But cute guys come, too," I'd explain, "our age!" Well, almost. Most of them were at least fifteen.

But these weren't like the guys at school. In Santa Cruz there may have been a Filipino surfer or two, maybe a pseudo-preppie here and there. But not in Salinas. There were no madras shirts to be found. No penny loafers, and especially no letter sweaters.

This was the early sixties, and Filipino boys were working on their cool look. They were hanging out with the Bloods, the Black Brothers, and their style came from the City. They wore sharkskin pants pegged tight, and black points instead of sneakers. They pomped their shiny black hair and wore black hairnets to keep it all in place — like the bad boys from Mission District. The style said: "I am *so* cool, I can wear a *hairnet*, and *still* look bad!" That walk, the way they moved, was honed to perfection: smooth as a Bach fugue. And they could dance. They had the flame step *down!* They had the slide, and the glide.

I wanted to dance like that! I studied their moves. I watched American Bandstand and Shindig faithfully every week. This was crucial to the future of my social life!

Some nights, a special band would be brought in from Oakland or San Francisco for the kids. These bands usually had car names: The Jaguars. The Corvettes. Sammy and the T-Birds. They'd be hired with the specifications that every once in a while they play something like a samba. Or waltz, so the older folks could take a breather.

On any evening a "car" band played, the teens would be there in force. They came from Alisal High School, Salinas High, E.A. Hall, and Watsonville High. The girls wore black minis and floppy mohair sweaters over cotton Woolworth blouses. Their hair was teased high into beehives and bubbles. The kids speculated on whether or not razors were hidden in the nests. Some of them had their hair dyed auburn to emphasize their mestiza qualities. My mother said they look cheap.

When the music started, it was always something like "Louie, Louie," followed by the latest from Wicked Pickett, or Junior Walker — something with irrational or minimal lyrics, but hard-driving Motown beat:

> "Ah said —
> Shot-guuu-uuun! DO it while you RUN now!
> Do the jerk, Baa-by
> Do the jerk NOW!
> We gonna —
> DIG poTAYtoes!

We gonna —
PICK toMAYtoes!
Ah said —
Shot-guuu-uuun!"

All the kids, many of whom had spent their week at stoop labor, chopping at cauliflower and brussel sprouts stalks, or in a cannery, sorting rotten vegetables, would strut out to the middle of the dance floor in one large, cocky group and start dancing. Everyone else would follow: old men in baggy suits, fat women wearing too-tight dresses, young Pinoys and Pinays, fresh from the Islands, wearing outdated clothes from the 50's, American-born Flips showing off their Mainland style.

I'd look around nervously; someone had *better* ask me to dance! I was still too young for most of those boys. I remembered with bitterness a friend reporting to me that an older boy I'd had a crush on had mentioned I was a sweet kid. The worst of insults!

Some old Manong would come along, and hold out his hand. What the hell ... I'd do the hitchhike, and my ancient partner would do a solo rendition of the jitterbug. It didn't matter as long as we were out there, moving.

"Are you Pinay?" an old Pinoy asks me.

"Yeah," I say truthfully. I'm pure Pilipina. It seems to make them happy. The question often comes up during a waltz, or anything slow enough to allow conversation.

"Born here — or in the Islands?

"San Francisco," the second-best answer.

"Ah, but pure Pinay — dat's good," he says. "Make the best wife."

Jeez, he's not thinking ...? Sometimes I wonder.

"Bye 'n bye, I go back to the Pilipinas, find a wife. Pinay the best!"

The band switches to a Latin number: Mauro's trumpet

blaring off-key, the drummer picking up the pace, giving it a little oomph here and there.

My partner grins, happy to remember perfectly the steps to match the rhythm, and all the dangerous and exciting nights through which he's steered his life.

"Aye! Come on!" he says, snapping his fingers. He lets go of my hands, motions to me to follow, and we make our way to the center of the floor.

ALBERTO S. FLORENTINO

A COLLEGE dropout from accounting school; went into writing for the stage, then for TV and the movies; ventured into book publishing in the '60s, turning out seventy-five titles; taught dramatic writing for TV in the '70s at the U.P. Graduate school (mass communication); published five books of his own plays; his first play The World Is an Apple *is a literary landmark in the Philippines, the most popular and most produced in a 1984 poll; winner of TOYM award in 1960 (the group included Ninoy Aquino); a Patnubay ng Kalinangan award from the City of Manila; five-time Palanca and two-time Arena Theater winner; traveled six times to the U.S. on travel and study grants; Philippine representative to the 1966 PEN Congress in New York; attended writing conferences in Denver and Aspen in Colorado and Vermont (Breadloaf); was regional editor for* Short Story International *(New York); moved with his family in 1983 to New York where he is now a permanent resident.*

On "Sabrina": Florentino's early (student) writings were poems and short stories. "Sabrina" originally existed in his head as a short story. During his stint as script supervisor for Balintataw *(where he doubled as a scriptwriter under various pseudonyms), he wrote it as a TV drama over a weekend. The "episode" was aired the next week on* Balintataw, *the much awarded TV drama anthology. Lately, "Sabrina" was written as a "period short story" for inclusion, with 20 other plays, in Florentino's definitive book,* Ang Daigdig Ay Isang Patak na Luha, *coming out in 1994.*

SABRINA

SABRINA is practicing the "moonwalk" dance being introduced by Chito Feliciano on his dance program, her eyes glued to the TV set. Above the sound of the music she hears the electric chimes downstairs. Without pausing from her dancing she shouts to the maid to see who is at the gate. Then she realizes the maid has gone on a day off, much to her chagrin — did she have to when her Mom and Dad are in Baguio?

She runs out of her room, down the stairs and reaches the gate. She twirls the lock open, expecting to find a bill collector or the mailman. Instead she finds a young American (John), in street clothes, standing in the sun, a gift-wrapped package under his arm, mopping his sweating brow with a khaki handkerchief.

Right away she marks him off as a Saigon-based soldier on R&R visit to Manila. Lately, she has seen a horde of them walking in and out of hotel lobbies with miniskirted bar-girls from Mabini or Olongapo. Somehow, these men are easy to pick out, like Peace Corps members, or U.S. Embassy personnel, or visiting American artists-writers. But what is he doing here in our house? Sabrina asks herself.

Sabrina: Yes?

John: Is this where Benjamin lives?

Sabrina: Yes.

John: Is he home?

Sabrina: I think so ... why, he — yes — yes, he's home — I think.

John: You must be his sister.

He stares at her palazzo pants, her hair strewn all over her face, looking like a model posing on a ramp as she tries to open the gate without touching ground.

Sabrina: Yes, I am. Won't you come in?

He bends low as he enters the service gate and clears the top, but being too tall his shin catches the bottom, almost pitching him forward.

Sabrina instinctively offers her hand for support, but he manages to stay on his feet. Embarrassed, he offers her the package under his arm and bends to chafe his shin. Limping, he follows her up the house.

Twenty minutes have passed and Benjie has not shown up. When Sabrina earlier announced the guest, Benjie had turned to her —

Benjie: An *American?* Let him wait.

He had turned back to his friends to resume his impassioned harangue. Now he *really* is taking his time, and Sabrina apologizes —

Sabrina: I'm sorry Benjie's taking his time — he's with friends —

John: It's not his fault. This is a surprise visit.

Sabrina: I'm also sorry Mom and Dad are away in Baguio. It's a yearly summer ritual for them — and for a lot of other people. But then, it's really Benjie you want, no?

John: Yes, but I'd love to meet *them*, too.

Sabrina: If you're staying longer in Manila, you'll get a chance to meet them.

John: I'm staying only a week. I have a snapshot of your family here.

He fishes out a worn-out sepia-tinted photo from his breast pocket. It is a duplicate of a family photo she once found in her Dad's wartime album, showing her as a little girl in bloomers, with a ribbon in her "ringlet" hair.

John: It was given to my Dad the last time he was here.

Just after the liberation of Manila.

Sabrina: Boy, am I glad Dad didn't give away a much *earlier* photo of me. You would have caught me without even a miniskirt on. It's incredible — you coming all the way from — where did you say?

John: Milwaukee.

Sabrina: From Milwaukee — by way of Vietnam — to give a gift to Benjie whom you've never seen except in a twenty-year-old snapshot.

She has risen from her seat to serve him a drink from the bar.

John: My Dad, as a liberation G.I. in Manila, befriended your brother, then seven years old.

Sabrina: Just like in a John Wayne movie?

John: Yes, and he promised to send Benjie a gift at the end of the war. But *unlike* in a movie, my old man forgot, until I wrote him lately that my R&R includes Manila. Then he *remembered,* and here I am —

Sabrina: An American bearing gifts!

John: Ah, yes, yes ... so ... so beware!

An embarrassed silence follows during which they realize Benjie has not come out and may choose not to.

John: I hope I didn't take you away from anything.

Sabrina: Oh, no.

John: You may leave me here. Or if Benjie's busy, I could just leave this. I can also return —

There is a commotion from the den below. Soon Benjie and his friends surface, still hotly arguing with each other over something. They see the American G.I. and they grow quiet, suddenly bristling with antagonism.

Benjie is infuriated and embarrassed before his friends because of the presence of a *white* man in his house.

Sabrina: Well, Benjie, start introducing your friends to John.

Benjie: John ... meet my friends.

Friends: Hi ... hi there ... howdy?

Sabrina: Let me start with Pete —

Benjie: I'm sure they are *all* glad to meet John here. But they've got to catch something before offices close. I hope you understand —

John: Of course, of course —

Benjie: I am supposed to go with them —

Sabrina: But, Benjie, you have a *guest!*

Benjie: I know, I know. That's why I *am* staying behind. But I can't stay too long.

John: Oh, I really won't take too long.

Sabrina: he's right — only long enough to hand you a gift —

Benjie: Oh, a gift? How interesting! What is it? A hunting rifle? To hunt *white* boars around Clark Field?

Sabrina: That's far from looking like a rifle, Benjie! John, my brother here has a *grim* sense of humor.

Benjie: You don't have to *apologize* for me, sis! I'll just see my friends to the door.

Sabrina: I'll see them to the door, Benjie —

Benjie: Don't worry, sis, I'll be back.

After listening in complete silence to John, Benjie starts saying his piece.

Benjie: Well, John, I'd suggest you do this: go back to Vietnam. Your *side* of Vietnam of course, although I wouldn't object you landed on the *North* side. Go back to your killing spree. Back to killing pot-bellied babies, back to your napalm bombs.

Then write your Daddy-O — tell him the brown lad he met in Luzon got through all right — wasn't mistaken for a wild boar, thank God! — I mean, thanks to trigger-happy American sentries. Tell him that *native* boy doesn't exist anymore. Someone's taken his place: a stranger he doesn't know. And return his gift to him. Tell him "address unknown" — no, rather, say: "believed to have changed, not his address, but his beliefs, his outlook towards Mother America."

Then Benjie executes a military about-face and bounds

down stairs humming "Oh, say, can you see ...?"

Benjie's outburst has caught John by surprise, even Sabrina who knows how Benjie feels about Americans but not how he would react directly to someone like John. They stare helplessly at each other. John fidgets with the gift.

Sabrina: Please sit down, John.

John: Thank you, but I really must go —

Sabrina: But you can't. Not this way. I don't want you to leave with this impression —

John: It's the *only* impression possible.

Out in the street, the sound of Benjie's Honda takes a long time dying.

John: I can't possibly return this to my old man. It'll break his heart.

Sabrina: Your Dad deserves to keep a happier memory. Let me keep it for Benjie. He might want it later. May I open it?

But she has started to open the box: a combination tape recorder and radio. She turns it on for some music.

Sabrina: Wow! Just what *I've* always wanted! I've been looking at one on Escolta and was thinking of buying one —

John: Then keep it please. I wouldn't know what to do with it.

Sabrina: But I'll never hear the end of it from Benjie!

John: Now, I must really be going, Sabrina.

Sabrina: Must you, John? Just because of what happened?

John: Anyway, I came just to deliver a gift.

Sabrina: Not really, John, no —

John: I got it plainer than if he'd written "GO HOME YANKEE" on a placard and hit me on the face with it.

Sabrina: But Benjie is *not* the Sioson family nor the Filipino people. He's not going to spoil what we've been known all over the world for — our hospitality. It's lunchtime. How about a bite at the Automat? It's only a minute from here.

John: I feel like going home.

Sabrina: At the Automat, you'll feel at *home*. It's in the

middle of our Little America.

John: Sabrina ... you don't have to make up for him—

Sabrina: I'm not making it up for Benjie. And I'm not letting you turn down a girl's invitation. How will I be able to live it down all my life?

Perhaps each has really been attracted to the other at first sight. Or perhaps they are slowly drawn to each other by the brother's antagonism. But from the Automat they drive around the city in Sabrina's car; and they spend the evening together at the Sulo Restaurant at *his* invitation and his turn to say she can't say no to his invitation. They end up at the Showcase, for some dancing. It turns out he has not gone anywhere else in the city and knows no one. Evening of the next day they are in the *Indios Bravos*, a place he has begun to like very much.

It is their third time at *Indios Bravos*. They have been hours in the cafe, starting in the late afternoon when they were the only customers, then staying on to watch the city go dark and see the people — habitués and tourists — go in and out. They stay late into the night until, again, as in the late afternoon, they would be the only couple left.

John is playing with his dry martini, twirling his drink with his small, thick finger, staring at it, tilting it, sipping it.

Sabrina sits across the table studying his eyes under the low light, his blond hair that half hides his face. His tongue has started to loosen and he begins a long monologue addressed more to his drink than to her.

John: I was plucked from my youth and placed in the midst of a carnage. When the draft board caught me — that's the word, *caught* — I was on the campus, I was in the middle of my last year in college, in fact, in the middle of a date — or if I may exaggerate — In the middle of a *kiss!* Oh, I've a number of girls but they were only part of my growing up —

in fact, part of American co-educational life. None of them really mattered much, and that, Sabrina, is my greatest fear; that I will die before I meet her who is destined to be my first, great love. I want so much to stay alive — long enough to meet and fall in love with her. Is that asking too much of life? I want to live long enough to leave a mark: on this earth, on my country, on my town, on my home. I want to leave behind a sign that will say that John Fergusson Cummings was born, grew up, wrote a book, headed a corporation, or won a trial in court. Oh, I will even settle for any mark: maybe robbing a bank. Thing is, I haven't done or created anything — good or bad — that will last twenty-four hours. I haven't found where my interest — or talent, if any — lies. Was I born and reared to drop bombs on thatched houses half a world away? To riddle thin, hungry natives with machine-gun fire — and die afterwards? Is that how I will make my mark, as a murderer? For murder it is, can't you see, all of you out there, can't you see at all it's stark *murder*? That word had lost its offensiveness, its real horror, and it seems only *we* who are there can speak of it truthfully. But we cannot because it is treason to do so. "Ours not to reason why ..." Oh, I write my Dad to tell him how it really is — somehow I get past military censors — but my Dad won't believe me. He says it is just like in Bataan and Corregidor. But it isn't, Sabrina, it is a different kind of war. Different from Korea, from Pearl Harbor and what happened after it. It's not even a war. Wars can sometimes be decent. Or even humane. But this, it's a carnage: a ruthless, bloody, senseless, endless carnage. And I am caught in it as in a vortex. God, I sometimes shout in my mind, can this be happening right under His nose? What is the meaning of all this? Where is the end? Is there even a God to hear me, Sabrina? Is there?

John grips his glass, almost crushing it in his hands, spilling the remainder of his drink on his hand, on the cloth napkin and the table. Sabrina takes his hand and slowly pries his fingers open, one by one, until she is able to free the glass. With cloth napkin she wipes his hands dry. Then she clasps his hands to keep them warm and dry.

A shallow falls across the table. They both look up and find Benjie towering over them, his friends behind him like aides-de-camp. By their looks they have been drinking the whole night.

Benjie: Good evening, sis. Or should I say "Good morning"?

Sabrina: Benjie, of course you remember John —

Benjie: Shouldn't my beloved sis be home at this hour instead of fraternizing with R&R —

Sabrina: Benjie, I think you've had more than you can carry.

Benjie: What are you doing in this questionable place with this questionable character?

Sabrina: Benjie, how dare you!

Benjie: How dare I what?

Sabrina: Benjie, I beg you, please …

She tries to catch his hand but he swipes her hand off, hitting a glass which breaks on the floor. John rises from his seat —

John: Benjie —

Benjie: Why do you stand up? We're not playing your national anthem …

John: I don't want to have to defend a lady from her own brother …

Benjie: But that's where you Americans are good at, defending Asians from each other.

John: I will have to ask you to leave her —

Suddenly, Benjie sends a blow across the table, hitting John squarely on the chest and throwing him against the chair. As if on signal, Benjie's friends starts to pummel John until he drops on the floor. Sabrina throws herself in the middle of the melee.

Sabrina: Stop it! Pete! Stop it! Somebody, please call the police!

Benjie tries to pull Sabrina out, but she pulls away with

fury.

Sabrina: Don't touch me, Benjie! Leave us now or I'll ask the guard to call the police!

Benjie raises a hand to slap her but Sabrina will not be cowed. Then Benjie and his friends file out of the place. Sabrina kneels down to pull John up.

Sabrina: Will somebody please help him to the car?

They are in his hotel room in the Hilton. With the little knowledge of first-aid that she remembers from her girl-scouting days, Sabrina dresses the wound on his lip — a mean one-inch cut — and the bruises on his face.

Sabrina: Oh, they really cut you up badly. Maybe we should have called the police and pressed charges —

John: Against your own brother? Oh, no!

Sabrina: Benjie's been spoiled by my mother. It's high time someone taught him a lesson.

John: I wasn't cut out to be his teacher in that respect. It's my fault, too.

She looks out the window at the cars lined toys in the hotel parking lot.

John: Sabrina, I appreciate your making it up for him—

Sabrina: John, I keep telling you, I'm *not* making it up for him. I am not being nice and kind only because he's been very *mean* to you. It has nothing to do with that.

He has stayed as far as possible from her after she had bandaged him up. Now he walks over to her and stands behind her, looking at the night sky.

John: You've even risked spoiling your reputation by coming to my room at this hour.

Sabrina: What reputation? I came because I like you, John.

John places a hand on her shoulder.

John: Sabrina, I wish I could tell you my own feelings. But there is so much between us. First, there is a whole globe, this — turbulent — world between us. Then blood and race and —

Sabrina: What I feel now has nothing to do with color or race. You might well have been yellow or purple. I'm color-blind.

She turns to him. She starts caressing his cheek: pink and clear like a baby's skin. She wonders if he has started to shave. He picks up her hand and kisses the tips of her fingers, closing his eyes.

John: Sabrina, I'm so lonely ... and afraid ...

Sabrina: Afraid of what, John?

John: Of this kind of life. I'm so close to death I can't even start to live.

Then they kiss, and she realizes how short she is against him — and she has to stand on her toes to reach his lips.

Sabrina sits at one end of the bed folding John's shirts and stuffing them into his suitcase. He comes out of the bathroom fixing his tie.

John: Sabrina, you don't have to see me off. I can take a taxi. I want you to go straight home.

He picks up the phone and calls the desk for a room boy. Sabrina sits quietly, thinking how she can slip into the house —

John: Will you be all right, Sabrina?

She rises and adjusts his tie unnecessarily. He gives her a peck on the cheek.

Sabrina: I can take care of myself.

John: I know it's hard to do it out there ... but, for your sake, I'll stay alive.

Sabrina: John, you will keep yourself alive, and not only for my sake.

John: Out there one doesn't know if the next day will find one — blinded — or crippled for life — or dead.

Sabrina: You will be all right, John.

John: I'm going up to put in a request to my commander ...

Sabrina: Request?

John: For permission to marry.

Sabrina: John, you're *proposing to me!*

John: But I have to propose to my commander first.

Sabrina: Yes, especially because I'm Asian. Asian wives pose such a special problem for the army —

John: Sabrina, it'll take some time.

Sabrina: It will give you time to think it over.

John: I don't have to. I'm quite sure about my feelings, it's you —

Sabrina: Like you, John, I live by the day.

John: I'll be back here soon, with permission to marry, God willing.

Sabrina: You mean Commander willing ...

John: Oh, yes. Do you realize the White House has to approve it?

The doorbell rings and the room boy comes in to pick up John's luggage.

From the airport — for she had insisted on driving him there — she makes her way home in ten minutes. She rushes up the house.

At the door of her room Benjie, having just heard her car drive in, stands guard, holding the morning papers.

Benjie: And where have been all night?

Sabrina: I stayed the night with Elena.

Benjie: You probably mean your white boyfriend?

Sabrina: Let me pass —

Benjie: I don't blame that whitey man for thinking my country is a whorehouse, but must you, my own sister, act like a whore —?

He drops the papers and tries to catch her hand. She pulls away, throwing him off balance, and dashes into her room, shutting the door behind her. Benjie pounds furiously on the door.

Benjie: Open the door, Sabrina! Open the door, slut!

John's absence has brought about a moratorium in their quarrel. It has not been difficult for each other to avoid the other in the house for they keep disparate hours: Benjie comes home past midnight, sleeps up to noontime, while Sabrina leaves for her office at seven thirty in the morning and is home by early evening.

One Sunday they catch each other at the dining table.

Sabrina: Why do you stare at me like that?

Benjie: I've been missing you for days. I was afraid something had gone wrong. You all right, sis? How is your world policeman? Doesn't he write you? Or is this the case of "hanggang MIA lang"?

She is debating with herself whether to retreat to her room without breakfast or to battle him across the table.

Benjie: Hey, sis, I'm talking to you! Or don't you talk to Indios anymore, only to Caucasians?

Sabrina: Benjie, you've been very beastly to me lately—

Benjie: If you must know, my dear sister, you're my responsibility. What will Mom and Dad say if they come home to find you've fallen into the bloodied hands of a murderer —

Sabrina: Don't call him *that!*

Benjie: Why do you get hurt? What's he to you, really?

Sabrina: A human being, so treat him as one.

Benjie: If he is one — and that's one big if — then it's high time he behaved like one, and not go around taking potshots at us Filipinos —

Sabrina: Benjie, he has nothing to do with what's happening in Clark Field. That's a different matter.

Benjie: They're all the same whenever they are. In Alabama, in Saigon, in Angeles, Pampanga. They shoot Blacks for simply wanting to enter a classroom. They shoot Vietnamese farmers trying to convince them democracy will grow in their land like rice. And they shoot us for trespassing on our own backyard. If we don't watch out, they'll decimate us. But, wait a minute. Why do I have to say this to *you?* Before you met him, we used to agree on a lot of things. Like on Vietnam — it being one mass murder, no different from what happened at Auschwitz. That we should, years from now, hold a Nuremberg trial — you even suggested Japan as the site of the trial.

Sabrina: Maybe I did — but I don't have to agree with you on everything.

Benjie: Oh, you've changed your mind about Vietnam.

Sabrina: Maybe not. But now I am more enlightened on it. I have met someone who is smack in the middle of it. It's different from reading a book about it. I've talked a lot with him and it has given me an insight into that war. I realize now that John and his friends are as much victims as the Vietnamese peasants. They're at the mercy of those above him — in Vietnam and in Washington. Of course he knows what he's doing out there.

Benjie: Then how can God forgive them if they know and persist —

Sabrina: It's not so much knowing as being unable to help what they're doing!

Benjie: Why then does he obey? Unless he *enjoys* it. Why doesn't he drop his rifle and leave the frontline?

Sabrina: Do you think it is easy for a soldier to do that? For a man you're naïve — it would mean court-martial, or death, or imprisonment for him!

Benjie seems to have run out of arguments.

Benjie: Better for him to die doing right —

Sabrina: That's easier said than done.

Benjie: It's cowardice.

Sabrina: It's a weakness more than anything else, Benjie. Helplessness. Don't forget that John's just a boy. He was only a senior in college. He's younger than both of us.

At that moment the doorbell rings. Sabrina takes the chance to break the discussion. It is the mailman bringing in the first of a number of cassette recordings which John mailed to her from Saigon.

It is an uncanny feeling, hearing his disembodied voice as if he were right before her, but hearing it all strange and foreign. Sometimes, she wishes he would go back to writing letters, even on military stationery, even in his unreadable penmanship.

Reads one tape:

"It is a fine morning here in Saigon. The fire trees are in bloom, a great sight to see. It is wonderful to see Saigon's women, pedaling their bicycles against the breeze, their ao dais billowing behind them like fish lanterns. And the girls — every pretty Vietnamese girl here reminds me of you, Sabrina ..."

The tapes come in almost every day. In between descriptions of the city and its people, and life at the barracks, he talks about himself:

"I've never been the same since our meeting. Before, I never cared for my life. I was ready to throw it away like garbage, as my own people have been treating my life. Now, I believe in life, love, faith, tomorrow, goodness, and all the good and beautiful. Pretty soon I'll start believing in God again. It is a short way — isn't it? — between believing in the things He made and believing in Him."

It had become a ritual: her daily communion with his words and thoughts. In the morning, around nine, the maid would bring in a new tape after the chimes. She would grab it, run to her room, lock the door, slide the tape into the recorder, and lie down to listen to him while she stared at the ceiling.

"Last night, in the lull between skirmishes, I played in my mind — like a cassette recorder — the days I spent with you. The memory of that week, in spite of your brother (I have spliced him out of it) is, to use a mixed metaphor, like a piece of cake I have hoarded — niggardly miser that I am — in the night under my blanket, relishing it bit by bit and always afraid the hoard will not last the time left of my life."

He suggests one day that she also send him her voice

on tape but she chooses to write him in the old manner. The idea of having to buy an empty tape and speaking out loud to it through a mike she finds quite embarrassing.

One day he sends this is in:

"We went through an ambush yesterday — the Vietcong are turning vicious, like gadflies, and I got out of it half alive. I spent a day at the hospital. My chum, whom I wrote you about, didn't make it."

At this point his voice seems to break:

"When we buried his remains, I cried like a little boy … and wished you were beside me."

In the next tape he complacently talks about his plans to marry:

"I wrote Mom and Dad about you. They're pleased you're Filipino. Dad feels a Filipino doesn't seem a stranger at all. Oh, yes, I was called by my commander regarding my request. He assured me he'll he hearing from Washington soon. Boy, perhaps LBJ himself will sign our marriage contract — and there's only a slight change from *martial* to *marital* contract — hehehe! — so don't be impatient — or am I presuming too much at this end? I do wish you'd let me know by long distance — I told you how to go about contacting me via RCA Manila — if I'm doing right in pursing this idea like mad. After all, it takes two to marry."

Towards the end of the year his voice sounds weary and lonely and afraid:

"Life in Saigon and the suburbs is perking up because of the coming Tet festival. But it is not as idyllic as your fiestas over there. The Vietcong have the habit of celebrating it with rampage — a mass amok I should say! Behind the joy and color of this festival is the color of blood, the specter of death. When one hears sounds of explosion, one wonders: Is it firecrackers or gunfire? Is someone celebrating life, or giving up life? … The Vietcong are strangely quiet. I don't like it. I don't like it at all."

Sabrina comes home with a cassette tape which she has received at her office. Running to her room, she finds the radio-recorder gone.

It isn't too difficult locating it, for music is coming from the terrace, from the radio-recorder perched on the low terrace wall. Beside it, Benjie sprawled on the garden chair, listening.

Sabrina: Why did you get that from my room?

She heads directly to the recorder. He clamps a hand over it before she reaches it.

Benjie: Why, I thought this was mine? Given to me by your soldier-defender of democracy in the Far East?

It is some time before she answers.

Sabrina: When he tried to give it to you, you refused it. You even insulted him.

Benjie: I'm sorry I did — I mean, sorry I refused it — but now I want it.

Sabrina fumes with anger.

Sabrina: All right. It may be yours — I'll buy my own— today — but the tapes are *mine*.

Benjie: What tapes? Oh, those magnetic love letters ... from your magnetic personality. Sorry, but I got rid of them.

Sabrina: How dare you —!

Benjie: I couldn't stand them. I listened to one and I almost puked.

Sabrina: That's like opening my letters: a violation of privacy ...!

Benjie: I found them in *my* recorder —

Sabrina: But you had no right to throw them away!

Benjie: But I didn't throw them away. I kept one. For Dad. He'll enjoy listening to this one.

He turns off the radio, presses the replay button and John's voice comes out in a shrill melodramatic tone.

John's voice: Oh, Sabrina, Sabrina, how I ache to catch the scent of your breath again. And feel of you —

She reaches for the recorder, but he slaps a hand over

it. The recorder stops.

Benjie: Won't Dad enjoy *that?*

Sabrina: You have no right to meddle —

Benjie: Why can't I — your brother —

Sabrina: My life's my own and only I can decide what to do with it!

Benjie: Even if you want to throw it down the gutter!

Sabrina: But I have *not!*

Benjie: You're free to do what you want with your life, but must you drag our family reputation —?

Sabrina: You sound very much like that brother in that Montano play! Besides, what have I done to be shameful?

Benjie: There's the tape —

Sabrina: What does it prove? And if I *did* give my body, it's my own body — and my own affair — and you've nothing to do with it. As I have nothing to do with *your* body!

Benjie: You're really a —

Sabrina: What? *What? Say it!* WHAT?

She glares at him ferociously, as she has never done before in all their life together. Benjie is struck speechless. Taking advantage of her upper hand, she pulls the cassette from the radio-recorder and runs to her room.

Benjie: Bitch!

Benjie is in his room listening to a program of Asian music on the radio. The program is interrupted by an announcement:

Radio: "A massive attack was launched early this morning against this beleaguered city during the height of the Tet celebration."

With a sadistic glee — for his encounter with her that morning has rankled him all day — he runs to her room (the door fortunately unlocked) and finds her primping sadly before the mirror.

Sabrina: Benjie! Even a brother has to knock —

Benjie: I thought you might not want to miss this:

Radio: "Concerted attacks by land and air were made against Saigon and other military key points in South Vietnam, resulting in heavy casualties among South Vietnamese and American troops and civilians."

She draws a heavy breath on hearing this, but she manages to shout:

Sabrina: I don't want to hear it!

She flees out of the room and into the terrace, Benjie at her heels, with the radio blaring:

Radio: "Damage to military installations and personnel casualties have not been determined."

Benjie: Let's hope your boyfriend survives this.

Sabrina: Why do you hate him so, Benjie? Why, why? You're a sadist. I thought I knew my own brother!

Benjie: I thought I knew my own sister, too!

To cool off she drives down the boulevard. Later, nagged by the news about the Tet offensive, she drives to the RCA office near the Luneta. She asks to be connected to Saigon and gives John's name and address and phone number. But the lady at the RCA tells her all civilian communications with the city have been interrupted since dawn of that day.

For two days she has no contact with John.

On the third day she is able to get Saigon but can get no news about John. After a week a cable from John's commander arrives:

"ACCORDANCE WISHES JOHN FERGUSSON CUMMINGS WE SORRY NOTIFY YOU HIS DEATH LAST JAN 31 69 IN LINE OF DUTY STOP OUR CONDOLENCES STOP PERMISSION TO MARRY GRANTED HIM THE DAY BEFORE HIS DEATH."

Holding the cable in her hands, she feels her knees suddenly buckling under her and the tightness grips her chest. Tears, in a hot gush, rush to her eyes with sudden burning sensation.

Benjie, who happens to be around, catches her arm and

leads her to the sofa. Not knowing what to do or say, he just stares at the cable on the floor. Sabrina presses her temple against the back of the sofa and kneads the cushion with her hands.

Benjie rushes to his den and returns with the radio-recorder and places it on the center table. He approaches Sabrina gingerly and sits down beside her. He lays a hand on her shoulder.

Benjie: Sabrina ... you really did liked him? Oh, I was really mean and beastly, wasn't I? Do you think you can forgive me, Sabrina?

She makes a slight turn to look at Benjie. She lets go of the cushion and starts kneading Benjie's hand. Benjie feels trapped and thinks: If she doesn't stop, I'll soon be in tears myself.

The jam session has been going for hours. Benjie and his girl have been dancing while Sabrina tends to the music. She is seated on the floor, her legs under her, her white knees showing amply under her miniskirt.

Benjie's friends are dancing with their girlfriends, or drinking and chatting in every corner of the living room and terrace.

Among them is a young awkward-limbed young man with intense eyes dark brows, seated a distance from Sabrina. A new recruit of Benjie's militant group, he tries to hide his shyness by leafing through an old magazine. Once in a while he glances at Sabrina, as if gathering courage to ask her to dance.

The young man breathes heavily, put down the magazine and rises to approach her. Sabrina looks up from where she sits on the floor and their eyes meet. She nods to his mute request (shall we dance?) and he lifts her from the floor.

Left lying on the floor is an issue of *Life* magazine, open on the spread where photos of 242 young American men who died in one week's operations in Vietnam are featured.

Among the deflowered youth of America in Vietnam is one John Fergusson Cummings, from Milwaukee, Wisconsin, killed in line of duty on January 31, 1969, at the age of twenty-two.

MICHELLE CRUZ SKINNER

I WAS BORN in Rizal, Metro Manila, in 1965. My aunts still have the car in which my mother rode to the hospital to have me. My father drove. It is a white Opel that sits under a tarp in the carport in Makati. My mother, whenever she sees it, likes to say that it is older than me.

We lived in Manila; Los Baños, Laguna; and Angeles, Pampanga. When I was five we moved to Olongapo and stayed. When I was seven, martial law was declared. The story "Faith Healer" is kind of about that. Like all my short stories it is partially from memory and mostly from observation and imagination. "Faith Healer" was part of the PEN Syndicated Fiction Project in 1988.

From Olongapo, I moved to Honolulu, Hawaii and received my Bachelor of Arts in English from the University of Hawaii at Manoa. The stories in my undergraduate thesis— "Faith Healer" was one of them—and some stories I wrote shortly afterwards were published as Balikbayan: A Filipino Homecoming *by* Bess Press *of Hawaii. I received a Master of Fine Arts in Creative Writing from Arizona State University. I'm working on a book. I'm married.*

FAITH HEALER

I WAS BORN feet first and believed that this made me able heal people. Grandfather seemed to believe this, too. Whenever a fishbone was stuck in his throat he would come to me and have me lick my index and middle fingers and rub his throat. It was a Filipino belief, he said. He was always very old to me and I remember the skin on his throat being loose and soft.

"Lolo, is it working? Is it loose?" I would ask and he would just point at my fingers to keep trying to clear his throat. It made me feel important when He would stand before me presenting his throat to my fingers. I wondered what else it was that I was supposed to be able to heal people of.

Mama said I was lucky. Being born upside down, I could have died before I got out into the world. That's why I was so serious, she said. Mama believed that children who had faced death in this way were either very serious or very lighthearted.

This didn't make any sense to me at the time. I knew that I didn't laugh very often, and I tended to think things over carefully. It seemed that I just didn't take life in as easy and reckless a manner as most other children. Maybe that's why I did not really care for the company of other children.

When I was alone, I would read or draw or makeup stories in my head. At Lolo's house I would mostly draw. This was because Lolo knew I liked to draw and always made sure that he had plenty of scratch paper and crayons in his study. I would sweat at his desk drawing pictures on top of the glass that had all of his notes and photographs and newspaper articles pressed beneath it.

When I got tired of drawing, I would pull a newspaper out of Lolo's tall stack of newspapers. The *Bulletin Today* always had a lot of pictures, but *Manila News* was smaller and easier for me to handle. Also, their articles were shorter and used smaller, simpler words that I knew.

Lolo had been a journalist until he retired. That was why he had a study and so many books and why he subscribed to so many papers and read them all. At least I thought that was why. He was proud of his reading. When he came back from the hospital, after his stroke, he tried to read a newspaper and realized that he couldn't. He cried for a long time at night. The next morning I crept downstairs and found him in his study surrounded by stacks of books and newspapers.

While he remained unable to read, he refused to see visitors. This was a problem for Mama and my aunts and uncles because Lolo had a lot visitors who inquired after his health and wanted to wish him well. Relatives and a lot of his former co-workers came by. We lied about Lolo's health and took the cakes and candies and fruit that they brought.

Lolo soon remembered how to read and the next time we visited him I brought him a book. Mama tried to talk me out of it. "Don't waste your money. He has more than enough books." But I insisted. "You're matigas na ulo, like your Lolo," she said.

One night when we were at Lolo's, when I was almost asleep, I was jolted by the shrill siren of an ambulance. I ran to Mama's room crying because I thought they were coming for Lolo. It turned out to be Mang Boy, the man who lived in the little one-room next door.

All the neighbors said he was an artist, but I had never seen any of his paintings. I imagined that he kept them hidden in his house and that when he died we would finally see them. He didn't die that night.

The next day, Sita, the laundrywoman, told us that Mang Boy had had a heart attack when he heard on the radio that President Johnson had suffered one. That was the first time that I had ever heard of President Johnson.

Lolo just said that President Johnson wasn't worth it. I believed Lolo because he knew more about President Johnson than I did. We agreed that Mang Boy was a very foolish man.

A few months later when we went to visit Lolo for his birthday he met us at the gate with a very weary and somber expression.

"Martial law has been declared," he said.

"Marshall who?" Mama said as she struggled to get out of the car. "Who's he?"

"No. Mar-tial law," Lolo pronounced carefully. "Military rule. Proclaimed by Presidential Decree just this afternoon."

"Oh."

"President Johnson?" I was confused.

"Nooo."

"Oh." I thought about a minute. "Did he have another heart attack and die?" Lolo said no again and then mumbled something about how he wished somebody else would die. For the rest of the day everyone was quiet and very serious. I was sorry we had come to visit. We all went to sleep early that night.

Lolo typed in his study all the next day. He moved the phone into the study with him and made a lot of phone calls in between his typing. I sat on one side of his desk and drew pictures while he sat on the other side and typed and called people. I was the only one allowed to keep him company. He shouted at anyone else who entered.

Mama and Auntie Perla, my oldest auntie, complained about Lolo's behavior at dinner. Lolo just continued to pick at his fish.

"You could at least behave better in front of your granddaughter," Mama said. Lolo looked down at my clean plate with the utensils neatly laid across it. Then he looked at me.

"Are you tired, girl?"

"Yes, Lolo."

"Give her a bath and put her to bed. But don't get her hair wet or she'll get a cold."

"Tatay, you're not listening to us!" Mama complained. Lolo finally looked at Mama.

"You're going home tomorrow, aren't you?"

"Yes."

"Take her home to her father. Keep her in the American School." Lolo finished by wiping his mouth on a napkin and leaving the table. I wanted to stay in Manila with Lolo, but we left the next day as we had planned.

A few days later Daddy came home with a Filipino newspaper. Daddy always had a newspaper with him, but it was usually the *Stars and Stripes*. He seldom bought Filipino newspapers and he bought only *Bulletin Today* when he did. This newspaper wasn't *Bulletin Today*.

"Lorna!" he yelled as he walked in the door.

"Hi, Daddy!" I called from the couch. He ignored me.

"Looornaa!"

"What?!" Mama yelled from the kitchen. "I'm here."

"Your father is in the paper!"

My mother came running out of the kitchen with blood on her hands. "Ay Dios ko! Why? What happened?" Mama always expected news to be bad.

"What happened, Dad?"

"Just look at this!" Dad held up a page of the newspaper to Mama and pointed to an article. "He's gone and criticized our, well, your, beloved President."

Mama grabbed the paper away from Dad, smearing blood all over it as she gripped the pages tightly. It looked like the newspaper was bleeding. Or maybe Mama was. "Ay! This is ... terrible!" she moaned as she read the article. "He's too old to be doing this sort of thing."

I was trying to peek at the article from under his arm, but I didn't know which one she was reading. She finished the article quickly and snapped the paper to the front page to look at the masthead. "My God!"

"I know."

"This is a radical paper. They're all UP radicals!"

"The University of the Philippines is your alma mater, hon."

"Yes, but we weren't like this," my mother replied indignantly. "How did you know? You never buy this paper."

"He called me. Can you believe that?" Dad shook his head. "He called me at the office this afternoon." I didn't see anything unusual about that. Since we didn't have a telephone, Lolo always called Daddy at the office when he wanted to tell us something. "He called and told me about it, so of course I went out and bought a paper right away."

"Well, what are we going to do?" Mama groaned. She walked into the kitchen and begun scrubbing her hands in the sink, trying to get the blood off. We stood behind her and watched silently. Dad didn't appear to have any answer to her question. We just listened to the water rushing over Mama's hands.

"We have to call Perlita and the others," Mama suddenly decided.

"Why do we have to call Auntie Perla?" I said. "Can't we just call Lolo?" Mama brushed me away from her skirt and brushed my question aside. She ran to put on some shoes. Dad had already gone back outside. I heard the car start and then Mama ran out.

"Can I come?" I yelled at her retreating back.

"Susan will take care of you!" Mama yelled. She climbed into the car and they drove off. Susan, the maid, dragged me away from the door and made me sit in the kitchen with her while she finished making the dinner my mother had abandoned. I remained sullen and pouted. When it came time for dinner, I refused to eat and cried instead.

Mama and Daddy came home late that night. Mama came into my room while I was lying in the dark and started packing my clothes. I watched her silently for a few moments until I could separate her body from her shadow in the dark room.

"Mama, are we going to Manila tomorrow?"

"Yes, honey. Go back to sleep."

"Is Lolo okay?"

"Go back to sleep, dear."

They carried me into the car the next morning before I was fully awake. Mama had packed some sandwiches and bananas and we had those for breakfast. We drove over Zigzag, through the dusty little barrios and past the small towns without stopping. We reached Manila, sore and tried from the long drive, a little after noon.

After we got there things happened so quickly that it seemed like everyone was whirling around me. Auntie Perla met us at Lolo's house and then the other aunts and uncles arrived one by one bringing all their kids with them. It was hot and noisy in the house and I become grouchy.

Lolo wasn't there when we got there. Later in the evening we all went to Camp Crame where Auntie Perla said Lolo was, but I never saw him. None of us saw him. All I saw were a lot of Army men and a lot of ugly brown buildings. I didn't know if Lolo was really there or not. I hoped not because the men didn't smile.

Daddy went back home the next day but Mama and I stayed. I really wanted to go back home. Lolo wasn't around and I hated my cousins who were so noisy and stupid. They never left me alone. And my aunts and uncles got angry at me for being unfriendly.

Lolo never came home. A week later Auntie Perla answered the telephone and screamed. We all came running and crowded around her quietly while she tried to talk to the person on the other end of the phone. She was frantically pulling out drawers and flinging open the doors cabinets searching for something. Mama passed her a small notebook and pen and, still listening to the phone, she wrote something down. We all left after that and drove for almost an hour through the heavy diesel smog of Manila traffic until we came to a large, dirty white building in a strange part of town.

It was a hospital. The nurse took us up to Lolo's room and then left us as quickly as possible. Lolo lay flat on a narrow bed with a white sheet stretched taut across him pinning him to the mattress. Even if the sheet hadn't been there, I don't think he could have moved.

His skin wasn't the wax-paper thinness that I remembered. It was almost transparent now. I could see not only the dark blue veins on his neck, but also tiny blood vessels. The skin on his neck looked even more loose and wrinkled than I remembered. He never opened his eyes, but just kept sleeping. I was afraid to touch him he looked so weak.

The nurses tried to make us leave, but there were too many of us to throw out. So, we stayed there for the night, sleeping in the few chairs in the room and out in the hallway. I wanted to stay awake, but I couldn't.

When I woke up the next morning, someone had already taken Lolo away. I believed that I could heal people, but I hadn't been able to help him at all. I found out that all I could do was remove fishbones from people's throats. And only Lolo truly believed that I could do that.

PAULINO LIM, JR.

THE EXCERPT is from the third book of a political trilogy which I began when I was a Fulbright lecturer in Taiwan during the 1986-87 academic year. Before then I had written short stories, as well as a Master's thesis on Bienvenido N. Santos at the Santo Tomas in the Philippines and a Ph.D. Dissertation on Lord Byron at UCLA. The latter was published in Salzburg, Austria (1973). Right after high school I had my first published short story. The turning point of my writing career came after a visit to the Philippines, when a short story I wrote in my hometown — Camalig, Albay — won first prize in the Asiaweek *1985 short story competition. The story, "Homecoming," has a political theme and forms part of the anthology* Passion Summer *(1988).* Asiaweek *published the story on 26 January 1986, a few weeks before the People's Power Revolution that ended the Marcos dictatorship and began the beleaguered regime of President Corazon Aquino. New Day has published the first novella of the trilogy,* Tiger Orchids on Mount Mayon (1990), *and also the second,* Sparrows Don't Sing in the Philippines (1993). *The third novel,* Requiem for a Rebel Priest, *has been completed. Mainly, I am a professor of English literature and writing at California State University, Long Beach.*

MICHELLE AND THE JESUIT

(An excerpt from the novel *Requiem for a Rebel Priest*)

AFTER YEARS of training for the priesthood, he had felt as comfortable standing on the pulpit as sitting in the classroom. That was before his Jesuit superiors sent him to study at San Francisco University in the late 60's and his whole life changed. He had not anticipated nor trained for it, not in the cloistered schools at Ateneo De Naga in the Philippines, or novitiate at Woodstock, Maryland, for the tertianship prior to ordination. The Jesuit campus at SFU was relatively calm compared to the turmoil in nearby San Francisco State and Berkeley across the bay. He quickly identified the elements of demonstration. Action was galvanized by placards waving above marchers, loudspeakers gathering cacophonous voices into frenzy, then breaking up when shots were fired in the air and smoke belched provocation and violence, and policemen's clubs began swinging at suicidal heads. He'd retreat to the chapel and his room in the dorm where he found refuge from the dangers of the streets of San Francisco, but none from his disturbed heart.

At the Jesuit community, where he stayed, he sought out his American Literature professor, Father Robert Jeffers, before the start of the semester. Father Jeffers greeted him with a diffident smile and said, "Welcome aboard, Gene. See you in class." Jeffers lectured from notes, speaking in clear phrases that Gene found easy to take down. He had the impression that Jeffers seemed to look through his students, rather than *at* them, more intensely absorbed in ideas than personalities. He'd welcome questions, restate the points of his lecture, thank the speakers, then move on. He kept humor and irony to a minimum; a favorite target for his jokes was the hippies, "denizens of Haight-Ashbury" as he often called them. In his introductory lecture on American Transcendentalism, he said, "They completely miss the mark, hippies who think they have found a guru in Thoreau." He did not elaborate, and simply added, "Wait until we read *Walden*."

Gene listened to the lecture with stereophonic attention, one for the language and the other for ideas. In his notebook he wrote pronunciations different from what he had heard in the Philippines: "couplet" pronounced "cuplit" and not "cooplit"; "allegory" stressed on the first rather than the second syllable; "connect" not fully articulated in "Connecticut." He did not trust his background knowledge of the country's literature, which he learned via courses in American history and literature, although taught by American Jesuits at the Ateneo; he did not know enough about Carlyle to pick up Jeffers' reference to the Victorian as he lectured on Emerson. But he had studied Kant in his metaphysics classes at the seminary and excelled in logic. He found it fairly easy to grasp the larger philosophical ideas; his lack of confidence in the spoken language was offset by his grasp of method and logic, and he prided himself at being able to disentangle skeins of thought, or bring down to earth a speaker's rhetorical flights of fancy. He found amusing the notion that Emerson substituted the unconscious for divine grace, found the locus of God in the human soul, and preached self-reliance. Jeffers gave an explanation for the Emersonian sleight-of-mind: "And this all become possible in the shift from allegory to symbolism as a mode of thought, from the Puritan thinking that nature is an emblem of God to the Romantic notion that nature is a revelation of God."

One night after supper, when most of the priests had left the dining room early to watch the final quarter of a football game between Notre Dame and Southern Cal, Gene said to Jeffers, "I'd like to do my paper on Emerson's essays as sermons, if that's okay with you."

Jeffers smiled. "Of course. Do they remind you of your own sermons, Gene?"

"No. Emerson is much more eloquent. Besides, in the Philippines we're preaching agrarian reform and liberation theology."

"So do our Jesuits in South America. A potent combination, I'd say. I'd like to go to San Salvador myself if I had the chance."

"My papers won't be purely a rhetorical analysis. I'm more interested in how he finds God's power in the human mind."

"That should be an interesting paper. You can extend that by showing how he equates the theological sense of grace with the psychological notion of the unconsciousness."

"I'll try. I remember, you mentioned that in class."

"You know, there's a Ph.D. Dissertation lurking in there some place, in case you're interested."

"Thank you, Father, but perhaps not."

"Call me Bob, Gene."

"Have you ever visited the Philippines?"

"No, I'd like to, maybe teach at the Ateneo, among the top three or four schools in the country, I hear. Is this your first visit to the U.S.?"

"No, Bob, I did my tertianship at Woodstock, Maryland."

Jeffers laughed and said, "I forgot we have a seminary there. Nowadays, Woodstock means rock concert, you know, that took place last summer."

Shortly after, a woman in class named Michelle entered his thoughts. At night in his study and the daily Mass in the community chapel, classroom images came unbidden. He'd see her whiteness against his brown skin, a soft profile in contrast to the sunburnt beach-blonde California stereotype, her upturned nose and blue, blue eyes. As the semester progressed Michelle's words gave voice to the mental picture, and he'd find himself trying to find flaws in her logic but getting lost in her laughter, her ideas quite different from his or Jeffers'.

Even Jeffers began to look at Michelle, Gene noticed. He recalled the time the class discussed "Days," a poem of eleven lines by Emerson. Jeffers was more interested in showing how the poem arrived at themes of self-reliance and return to nature. Tropes of days seen as hypocritical daughters of Time and as dervishes that offer gifts. The speaker spurns gifts of riches and fame, content to take a few herbs and spices from his pleached garden.

"Now, you can see why hippies love this poem," Jeffers was saying, "thinking they can subsist on apples and herbs, the kind that you smoke."

After the laughter subsided, Michelle's hand went up. "I find amusing the gender that Emerson assigns to days. I believe the poem is quite disparaging, somewhat contemptuous of women."

"But dervish is pretty neutral," said Jeffers.

"Perhaps, but the fact is the hypocritical days are depicted as women offering gifts to men, each after 'his will,' as Emerson puts it," Michelle said.

"It would be unpoetic to say 'his' or 'her'."

"True, but to take the other image, as members of mendicant religious groups, dervishes are much likely to beg than offer gifts."

The class broke into the iconoclastic laughter at a revered thinker making a fallacy. Gene chuckled, thinking, All right, Bob, admit a possible contradiction in the poem and the laughing will cease.

"I suppose, Michelle, you'd like to do a paper on Emerson's misreading of Eastern philosophy," Jeffers said, trying to make an ironic recovery of the ground he had lost during the exchange. It was a mistake.

"No, sir, not interested. I don't want to do my research at Tessajara."

"That might not be a bad idea. Jesuits at the St. Sophia University in Kyoto often go to Buddhist monasteries and have retreats conducted by Zen Masters." Another mistake, a non sequitur, Gene thought.

"In the interest of ecumenism, I suppose," she said, matching his understated irony with a smile, and no hint of rudeness.

Wisely, Jeffers began talking about the poem "Each and All" but Gene saw that his professor was rattled. The other students, inspired by Michelle, began to tear the poem apart.

"The theme of the poem sticks out like a sore thumb," said Brajnikoff, a reedy, emaciated student. "Take a look at the couplet 'All are needed by each one;/Nothing is fair or good alone.' It doesn't even rime."

"Come on, it's a visual rime."

"Visually inept, I'd say. And take a look at what follows. The speaker brings home a sparrow in its nest to listen to its singing. It's worse than Tennyson plucking the flower from the crannied wall to extoll its beauties."

The bell rang. Gene saw his professor smile, a wan smile, and felt that he'd survive, wiser but for the humiliation of being taught by his students. Emerson, too, would survive.

Michelle and Gene had conversed as classmates halfway into the semester; they were ready to treat each other as friends but he had not mentioned he was a priest. Was it too late to do so? Would she construe it as a warning of sorts and take it as an insult, that he saw the possibility of their relationship becoming more intimate? That would be presumptuous. After waiting this long, he wondered what she'd say. I thought there was something prissy about you, now I'm not surprised. Or, how nice of you to warn me; am I supposed to put up an emotional guardrail?

When hr told her his term paper project, she groaned, "Yuk! 'Emerson's Essays as Sermons'! What on earth made you choose that topic?"

He checked his first response, "Nothing on earth made me do it but perhaps something in heaven did." Too easy a ploy for a cheap laugh. How much of his thinking oscillated between the polarities of heaven and hell. Too many Filipino puns in English relied upon bilingual awareness, for instance, collapsing the phase "traditional politicians" into "trapos" and recovering its Spanish meaning of the latter a "dirty rags."

"I'll do a rhetorical analysis, you know, look at stylistic devices, figures of speech, that sort of thing. Structuralism is the rage these days, you know."

"Have you taken courses in classical rhetoric?"

"Some."

"I envy you here. Here at SFU?"

"No, at Woodstcok."

"Really? Where they had that fantastic rock and roll concert?"

"No, this was a Jesuit school in Maryland."

This was the moment to say he had studied for the priesthood at the seminary, but he didn't, withholding information as crucial to a woman as knowing that a man she likes is already married. Sensations he remembered, or his body remembered, clustered around defiance. Twice in his life he had felt it: when he resisted family to take up the favored careers of his family, law, medicine and foreign service; and when he resisted his superiors' advice to tone down rhetoric when he began preaching that the Bible did not absolutely forbid violence to right wrongs engendered by unjust social structures. He knew the feeling, bracketing action and thought with remorse or triumph at the end, with no one to blame but himself. He thought of Filipinos, afraid to be exposed as illegal aliens and face the ignominy of being deported, lying their way to respectability. Among Filipinos they were called TNT, the explosive acronym for the Tagalog "tago ng tago," literally, "hide and hide."

"Gee, you must love the Jesuits."

"Don't you?"

"Not really. Berkeley was my first choice," she said, an elfin smile on her face. "I guess, I didn't make the quota assigned to whites."

"How about you, what's your research project?"

"Definitely not Emerson, too transparent. I'm going to

do mine on Poe, all that murky uncertainty of his tales."

"You'd rather be mystified than enlightened."

"That's nicely put. Now I see you wanna do rhetorical analysis. You and Jeffers are on the same wave length. You both want to wrap things up, define themes, analyze rhetoric."

Gene laughed and said, "That's Jesuit education for you. Don't knock it though. I did read someplace that Hitler used St. Ignatius Loyola's training manual in his youth campus."

"No kidding."

"Must be apocryphal?"

"Oh dear, you even talk like him."

"No, a Filipino and American may speak the same language but they're not saying the same thing."

"Is that so? That means I just have to guess what you're trying to say to me."

"That's easy. What are you doing Friday night?"

"I like the way you sprang that on me. If you really want to know, I'll be waitressing at the Beacon, a seafood place at the wharf."

"Are you busy, then?"

"I'll be done by about eleven. Come thereabouts and I'll take you to a party across the bay."

He ordered beer and watched Michelle. It surprised him. He had not really watched women work. He had gotten used to maids who did their self-effecting chores, like the black-clad figures on the Japanese stage, who helped kabuki players change costumes and move props. In class Michelle was all mind and speech, here all motion and body language. It took a while to put the two images together, her fluid and brisk movements, her throbbing bodily presence with her mental energy and gift of tongue. Without his being aware of it at first, his body responded as if trying to match her action, stopping at tables, taking orders, disappearing behind the kitchen door, and bringing in trays of salmon, clams, and lobster.

"Howdy, stranger," he heard Michelle from behind, "ain't you gonna buy me a drink?"

Unfamiliar with barroom banter and dating, he was tongue-tied but managed a smile at the moist face, teasing him with an attention that was almost surrender.

"Shall we go, Gene?"

He paid for his beer and followed Michelle trailing a smell of cigarette and liquor. Outside, he wanted to guide her by the hand but could not decide whether to hold her elbow or shoulder. They got into her Volkswagen and drove a few blocks down Mission Street before getting on the freeway. Across the Bay Bridge, wind swept the restaurant scent away and Gene felt the nearness of a body, sweaty and warm, in space as tight as the confessional with no grille or curtain to hide her white arm and leg working the stick shift and pedals.

Michelle squeezed the VW between a Buick and a Ford, as if sidling between crowded tables. She said, "How's that side?"

"You're fine."

"Great. We'll have to walk a bit, couple of blocks up that road."

"What's the occasion for the party?"

"Nothing, really, just four Berkeley guys sharing this old Victorian home inviting their friends to a Friday night shindig."

The porch of the two-story house extended from the main structure, with the stairway close to the sidewalk. Gene followed Michelle into a living room, canopied with a thick smell of pot and human bodies, whose individual chatter became intelligible within a radius of two feet above the din and the sitar. A few said hi, as Michelle took him to a basin of iced drinks in the kitchen. The circle of their intimacy drew tighter than the confessional nearness of the Volkswagen, her hair upon his face.

"Help yourself, Gene," she said, as she picked up a bottle of orange drink. "The success of this party is entirely up to you."

"You bet," he said, opening a beer and raising it to Michelle, but she was already talking to man sporting the evening stubble of a shaved head and a Nehru jacket. He started back to the living room, checkmating bodies along the way, pausing to eavesdrop on conversations and giggles.

Two Filipina students were comparing notes. One said, "I can't speak Tagalog now. We came here when I was a kid, but still know a few words, for instance, 'tabungaw' for squash, or 'ampalaya' for bitter melon."

"Have you eaten ampalaya cooked in coconut milk and seasoned with bagoong and hot pepper?"

They noticed him listening and he quickly said, "Hi, I'm Gene, couldn't help overhearing your culinary conversation."

As if on cue, they shot a glance at each other. I wonder if it's how I said 'culinary'; it could be my textbook English or my accent.

"I'm Andrea, this is Jasmine. We're both from the Philippines. Should we try to guess where you from?"

"I think you already have."

"You don't fit the stereotype, Filipino guys are supposed to be crazy about blondes. You've come with a brunette."

"You must admit, Jaz, still a very white chick."

"No offense, Gene, we're just teasing you."

He said with mock longing, "I sure miss ampalaya cooked in coconut milk, seasoned with hot pepper."

Andrea and Jasmine giggled and put their hands to their mouths. Ah, the Pinay's giveaway gesture of modesty.

He saw the man in the Nehru jacket again, this time talking to a group of men. He was saying, "A dropout, twice. I dropped out of the investment business and now Tessajara."

"What happened?"

"I don't see eye to eye with the jikijitsu. He hates my guts. He's being groomed to run the place when the Zen Master goes to Florida. We've just bought a huge piece of property down there."

"Why does he hate your guts?"

"Oh, he's a pompous ass. We were discussing koans one day and he really blew his top when I asked, 'What happens to the nails that we cut off our fingers and toes?'"

"A dumb-ass question."

"Perhaps. I was making a point about koans. You know, riddles the Zen Master gives you, such as what's the sound of the hand clapping. You're supposed to come up with an answer that satisfies him. Something experienced rather than thought of."

"That sounds reasonable. An answer arrived at between thought and action. Must be the stuff of life itself."

"No matter. Trying to answer koans is as dumb as figuring out how many angels can dance on the head of a pin."

A man kept mumbling, "Hit, man, hit."

"There is a common denominator at the base of all religions. Therefore, as to the question, can a man eat at McDonalds and experience mysticism, the answer is yes. Except perhaps it's a much more difficult for beef eaters to experience mysticism than vegetarians."

He'd bump into Michelle on his way to the kitchen for beer, and held her on the pretext of steadying her sway, curious whether the toned firmness extended beyond the arms and waist. She didn't mind the narrowing circle of their intimacy as the past-midnight hours brought tedium and began to scatter the guests.

"What do you think, Gene?"

"I'm ready when you are."

He had his arm round her shoulders as they walked to the VW. The Buick and the Ford were gone. Michelle unlocked his side, he got in and opened the driver's side. She eased the VW down University Avenue toward the freeway. In mistied distance the lights of San Francisco seemed unreal as the reflections on the bay. He touched her thigh; she let go of the stick shift and pressed his hand against her skin, sending shivers down his spine.

He woke up dreaming of Michelle's bed, expecting to see the San Francisco light gathered by the curtained alcove of her Victorian house. Then he heard Berlioz bark. He kept his eyes closed, reluctant to let go of Michelle, whose body contoured sexuality in the uninhibited surrender of her embrace. God, he thought, that was twenty years ago. Then he heard a glass door slide open, and his wife Helen perching her voice to the decibel level of a growl, "Berlioz, shut up!"

He opened his eyes to the epiphyllum on the still, breaking the rectangled monotony of the tract house window, and slipped out of the carpeted bedroom, down the hallway, past the living room to the kitchen. Reading the morning paper, Helen gave the habitual tilt of her head, so he could kiss her cheek, then said, "Your damned dog kept me awake all night."

Both did it, referring a child or dog that caused annoyance as "your daughter" or "your dog," inviting argument or a placating apology on behalf of the absent child or the mute dog. He chose to remain silent, already won to the idea of taking Berlioz to the Philippines. If this were the usual paid vacation, which marked the beginning and end of an office worker's calendar year, Helen would have been clipping travel information about weather, bargains, festivals. Not much word about travel to the Philippines, especially after military extremists attempted their sixth coup and staged it in Makati, Manila's financial center; this got worldwide television coverage and scared tourists by the thousands away from the country. Instead she was clipping items about Japanese workers being kidnapped by the communists, a congressman caught with three hundred fourteen firearms he was trying to get past customs at the Ninoy Aquino International Airport, and the United States recalling its two hundred sixty Peace Corps volunteers after one was kidnapped in Negros. She had a clipping about the breakdown in the country's "infrastructure," shortages in water and power, and shoddy telephone system; multinational corporations were drawing up plans to relocate to Hong Kong or Singapore if things got worse.

"Fresh doughnuts!" he said. "You must have been up early."

"I was awake before six and walked to the other corner. Those Vietnamese are certainly doing well with their doughnut store."

"I see four of them, a man and three women. Must be a family, else they wouldn't survive if they were paid regular wages."

"I'd be curious to know what they were back in Vietnam."

"You're always curious. Are you thinking there might be priests among the Vietnamese vendors and green grocers?"

"Helen."

"Sorry. Well, for one thing, they might be ethnic Chinese. They are the most successful of the Vietnamese immigrants. They've muscled their way into Chinatown in L.A. and now own fifty percent of the business there. Heard that in a lecture at Irvine."

"Not to mention Little Saigon down the freeway. I'm not surprised."

"That reminds me. A group of us are going to Little Saigon tonight to check out a new seafood place. Didn't you say you're going to have choir practice tonight?"

"Yeah, a final rehearsal on Friday."

"You've told me, but I forgot where the concert on Saturday is going to be held."

"At the Lutheran Church in Long Beach. The Protestants have adopted the Latin Masses discarded by the Catholics, who are busy singing their folk Masses."

"But you're doing Fauré and Schubert."

"Oh, well, French and German, a regular Mass and a Mass for the dead, a celebration and mourning. I doubt whether anyone sees the irony."

"Except you, of course," Helen said. "What's that phrase of yours again, 'a time to sing and a time to cry'?"

He shrugged off her remark and scanned the front page of the *Los Angeles Times.*

"If you just have a snack after work," Helen said, assuming wifely concern, "I'll bring home food from the restaurant."

"It's okay, there's crispy pata in the refrigerator."

"Yes, but heat it in the regular oven, not the microwave, if you want it crispy."

Of the rituals of the day, coming home to an empty house brought back the twilight gestures of priesthood. But for him the difference between a priest and a married man was that priest came home to an empty house, a room or cell. Alone he faced anxieties and stirrings of his libido with distraction or prayer, a book or music; sleep and dreams did the rest, dreams for which he felt responsible only if relished too long into waking.

He thought of not coming home after work and said, "I think I'll go to the barber after work, then drive over to the Lutheran church."

"Which barber, the Filipino or the American?"

"Diego, the Filipino. Bill's retired now and works only on Friday."

"I think Bill cuts your hair better than Diego."

"Well, Diego insists that he isn't really a barber but a hairdresser. He styles women's hair, too, charges only six dollars, Bill eight. Add two bucks for tip and there goes your ten."

"I wonder how much a haircut in the Philippines is now?"

"Less than the equivalent of a dollar, I'm sure. Diego gives you the works, massages your neck and scalp. Oh, but he talks."

"All about his being an illegal alien for over twenty years."

"He now has a green card, one of the first to apply for amnesty. I notice his speech is slurring though. Could be the open-heart surgery that he's had."

"Oh, you haven't told me about that."

"That isn't what's interesting. Apparently he had a salon somewhere in Wilmington. Lots of Filipinos and Mexicans there. He sold the business before he had surgery, so he could qualify for government help."

"Oh, dear, twenty years of subterfuge, he's learned how to beat the system," said Helen, gathering her coffee cup and teaspoon.

"Just put them in the sink. I'll wash."

Helen had twenty-two miles to go on the freeway to Irvine, six for him on surface roads. He recalled when a city planner in Los Angeles proposed adopting the jeepney as a solution to the city's traffic woes. Not surprising, another also suggested shipping garbage to the Philippines, adopt Manila as a sister city of trash, where thousands make their living off a dump site known as Smokey Mountain. He remembered when Cambodians from downtown Long Beach appeared in the tract on mornings trash was collected. The people living in the tract homes did not mind them picking up discarded appliances and lumber, but when they started opening up trash bags, the housewives complained. They called a meeting at the recreation hall in the park, invited their councilor and police. "I don't want them poking their sticks into my daughter's tampons," one woman said.

At work he must remember to tell Eric he was going to the Philippines. He had been responsible for getting the younger man a job in the educational research company; with Filipino population approaching the half-a-million mark in Southern California, there was a demand for teaching materials on the Philippines from the school districts. They had met in church and became friends. Eric had attended the seminary of the Society of the Divine Word but left before taking Holy Orders. Not quite an ex-priest, he showed traces of theology, Latin and German that the Deutschland S.V.D. Fathers had left him.

They often compared notes about their days in the seminary. After a few drinks, Rod would say, "The difference between you and me is that I reneged on a promise and you broke a vow."

Gene would counter with an ad hominem, drawing from his repertoire of seminary jokes. He'd say, "Listen, ex-SVD cleric, you hard so-vee-drinkers are not supposed to make that fine a discrimination. Leave the hair-splitting to the Dominicans."

"What do you say is the difference than?"

"Timing, hijo, timing. You left before you were ordained, I left after. You must admit we both feel guilty about it."

"Shall I call you Papa now that you've called me hijo? After all, you became a Father with a capital 'F.' I only became a parent."

They'd laugh. In quieter tones, they'd talk about what they missed the most about priesthood. Not the authority to unite couples in matrimony, baptize, consecrate the host at Mass, but the power that the church bestowed upon the authenticity of their words.

"It's the same power that commands the Church attention whenever it makes a statement on anything, even if people don't agree."

"And the Church confers upon you that same power as a priest — is that what you're saying?"

"Precisely."

"I never experienced that," Eric said, "so I wouldn't know."

"However, in interpreting the word from Rome or the Gospel, the priest does something, suit the homily to the audience, for instance. To the poor he offers consolation, but he won't castigate the rich, especially if he wants them to put more money in the collection box."

"Well, you should know. To keep the bishops in tow, I hear that Marcos would threaten to tax their lands and educational institutions and pass the abortion law."

"Ruthless Machiavellian that he was. That's the power of another hue, the kind that corrupts."

"Are you sure the power the Church confers upon priests does not corrupt?"

"I don't know the answer to that one. Saying it's the abuse of the power that corrupts is too easy. But perhaps I'll never know the answer, since I'm no longer a priest."

"Do you know the answer as to why you left the priesthood?"

Michelle? He had reached the limit of confiding; he wasn't going to tell Eric about her. It was as if her love was locked in his mind with the sacramental power of the confessional.

SAMUEL TAGATAC

IN 1948, two years after my parents came to America from Laoag, Ilocos Norte, my brother and I boarded a President Lines ship called SS President Walton. We disembarked in San Francisco, to Lodi, California, and then to Santa Barbara, enrolled in an elementary school called Wilson, where we began our Americanization and left our Iloco habits in the back-burner.

After high school, I wanted to be a fighter pilot, only to find out I was too short, or too Filipino. I never did find out which, but I accepted the former. Then I went off to college in San Francisco, studied medicine and psychology, had to enroll in ROTC and was told by a Korean veteran captain to put Mongolian for my race. All the while, I kept on writing, mostly not knowing what my subject was, imitating writers that I liked such as Hemingway, Steinbeck, Shakespeare, Dostoyevsky; but no Filipinos. I thought Filipinos were good for doctors, lawyers, and politicians ... and farm workers. Three and a half years later I got married, quit school, had a daughter, and divorced in the late '60s when I was back in college majoring in English. It was there in the San Francisco State strike of 1969 that I found out who I was; and my writer-self was born through the dynamic encounter and dialogue of a group of writers who lived in San Francisco and who tried to make sense of their place and inheritance in the civil rights movement spawned by the Blacks. I was fortunate to be at a historic place and time associated with such writers as Bayani Mariano, Serafin Syquia, Oscar Peñaranda, Juanita Tamayo, Emily Cachapero, Jeanette Lazam, Al Robles, Russel Robles, Bill Sorry, N.V.M. Gonzalez, Juaquin Legaspi; and artists who contributed to our dialogue such as Carlos Villa, Orvy Jundis, Edna Jundis; and scholars of ethnic studies such as Dan Gonzales, Dan Begonia, Lou Seballos, Ed dela Cruz, Ted Hipol, Richard Licong, and others.

Serafin Syquia said it best in the introduction to the now historic Flips *anthology: "... Most importantly, we are influenced by each other; in our encounters with racism — in our search for our roots — in our nostalgic remembrances of growing up in America." So it is this roots "eyeglasses" by which we see and write about ourselves.*

In the early '70s I taught creative writing and film at San Francisco State, and also at the University of California, Santa Barbara. During this period I was also an independent filmmaker in San Francisco contributing to the then new concept of Asian American Filmmaking. I got married, had two more daughters, left teaching, and became a restauranteur until the late 1980s when I left that endeavor. My writings have appeared in P.E.N. International, Kenyon Review, Asian American Authors, Liwanag, Amerasia Journal UCLA, Aiiieeeee! An Anthology of Asian American Writers.

At present I am at work on a novel, and Filipino American ballet, and producing a television documentary for public access TV in Santa Barbara, California.

SMALL TALK AT UNION SQUARE

HE SAT under the Dewey column that rose above him. On the pinnacle stood a worn-out concrete cast of a Greek-like goddess of sorts triumphantly pointing a sword at a deep blue windswept San Francisco sky. At the foot of the column, the pigeon-dropping-stained likeness of Admiral Dewey followed by a host of officers and men still stalked Union Square, the one-block square combination park and underground parking lot smack in the middle of downtown where on the Powell side of the park stood the majestic St. Francis Hotel constantly being wooed by the charm of cable car bells, and perhaps, also hollow tributes to past heroisms.

He shifted his position occasionally as though to let air circulate through his heavy coat pulled over an old sweater. It was not a cold morning. But it was his custom, now that he was crippled, to wear the old coat and sweater that he once wore only on his best days, and certain special occasions like walking on a Sunday afternoon in Golden Gate Park in the aquariums among the tourists and families. He watched the pigeons beginning to gather for their morning stroll across the plaza. His face sagged, cheeks loose from enervated facial nerves that had lost their function since his small accident.

At the opposite end of the plaza, from the Geary-Powell interchange, a young Pinoy was just entering. He was tall, Stateside born, thin and athletic, college-bound, with a springy gait, wearing glasses which belied his athletic stride, giving him a studious air. But he was dark-skinned, natural lasting tan, confident as he walked in the full morning sunlight. He waded into the pigeons, enjoying the startled flapping of wings as they rushed out of his way. Upon seeing the old man, his face suddenly brightened.

"Dom," he said, "what're you doing here?" Asking a question the answer to which he already knew.

The old man, broken from his trance, said, "… you." He leaned his weight to one side. "What does it look like I'm doing?"

"So, how are you?"

"Lousy," the old man said with gusto. His face flinched under its impaired condition. With his good hand, he pulled his cap off to scratch his head. There was not much hair left, only a pale scalp, a few scars from falls or fights. With his cap back on he looked like an old club fighter from a tenderloin gym, or a defrocked monk gone the way of the street.

"Nice day," said the young man, looking up at Dewey. Across Powell, the flags of the St. Francis stretched. Bells rang, and old St. Mary's in Chinatown rang a chorus.

"What's it good for?"

"See," the young man looking around past the skyline, past a United jumbo jet fastened on the top of a building advertising its low-fare junket to somewhere, "it's a great day for flying."

"Hell ... what's good about it, Franky?" The old man stared at the pigeons starting to gather around them. "What's good about it?"

"To see. Enjoy." The young man took a deep breath and stretched his arms out in a graceful arc that formed a cross with the shadow of his body on the cement. "Smells good! Fresh from the Golden Gate."

"Golden Gate, hell! Not for me," the old man said. And his face became tormented in a shadow of painful annoyance as he moved his body.

"You shouldn't feel that way."

"I'm no liar. It's the way I feel."

"You hurting?" The young man really wanted to know.

"Yeah ..."

"Your arm?"

"All over."

"Can't you do anything?"

"Nothing."

"No doctors?"

"Nothing."

"Why not, Dom?" said the young man. He removed his light summer jacket and swung the jacket over his shoulders. "You can't give up!"

"No good." The old man cried under the late morning sun. The shadow of the goddess moved closer to him.

The pigeons, having moved away, left wet white droppings. They hurried towards the far corner of the plaza where a fat grey woman dug into a paper bag full of bread crumbs. She flung the bread with great energy.

"No good." The old man cried once more. "Can't do nothing for me."

"Oh ... you've seen one," said the young man in a subtle inflection of relief.

"Yeah ..."

"What did he say?"

"Stroke!"

"What?"

"STROKE!" The old man shifted his body in annoyance and glared at the young man. His breathing became labored, his eyes wet, but not from crying. Then he said, "What the hell's the matter with you? Can't you hear?"

The young man smiled in an awkward pose of self-embarrassment, grinning a half-moon from ear to ear, then to a sheepish almond as he apologized. "Sorry ... I didn't get you at first."

"So what the hell you ask for anyway ... can't you see?"

"I don't know," shaking his head incredulously as though he had suddenly broken through a thin pond of ice. "Sorry ... sometimes words just tear loose."

"Yeah ..." the old man said, his head lowered as though he was the one being sorry. The shadow goddess' sword lowered itself between the two. At the far corner of the plaza the bag lady, finished with her kindness, sauntered off and disappeared into the tumult of traffic, while the pigeons flew in an upward spiral, some to stroll on the window ledges of St. Francis, and some on the head of the goddess above.

"You college boy."

"Right," the young one said.

"Books in your head." The old man pulled out a soiled handkerchief and blew his nose.

"Everybody reads."

"But you didn't see anything."

The young man stood back and took stock of the old man. He peered intently through his glasses as though he was at the site of an archeological dig trying to decipher a living hieroglyphic. His eyes grew owlish behind his horn-rimmed glasses which he pushed up on his bridgeless nose. At the opposite corner where the bag lady stepped down into the traffic, a street evangelist rose up with his time-is-near-and-repentance message printed red on white plywood draped on his chest back. It was obvious that he was taking a shortcut to the Powell Street side, the tourist side where they were launched up the hill on their way to Grant Street Chinatown, and all the way to Fisherman's Wharf. The street evangelist was in no hurry as though sure of his own destiny, and just as sure of his message, and the need for harvest. He was no John the Baptist although he walked on the straight and narrow, and spouted the same message as he passed by the old man and the young man, disappearing in the Powell Street orchard.

"… don't know nothing. I know you," the old man complaining, suggesting more than he knew.

"Me?"

"I see you." He wiped the loose sinus fluid coming down his nose and dripping down his lips. "Hanging around that O'Farrell Bar crowd, you know what I say will stay in your gut."

"They're okay. They're your old friends, aren't they?"

"I know they talk about me."

"They feel bad for you."

"So why the hell do they have to whisper when I'm around?" The old man's useless hand dangled and flapped on his side in futile protest. "They look, and smile, and whisper." The old man fidgeted, unable to perspire. "Hell, they don't know me no more. They don't want to know. They hate me coming around. They don't want to see."

"It's crazy. You gotta be wrong, Dom," said Franky.

"I'm right. I'm a cripple, ain't I? But I ain't as blind as I was."

The rough thunderous steel wheels of a cable car rumbled over the plaza like the guns of Dewey's Asiatic Squadron pummeling the Spanish Fleet trapped in Manila Bay. Then the jazzy chiming of cable car bells rose over the din and traffic horns. The goddess, awestruck, a frozen deteriorating memorial was now littered with competing pigeons.

"I know those bastards," the old man said. "I showed them how to drink." The old man opened his mouth to gasp for air, his cheeks pale and frosty with sinus. "And you're a punk."

"What!" said the startled young man.

"A punk. I know. You think they're hotshot steel workers riding steel broncos high above the world. I know. I was up there."

"Did you know Red?" the young man said.

The old man looked past the young man's shoulders, into the distance where he could see the steel framework of another high-riser above the other high-risers. It was deeper and higher than all the rest. Plumes of clouds began to appear in the East Bay sky. "He got me started," the old man said.

"He fell."

"That's right." The old man's annoyance showed in a subtle muscle twitch in his eyes, and rubbed his dull shoes together like a little boy in a confessional box doing penance. "That's the way he wanted to go. Damn Indian."

"He got you started drinking?" The young man smiled. The morning was hotter in spite of the cold wind, and perspiration made him irritable. His eyeglasses slipped on the tip of his nose again; he took them off and wiped skin oil off the frame.

"Hell, no, we all drank in the same place," said the old man. "Iloco boys, Visayan, you name it, every Saturday night when we came in from the fields. One night he says for me to meet him at work on a Monday morning, and to look like a Navajo, and he would tell his foreman that I was his cousin from the reservation."

"Did you?"

"Did I what?"

"Look like a Navajo."

"Hell, no. I went the way I was."

"Were there others?" The young man strained under

the hot sun and began to shade his face with his hands. The drone of the bumper-to-bumper traffic jam on the Bay Bridge was thick soup. Somewhere on the bay, a tugboat still pulled on its foghorn. The sky over the East Bay slowly paled to heated industrial gasses from ships and factories, Alameda's US carriers sprung loose jet fighters and coded signals. Dewey's triumph remained in stone.

"No "Iloco boy. No Visayan. Just Red and me put back that Zellerbach Tower." And he seemed to move his useless hand as though he wanted to point to the sky.

VIRGINIA R. CERENIO

VIRGINIA R. CERENIO is a second-generation Filipino American. Her poems and short stories have appeared in numerous publications including Breaking Silence *(Greenfield Review Press),* Without Names *(Kearney Street Workshop Press),* East Wind Magazine, Bridge Magazine, Berkeley Fiction Review *(U.C. Berkeley),* Asian Journal Columbia University), *and* Liwanag.

Virginia Cerenio's first collection of poetry, Trespassing Innocence, *was published in 1989 by Kearney Street Workshop Press.*

Trespassing Innocence *is illustrated with black and white photography by Tony Remington and designed by Lenny Limjoco, 1987 winner of the Philippine National Book Award for* Kasama, *a book of photos. Mr. Limjoco was artistic designer for Kearney Street Workshop's previous poetry publications:* Without Names *(Bay Area Filipino American Writers, 1985); Jeff Tagami's October Light (1987), and Genny Lim's* Winter Place *(1989).*

Ms. Cerenio received her B.A. In English and M.A. In Education from San Francisco State University.

DREAMS OF MANONG FRANKIE

> manilatown memories
> too many
>   to fill
>   one photo album
> pages cannot hold the music
> of clapping hands and dancing feet
> "such foolish things
>   remind me
>   of you..."

summer/Chinatown

the cable cars danced up california street, a slow samba line of tourists hugging cameras. bell sounds flew in the air like quick bird wings, a sunlit afternoon poured like gold rush into the cool brick alleys of chinatown. i walked out into the sidewalk. fish swimming upstream, scales glistening in noon light.

then i saw him, lumbering slowly up the river of sunlight like a lazy carabao in the warm day, fish scattering in his wake.

"Ay, Virgie! ... my beautiful pinay ... by golly girl ... whatcha doing here ... I been looking for you so long my eyes hurting me already." his hands big and leathered swallowed my slender ones in their darkness. manong frankie, fast frankie, one-hundred-miles-per-hour-on-his-feet dancin' frankie, hizzoner commisioner frankie, five-wives frankie, my dear heart frankie, how are you?

"Well ... I'm doing all right for an old man. Where you been? I thought you're hiding from me ... ahhh ... you work too much ... where you going now? ... are you busy? ... would you like to take a walk in the park with an old man? ... it's a beautiful day."

we held hands like teenagers, the carabao and the rice-bird playing in the sun and shadow of chinatown. anyone would have thought we were a loving grandfather and granddaughter. little did they know that the grandfatherly old man was in love with the thought of being in love again and the young woman was regretting being reincarnated too late in life. so, frankie, what have been doing again?

"... going crazy without you ... just finished dancing at Manilatown ... then I'll go for the pinochle game at St. Paul's ... then dinner, then to bed early, cause I got to be dancing all weekend!" he squeezed my arm with enthusiasm of someone who never tired of doing what they did best. smiling, i maneuvered my precious cargo across narrow streets, between parked and moving cars, through the flowing streams of tourists and chinatown residents.

all during our walk, manong frankie behaved like a lovesick teenager — squeezing my hand until it felt like one of those bruised bananas, left loose and single on sale, murmuring "oh, Virgie, who've you been seeing ..." and yet like a gentleman walking me down the street with all the dignity 79 years could carry.

swimming downstream to clay and kearny streets we ended up at portsmouth square park for the proposed walk. of course, this wasn't just any casual stroll, but a chance for frankie to walk me around in full view of all his kababayans, amigos, pungyao, friends. showing off his girl. "Ay, talagang Frankie! Magandang babae!" frankie waving, walking slowly and proudly like a datu surveying his barangay. the sunlight of surprise and curiosity appearing in faces lined with past winters, old men sprouting like dusty mushrooms on park benches, clustering around the card games. all of them like village elders whose responsibility of age has made them idle and called them wise, carrying on the recreation of men with nothing to do — smoking gambling, drinking, storytelling, ogling. and manong frankie was giving them a chance to practice the latter by parading me through portsmouth square. "Hey, Frank! You sonuvagun! You always fooling around with those women! Don't you know? Old men aren't supposed to do those kinda stuff!" frankie would smile quietly, the silence of his proud walk giving enough response to the remarks of the park bench crowd.

"Frankie, really!" I protested. "You're embarrassing me!"

"Don't worry," he said, patting my hand. "I'll just tell them you're my granddaughter."

autumn/portsmouth square playground

the breeze like cool careless fingers brushed through chinatown, leaves and litter danced waltzes in the sidewalk squares. the old women and bums wore layers of clothing like cocoons, eyes peering out beneath hats, between folds. only the occasional hooker dared to show her long pale legs, pedestaled on four-inch heels and shivering slightly into her short woolsworth's trenchcoat. the breeze carried the stale smell of the city, a faint hint of oceans a hill away, a dream of rains and the winter to come.

"Egypt," frankie said.

"What?"

"Alexandra, Egypt. that's where I learn palm reading."

"Frankie, you know how to read palms?" i was incredulous, especially after i had been told by my friends not to believe any of frankie's stories, because even he believed in the myths he had created about himself.

"Oh, yesss. I was in the merchant marines, you know, we went all over the world. And I met this old lady there in Egypt, who knows the secrets of palm reading and she taught it to me. I can tell your past and your future."

"Really?!"

"I'm not kidding. Here, I'll read your palm." we walked

over to a park bench and sat down, causing a mass exodus of pigeons. frankie held my hand, palm up, peering with the concentration he usually reserved for a keno ticket at reno, smoothing my palm with his thumbs as though it were a map of wrinkles. silence. another cool breeze shimmied through the park. "Your boyfriend is coming from far away. Maybe from the Philippines." frankie looked at me with a twinkle in his eyes, awaiting my reaction ... *oh, frankie, that happened a long time ago ... broken hearts never mend, they just cracked* ... "Maybe this boyfriend is already here. Your palm says it's someone maybe you know, a friend, someone who lives close by, maybe in your own neighborhood." frankie seemed very pleased by his pronouncement. he looked at me. "Hmmm ... you better be careful ... there's a married man in your future. maybe someone you know is trying to fool you." he looked at me with concern.

i laughed. "Frankie, you're too serious. Tell me, how many children will I have?"

he turned my hand into a fist, reading the wrinkles cornered below my little finger. "Four children ... but only three will live." the solemn tone of his words got carried away by yet another chill breeze, winging over a pyramid. his hand held main in comfort, already mourning a dead child, not yet conceived.

frankie had sad stories in every pocket today. "C'mon, Manong. It's almost time for lunch. It's too cold to be sitting out here." the chilly breezes chased us back to the warmth of manilatown. the pigeons reclaimed the park bench giving no respect to the art of palm-reading.

winter/manilatown senior center

"... hernando's hideaway, ole! ..." the melody drifted up from the basement onto clay street, being washed away by the chilly winter rains into the sounds of a wet city. the sharp slick sounds of city traffic were exchanged abruptly for the latin rhythms and crying clarinets of the manilatown senior center band. the band played as loudly and raucously as possible to compete with the sounds of the lunch crowd — shouted conversations into deaf ears, plates and tablespoons clattering in rhythm.

frankie, always the picture of sartorial splendor, was dressed in green polyester slacks, matching double-breasted jacket, tie. his tie had the remains of lunch — chicken adobo, squash, rice, sabao, fruit cocktail for dessert. not bad for a sixty-cent lunch.

frankie, as usual, was dancing. he loved to dance, would dance with anybody, for he was as he put it "a dancing fool."

"Virgie, you just in time to dance!" frankie greeted me with glee. there was no escape now. "I've been waiting for you!" he took my hand and led me to the small space between the band and the dining area. scattered applause and shouts of admiration for frankie's boldness. frankie led me gracefully into a foxtrot, while I tried not to step on his feet or bump his belly.

dancing with frankie called for maximum concentration. he would stare into my eyes with all seriousness and romantic drama, barely smiling, while his large hand pressing into the small of my back brought me ever closer to his embrace. for all his grace, his dance steps often did not match the music. there was always one point during the dance when he would show off his fancy footwork — his feet would move at about ninety miles per hour in a figure-eight shuffle making his rotund body move like a gaily dancing balloon. it did not seem to matter that his dancing partner could not keep up with him. but that was frankie — always dancing to the music inside his head.

> the oldest pinoy around manilatown
> 79 and still dancing
> since 1917 found him
> waltzing his way

into the heart of america
chicago's marathon manong
he latined his way into the navy
not seeing the world
but only as a blur thru finely coiffed hair
a perfumed shoulder
an upturned face
lip smiling promises
dance with me always dancing
never a misstep
but one-two one-two cha cha cha
thirteen grandchildren later
"one of them had to come out looking filipino
dark brown, flat nose…like me"
a wallet full of memories
i hear his voice whispering
now he's asking *me* to dance …

autumn/home

the phone rang one sunday afternoon.
  "Hello?"
  "Hello? Virgie?"
  "Yes—who's this? … Frankie, is that you?"
  "Yeah, it's me."
  "Frankie, is everything all right? where are you?"
  "Chinese hospital. But I'm okay, don't worry."
  "What are you doing in the hospital?"
  "You know old men need to tune-up once in a while just like cars. So I tuned up and I'm leaving tomorrow."
  "Are you sure everything's all right? What did the doctors say? Do you want me to come see you?"
  "Of course, always. But that's not why I called."
  "Okay," I said patiently. "Why did you call me, Frankie?"

"I just wanted to tell you … you're not going to forget me, are you?" *oh, god, frankie — don't talk like that, being in a hospital doesn't mean you have to die.* "I know I'm just a crazy old man, but don't forget — I love you."

"Frankie, don't be silly, of course I won't forget."

"Do you still love me, Virgie?"

"Of course, manong. Listen, don't worry. I'll come dance with you next weekend at Manilatown."

He laughed. "that damn doctor told me not to dance, but he's so young, what does he know? Dancing is good for the heart. It's good for an old man." he was silent for a moment. "Okay … do not forget me now."

no, manong. i won't. i can't. because i have dreams about you. and i never forget my dreams …

dream

he reached into one of those mysterious pockets men always have and brought out his wallet. he took out his photos, neatly ordered and fanned them like playing cards in his hand. the photos ranged from sepia-tone to color. in each one was frankie, a girl friend — blonde or redhead—or a relative. he invited me to look at them and i bent closer to see

one photo, black and white
a nightclub dark
cigarette smoke
frankie smiling
with his arms holding
his dancing partner
not a blondie, but me
with soft curls and
cadillac-red lipstick
holding on to my carabao

in the storm of music
darkness and light
we moved in a precious bubble
dancing in that merry-go-round
of people, knowing that if we
stopped dancing, the dream
would end and we would be
only a photo in frankie's wallet.

i held the small photo in my fingers, wanting to see the couples dance to the silent music. frankie put his wallet away, and looked at me sadly, shaking his head, then held my hands like china cups in his big dark hands.

suddenly he put his hand to his head as though he were in pain and started doing a clumsy but graceful step across the sidewalk, bumping into people as he went. he danced to the throbbing of pain inside his head, his hands trying to contain the loudness which seemed to be deafening him. the crowd of tourists waiting at the corner became his last obstacle as they parted like a gate to let him race onto the street like a horse with a broken leg. a cable car, coasting down california street, stopped too late and as the crowd cried in horror, the silent music frankie had been hearing inside his head came to an abrupt halt.

and in the photo, everything had gone dark, as though the band had stopped playing and the drunk swaying couples had gone home to sleep and could dance no more.

JULIA L. PALARCA

I AM a graduate of the University of Santo Tomas (Litt. B. in Journalism; M.A. in English) and did post-graduate work at the University of Wisconsin and Columbia University. I taught for a few years at the Far Eastern University Graduate School; Arellano University; and in the graduate department of my alma mater, the University of Santo Tomas.

I joined the Philippine Foreign Service where, after serving as Chief of the Office of Cultural Affairs in the Home Office, I was assigned as Vice-Consul to the Philippine Embassy in Washington, D.C; and finally as Deputy Chief of Mission (Ambassador) to the Philippine Mission to the United Nations in Geneva, Switzerland.

At present, I reside in a serene neighborhood in Mt. Laurel, New Jersey, where I read, write sporadically, and watch my roses grow.

IN AMERICA, RESTAURANTS ARE CROWDED

THE BROWN slant-eyed girl smiled as she took one of the revolving stools encircling the greasy counter. Wipe marks on its surface failed to mask the fishy odor which rose in a faint unpleasant cloud. She held her breath deeply then assumed an air of brisk confidence.

The lone waitress gave her a swift glance and continued washing cups and dishes in a sink under the counter. Dunk in soapy water, dunk in not-very-clear water, let stand. The young girl waited but no one approached to take her order.

So she looked around with amused understanding. I know, I know.

In America, restaurants are crowded. Ages before one is served. With elaborate casualness, she removed her beige car coat and laid it across her lap. Without her coat on, her arms looked fragile and dark beside the hairy whiteness of a man seated next to her. In quick self-consciousness, she drew farther away and clasped her hands together.

"Will you pass the menu?" she asked him softly.

"Sure."

Breaded pork chops, four seventy-five. Fried wall-eyed pike, two dollars and ninety cents. Her eyes traveled swiftly down. Macaroni and cheese, a dollar-fifty. Yesterday and the day before she had the same thing. She would have it again today.

She looked at the waitress expectantly with a bright smile that later stiffened into an impaled curve on her mouth. The front cover of the menu card carried the picture of an American in shirt-sleeves, sipping beer from a can. He was golden, strong, very sure. She ran a long finger across the ad, sensuously aware of its cool smoothness.

When the waitress finished cleaning the dishes, she started rearranging the cereal boxes lined up in rows behind her. The girl's cheeks burned. Twenty million little pins pricked her face, first on the forehead, then ran in a pitted path down to her chin. Oh, please, Lord, don't let it show.

She turned towards her neighbor who was staring ahead uncomfortably. "Don't they serve foreigners here?" she asked.

"She's crazy." He called out in anger, "Hey! Come on over, will ya?"

People looked up curiously. The waitress walked up to them as if it were only now that she noticed a new customer. Her uniform was neatly starched and the little cap on her head stood out like a crown.

"What will you have?" Pencil poised over a small memo pad.

Under the stare, the pins viciously renewed their attack. So the girl cupped her chin with her palms and dictated with tolerant humor. "Chicken soup, macaroni and cheese, and coffee."

As the waitress turned to leave, she added, "And oh, yes, make it black. No sugar." But the flush would not subside.

When the bowl of soup arrived along with biscuits wrapped in cellophane, the girl leaned on the counter and faced the man beside her. Lithe, tall, invulnerable. Beside him were three Chemistry textbooks. Great! He was a student like herself.

"I see that you are from the State University."

He nodded warmly. "Just like you."

At this, they both laughed a little. She noticed the waitress looking at them so she edged closer to him. "Would you care for some biscuits? Honestly, I can't finish all of them."

"Okay. Thanks. What course are you in?"

"Creative Writing 1." She looked up at him. Go on, ask more questions.

"First year?" he asked.

"Uh-huh. First time in the States, too."

"Well!" Others she had talked to always used the same wondering, admiring tone. "You look awfully young!"

"I'm nineteen."

She bent over her soup. Thick Campbell's chicken soup which would go deliciously down the throat. Steam rose slowly like a gray curtain. It undulated upwards, stretched, then disappeared. She watched the thick liquid whorl, dimple, and burst into soft little puffs. On each swollen bubble were the faces of all those she loved. There was Mother waving goodbye at the airport terminal, sending a blessing from across the wooden barricade separating guests from departing passengers. Her eyes were filled with a loneliness more poignant then tears. Close by, Father carried Pride like a flag. Bye! Take good care of yourself, child!"

Strange how dry-eyed she had been as she walked towards the check-in counters, the immigration booths, and finally into the luxurious waiting lounge. She savored the feel of unabashed excitement that flowed out and around her. When it came time to board the huge 747, there was pushing and jostling for space. Hand-carried native bags overflowing with gifts for overseas relatives and friends bumped into one another. She had almost nothing except an airline overnighter containing clothing change, her favorite hair brush, a pair of shoes, and all the dreams of many years. Aloft, the plane gradually gained air speed, quickly leaving behind the familiar landmarks. Outside her window, the clouds were incredibly soft, contoured by a magical hand into constantly changing patterns.

The girl's eyes traced the alternating green and white lines decorating the lower rim of the bowl. They went around and around interminably ...

Both she and the young man stood up simultaneously. To her surprise, he helped her ease into her coat with one hand, the other clutching the textbooks.

"Thanks." She flipped her long hair outwards and allowed it to fall back like a mantle of black silk. "I have to get used to wearing coats," she remarked ruefully. "Back home, it is too hot for one."

When he laughed, she could smell the coffee in his breath, but his voice was kind and friendly.

She stood behind him as he made his way to the cashier's cubicle, opened a leather billfold, and handed out five crisp notes to a jaded woman behind the register. A red-tipped finger jabbed the keys, a bell rang, and loose change coasted down into a round receptacle within one's reach. He waited for her to go through the same ritual.

"Look," he said afterwards as he opened the door for her on their way out, "you don't have any evening classes, do you? I mean, well ... it's almost six. Let me walk you home."

He reddened at the astonishment on her face. "I'm sorry," he blurted out, "my name's Karl. Karl Effron."

"Hi, Karl. I'm Antonia. Toni, for short." She glanced up at him. "German?"

"Yup. German Jew."

Then the words came out like a rush of angry waters, bitter with pain. "What a rotten thing to do! Don't ever, ever allow anyone to treat you like a lesser human being. Least of all, not an arrogant, stupid waitress." A dark shadow crossed his face. "Come," he said. "Where do you live?"

It was going to be a lovely walk, she thought happily. The air was cool and fragrant, full of singing, shining secrets. She wanted to fling her arms out and dance. Truly, America was a wonderful world to live in!

"I like that," he said.

"What?"

"The expression on your face a moment ago."

He placed an arm around her shoulders and both walked deeper into the night.

The girl's fingers caressed the rim of the bowl as she noted the graceful circle under her touch.

"Your soup's getting cold," the university student observed, as he stood up to leave. "Well, so long!" He added with sincerity, "I'm glad to have met you. And say, thanks for the biscuits."

"Not at all," she replied. "Bye!"

She bent once more over her bowl of soup. The unfinished portion lay quietly on its bed, unmoving like a sad thought. She tipped it slightly to one side but the little puffs did not swell. Behind her came the sound of a tiny bell ringing. The door opened and a blast of cold air from outside sent tiny goose-pimples through her.

The waitress brought the macaroni dish without saying anything, and the young girl told the silence beyond her, "Mmmm ... this looks good!" She picked up her fork, twirled the limp slender tubes around its tines and started to eat. But she knew that if she continued her meal, she would vomit.

And there was the cup of coffee still.

OSCAR PEÑARANDA

I WAS born in a house (actually under it), long in its ruins on an island called Leyte in the Philippines, went to school in Manila till the sixth grade, returning to Leyte every vacation time (a set-up insisted upon by the elders of my barrio to almost every young child who went away for an education), and at age of twelve went to Vancouver, Canada, with my parents, brother, and sister. Spent five years there.

Then we came to San Francisco in 1961. I was seventeen. Except for a few months in Hawaii, Alaska, Seattle, and Las Vegas, I have been in San Francisco ever since. But not quite able to dispense with my vacation habits, I still leave the City every summer. In Canada, I went to the virgin woods — hunting, fishing, camping, and picking fruits on farms. In California, I also picked fruits —I n Fairfield, the Suisun Valley, Putah Creek, and Winters. Every kind of fruit imaginable growing in California it seemed I picked. Even vegetables. That was for three summers. After that I went to Las Vegas, worked as a busboy and waiter for two summers. After that I went to the Alaskan fishing canneries for fifteen consecutive summers. I am now in the process of writing several works — short stories, poetry, novels, plays, film/TV scripts and nonfiction historical pieces.

I have taught at San Francisco State University for twelve years. I have been teaching at Everett Middle School in San Francisco for eight years. I was also the first president of the Filipino American National Historical Society, San Francisco Chapter.

I write mostly of the complex and diverse lifestyles and characters of the Filipinos in the U.S. And in the Philippines — from the sages and gods of the village where I was born to the cities of my present surroundings, their customs, their puny little heroic dreams, their brave visions; their stories of long ago and far away swept me. I found out (much later, of course) that I was pretty well molded in values because of these. All this before I was twelve. Whether it is a credit to that richness or a defect in my ability of growing, I have not learned much since. Probably, a little of both. I speak Tagalog, Waray, and sometimes when I have to, English.

"The Visitor" depicts a major Filipino American experience — the Alaskan Fishing Cannery life — although this particular story spans after everyone in the cannery had already gone back home to their respective abodes in the "lower 48." The lingering, nameless loner of this story finds himself wandering into the lives of past friends (Native American Indians) that he made during that cannery experience.

THE VISITOR

–HELLO?

–Hello. He hesitates a bit; the husband answered. He didn't know the husband. Hello, is Clara there? (He'll talk to her first since it was her house.)

–Yeah, the husband says. Just a minute.

–Hello? Clara says, hoarse and harsh as with a cold, the sound of her voice as he remembered.

–Hello? Clara? Listen, I was just on my way down south and I —

Clara screams a bit, elated, surprised. And then, How ya doing?

She says his name.

—How'd you know?

—I remember. How you been? She was chewing gum or something.

—All right. Listen, is ... George there?

—Yeah, he's right here. Just a minute.

—Hello? George says.

—Hey, what's going on, punk? (That's it, joke it out.)

—Hey, hey, hey! What're you doing this late time of year? He pauses. Are you in town?

—Yeah, I just got in. From Kodiak. I'm on my way —

—Kodiak! You mean you just leaving for home now?

—Well, for south, yeah.

—All gone now.

—You mean you been in Alaska all this time since June? (It was November.)

—Yeah, I just wanted to say hello. In passing. He hears noises in the background. He starts vying for attention.

—Wait a minute, George says. His heart starts hammering now. Stifled sounds are coming from the phone. Must be cupped, the mouthpiece.

—Hello? says a voice, a girl's voice, the familiar tinkle he slightly dreaded, not knowing why. Hello? she says again. A flood of images, scenes leap across his thoughts. Play it cool now. It's no big thing. Joke it up, laugh it off. Start rapping and keep rapping. Just assault her, render her defenseless.

—Hi, sweetheart, he says. How's the tea to my coffee and the cream to my sugar oops didn't come out too good but you know what I mean. (Damn, screwed it up.) She screams. Not as Clara her sister screamed, but a little girl's scream, fragile as dreams. And then like a jingle of Christmas bells, she screams his name. How are ya! Gee, it's so good to hear from you! Where are you? Where'd you come from? Are you alone? (She's taking over the conversation, fool. Watch it. Get loose. Get loose. Take command of the situation. She's rattling on and on. Ain't that just like her.) Gees, it's nice to hear your voice. Are you in town? Is this long distance?

—Hold it, hold it! Jesus Christ, Katherine, breathe! I

199

wanna see you still alive when I get there.

—You're coming over! Wow, how nice! She laughs. A girl's giggle again.

—What do you have there, a family reunion?

—Sort of. Everybody's here. Kind of get-together. Where are you?

—At the airport.

—At the airport? You gonna take a cab here? Wait. Don't do that. I'll get someone (George!) someone with a car, and I'll go with him to get you. (That's what he liked about her. No one else would do that, say that right without even knowing how she was going to get down there. She was never afraid to take chances, and if she had to, lose.) Did you hear me?

—I heard you. (But I gotta play it cool. The gentleman bit. Noble. Masculine. Stoic.) That's all right, though. It's no problem, Katherine. Got one already waiting.

They were both quiet for a while.

—O.K, she says. Her face swims before him every time she says that. O.K. With a smile. Expectant. With a glow.

He gets out of the cab and goes up the porch and knocks. There were some trees along the road he came up on and through their leaves he could see blue black mountains with their backs pinned against the sky. It was green country. The Last Frontier, they say. The Great Land. Someone lets him in; he doesn't know who, for they have some sort of party going on. The living room is in front of him, the kitchen to his left. Clara comes out of the kitchen, looks around him, behind him. Where's your stuff? Don't you have any luggage? Or are you traveling light again (a wicked smile breaks from her lips) and fast?

—I left them at the airport. Locker.

—Well, come on in for Christ's sake. She takes his hand and leads him through the kitchen, by-passing the living room, unseen because of the wall that separates the two rooms. She lets go of his hand after they pass the bathroom and points to a room. There, she says, she's in there.

He goes in the room. (This is ridiculous. I feel like I'm going to a damn whorehouse for the first time.) He sees her sitting on a corner of a couch, her legs tight together, knees drawn up, head bent down, her hair in black tresses, falling fluffy on her thighs, fixing something on the baby in her arms. She looks up. Smiles spring from her face and then she glows.

–Hiya, stranger. Whatcha been doin'? What brings you to town? Sit down.

He is standing in one spot and looks around for a while not moving his legs, then feeling for a chair behind him, he sits. (Nothing to it!)

–Boy or girl?

–Girl, she smiles.

There is a rustle in the next room, a dragging or shuffling. He looks there. How's your Mom?

–That's her you hear. Christ, she's been waiting for you. Once in a while, Katherine gets a serious sweet-faced expression, but only for a brief moment. This is one time. She likes you (then she perks up), always did. (That smile. Goddamit, I'm gonna blow it.)

–I only met her once, he says humbly.

–Yeah, but she talked to you for ten hours! She laughs. Her laugh that begins with a giggle. Then she pauses. Just enough time to let the girlish wrinkles settle on her face again. She knew you before that, she says.

–I'll go in and see her, I guess.

–Katherine! the mother calls.

She gets up. Goes to the next room. In passing he takes the baby from her.

–May I? he says. She hands her to him and he gathers her carefully.

–There, she says. Be back.

He was looking at the baby, rocking it clumsily, when she returns.

–Ain't she pretty?

–Um hmmm.

–She told me to fix you something to eat.

–No, that's all right. I already —

–I told you. She likes you.

–She hardly knew me.

–You can't tell her that. Besides you gotta way with people (squinting a bit, her left hand stiff-armed pointing, mimicking an indignant accuser) and you know it, she says, with a pout. She leaves for the kitchen. He leaves for the other room.

As he enters, he says, How are you, Katherine? They had the same name. It was a loose translation of their Athapascan Indian name, Tatinya. She was coughing, lying down in the darkness.

–Sit down, sit down, she says. Hand me my cigarettes over that table, will you (she calls his name). They talk for a while, his head now and then bobbing in the different shades of darkness, listening in the deep and profound discomfort of not knowing what to do with a secret bequeathed.

They were exactly like this, in these same positions, as in a tableau, when they first met in Two Rivers, an Indian village around Lake Iliamna when he went to visit Buffalo Boy his friend, Katherine's cousin but in reality it was of course to see her; he, who in the village people's eyes hungry for romance, had come from a distant land, with a different walk, a guest, a visitor, a sojourner, a stranger in a strange land, come to see their jewel, their princess of the sun; for they were hungry for romance, for something to tell their grandchildren or maybe just any hint or shadow of a possibility of a legend in the making, hungry without knowing it, craving for the miracle, for something of the old days, the great days, rightly or wrongly some tinge of robustness and lustiness and magic, instead of this juiceless, toothless, verbless indefiniteness and nonvocational grayness of everyday living which they, *and* he, had somehow found themselves wandering in today.

They were willing to build a house then, that is, little Katherine was building a house for her mother, unfinished from the inside, with all the unasked-for-help from anybody, for all her brothers then (one in prison, one fighting fires, one in Anchorage settled, and one in Sitka adventuring) and two sisters (one in school in Oregon and one married in Anchorage) were away. So once in a while he and Buffalo Boy helped, along with the other regular helpers, courters in disguise, too. He and Buffalo Boy stayed in an empty house, his uncle's who had just died, though Buffalo Boy's parents lived in the village also. But he was his (Buffalo Boy's) guest, his friend, and therefore deserved fealty and attendance. But most times he went hunting and fishing, and just loafing about, doing whatever Buffalo Boy said, for Buffalo Boy was his host, his guide, his friend and therefore deserved decision-making responsibility. So, when he finally saw her in that village, in a meadow on a slight hill, sitting down, digging on something, fighting the earth, looking for something there, her hair black, thick and wavy, her hair that frizzled to the touch of raindrops, tumbling down unharnessed into brave profusion, he did not call her or even look at her that long, but kept on walking with Buffalo Boy till he heard light thuds of footsteps behind him that suddenly stopped (it was stopping that, without putting down his gear, made him turn), "Hi, stranger," she had said, softly brushing her hair aside, her hair that had blown wild in the wind. And he left his hat there, too, at her house. That was two years ago.

—Yes, I understand, I know how it is, he mumbles to the mother. He is still nodding when she walks back in.

—I'm taking 'em to the kitchen, Mom. It's ready. Oh (to him), let me take her, extending her arm. The baby, she says.

—Oh, yeah.

—Go right ahead, Little One (her nickname), the mother says. He's hungry, I know.

—What's her name? (This is when they are out of the bedroom) — The baby?

—Karina.

—Karinaaa? stretching the last syllable, like holding the

last note in a song. Karinaaa? She didn't get it, he thinks. Karina what? What's your husband's last name?

—Oh, she says. Wentworth. Earl Wentworth. He's in there, pointing to the living room. We'll see them later, O.K? Let's go to the kitchen first and you'll eat while we talk. Two years, huh?

—Around there.

They sat down at the kitchen table. No one was there, he eating systematically, fork to mouth to plate to mouth and then to plate again rhythmic, not seeming to swallow.

—Did you get that card I sent you?

—Yeah, he smiles. Prettiest thing I've seen in years.

—Pretty, huh? The lovers, the drawing. I liked the style, didn't you? Reminded me of you and me. I dunno.

He looks around. (She said that kinda loud. Jesus.)

—I waited, you know. The quiet look again. Fork to mouth to plate to mouth, this time without the food. (Shit!)

—Who am I kidding, she goes on. I tried, eyes flickering, lingering this time a moment too long in closing. I —

—I know, I know. I mean let's not talk about it you didn't have to say that I understand we lived too far from each other I mean the distance we had to respect it somehow summers were all we had and not even that so explanations are not needed believe me that's just the way things turn out sometimes two different worlds and all that it's not the first time kid I'm all right I'm fine —

—I dunno. We're not so different, she shrugs.

—Yeah, well, let's drop it, Katherine (he looks around). For Chrissakes, what's with you, anyway?

She smiles, candles in her eyes.

—O.K. I'm sorry. Eat. You missed the cadence again.

After he eats, he gets up with his plate in his hand.

—C'mon now. Taking the things from him, Leave those alone, will you? She takes his hand, Let's go to the living room, shall we?

He feels his blood ascend, rising to his head and beating madly at his face to get out. But as they walk in, there is no formal introduction. George and Buffalo Boy are there. He is glad. He is glad, for though those two were very different from each other, they had one thing (and only one) that came in handy at that time for him: they both made him feel at home, comfortable. The talk in the room was nothing.

—You gonna stay awhile? Clara's husband, the one who answered the phone, the one of many that he did not know. Have a beer, why don't you?

Katherine says, He's got a flight to catch.

—Oh, there's plenty of planes leaving Anchorage, man. Not as many as Frisco but —

Katherine says, He's gotta go and smiles at them.

They talk for a little more, mostly of questions and remarks about San Francisco, mostly of things he really does not feel like talking about because he really did not feel like talking at all, but what can you do, you gotta fake it if the hurt is worth the faking and so the talk in the room was mostly of nothing.

Katherine gets up suddenly, running the palms of both hands down along the curvature of her buttocks to smooth down the plaid skirt she has on. Well, she says, he really has to go.

He gets up and smiles at everybody goodbye and says 'later' to George and Buffalo Boy and heads back to the mother's bedroom.

When he comes out of the bedroom, Katherine is waiting for him and she takes his hand as she leads him outside. She stays at the door.

—Well, goodbye, he says, and starts walking out, already along the path to the gate.

She calls his name. He knew it. Goddamit he knew it! He knew this would happen. He didn't turn, thinking I will turn when she starts telling me what she wants to say. His heart starts acting up again. She calls his name once more.

Oh, no. not this. Jesus. His heart is pounding now. He turns to her. She says nothing. She is still looking at him. Waiting. I'll start walking up to her when she starts talking, he thinks. But she remains on the porch motionless, legs together, stiff on her toes, her hands on her back. He walks up the steps toward her, and she looks down on him as he climbs up then looks up now as he reaches the porch.

—Don't you ever say that.

—What?

—That ... word to me. He starts thinking, what the hell did I do now? What word? All I said was ... the last thing I ... now he remembers.

—Oh, he says. That word, he starts nodding his head.

—O.K.? she says. There, now I can tell myself I'm special. I've kept you a moment longer than the rest.

—O.K., now he is shaking his head, smiling a little. I'll see you around.

—I won't kiss you. I know how you shy away from clichés but I want you to know that I wanted just the same.

He laughs a little.

—See you around, stranger, he says. And she puts something on his head. It was his hat. That he left at her mother's house at the village two years ago when they last saw each other.

He walks out of the house and steps into the empty street of the city of Anchorage and lets the faint mist of nighing evening seep through him. Rain is in the air and the wind is damp; no stars are dancing tonight; not one note from a bird singing yet he feels the beauty of sadness swelling inside him. His left hand fishes a cigarette from his jacket and stabs his mouth as the other one lights it. With the night the smoke rushes past his throat and deep within his lungs. He feels good. He is alone, one, but at one with the world, though the air feels damp with doom and he is miles and people and things and mountains and rivers and seas away longing for deliverance in a pair of sparkling eyes; he feels good inside. Christ, I never even noticed which one *he* was, he thought.

ERLINDA VILLAMOR KRAVETZ

*I'M REALLY a newcomer to fiction. I worked for about twenty years as a journalist (*Manila Times, UPI, AP, *and others). Four years ago I quit my full-time job with a New Jersey daily and for the next two years continued to freelance for newspapers, including the* New York Times *and other publications.*

I did my undergraduate at St. Theresa's College, and obtained Master's degrees in English from New York University and in Journalism from Columbia University.

Switching from journalism to fiction is not altogether uncommon. In my case I had trepidations about going into fiction this late in my writing career. But I now wish I had plunged right into it because creative writing requires no less than total immersion. It took a while for the basics of creative writing to sink in — not until I had agonized over scores of stories, most of which I wound up discarding even after countless rewrites. I learned more from those tentative efforts than from all the how-to books I studied and workshops I attended. I also read a lot of quality fiction.

"Song from the Mountain" grew out of an exercise piece. It is my first published work of fiction.

I have spent the past two years learning the craft of novel writing.

I wish I could say "writing a novel," but that would be too presumptuous on my part.

My story "Reunion" won first prize in PALM Council's first short story competition in 1989. I direct a fiction writing workshop in Monmouth County, New Jersey, where I live with my husband, Michael.

SONG FROM THE MOUNTAIN

TWO DAYS after Augusto and I eloped and were married by the town mayor, I almost became a widow. Only his reflexes saved him from his would-be assassin, my father. Father was normally a calm, even-tempered man, but something in him just snapped as soon as word about our elopement reached him. It was a hot, blistering day and we had taken the three-hour bus ride to my parents' town to ask for their blessing. As we got off the bus, my new husband held a red and orange umbrella.

On the street, my father accosted us, brandishing a three-foot long machete, and I knew right away he had gone berserk. Eyes flashing, clothes disarray, he lunged toward my husband, like a clumsy matador. Augusto sprang back and sprinted to safety. People scampered out of my father's way until he was subdued and disarmed by the constabulary police.

My parents had promised me in marriage to another man, whom I did not like — an older man, a civil servant. I shamed my family by running away with my high school sweetheart. My father was not arrested for the attempted murder. He had done what was expected of him: save face, salvage family honor.

Nothing was said of the incident after that. My parents still do not talk to us, refuse to give us their blessings, and have not acknowledged their grandchild, our son Butch, who is now five.

Augusto and I lived in Baguio at the time, a pokey

mountain resort town carved out of the Cordillera in Central Luzon. It had a large American community, which had been drawn to the place by its spring-like weather and the gold mines. The Americans had transformed their part of town into a gaudy colonial enclave. In high school some of my classmates were American boys and they were a great distraction. I fell secretly in love with every one of them. But I was shy and my parents disapproved of any familiarity with the American boys. Girls, my mother told us, cheapened themselves by associating with white boys. We, from a peasant family, were made to feel virtuous and respectable with our own kind. We gorged on pride, honor, loyalty. With love, we were frugal: a little went a long way. A furtive look from a beloved splintered into a thousand meanings.

In secret, we, the young ones, succumbed: the foreigners turned us into a generation of covetous voluptuaries poised between two cultures.

"I can't imagine spending the rest of our lives in this backward country," my husband said as we sat on a concrete bench in Burnham Park, admiring the perfect rows of imported zinnias, daisies and marigolds, leaves and petals singed by the tropical sun.

"We will never amount to anything, just like our parents. There's no use working hard," he went on.

The Americans had built the park in the center of town and planted it with trees and flowering plants shipped from the United States. We walked beneath a row of willow trees, pensive. Our thoughts pierced through the clouds, beyond the mountains girded by rice terraces that shimmered in the sun like a gigantic garland.

A year after our marriage, Augusto left for the United States on a student visa and immediately acquired a new first name: Gus. A college graduate, Bachelor of Arts in Economics, summa cum laude, he was filled with ambition. I was seven months pregnant then with our first child. I could not join him because his visa did not allow the spouse to come along. But he would send for me and our child, as soon as he had a permanent visa. I wasn't sure how he would work out the visa problem because immigrants' quota from our country was way overfilled. America considered us superfluous, unless we were nurses, doctors, and medical technicians.

But my husband is a resolute, enterprising man. I can tell you stories of how he survived in New York hustling, using his wits, maintaining his equanimity. He was like an animal raised in captivity let loose in the land of freedom. He wrote as soon as he arrived in New York in the winter. He had no job or money to make a deposit on an apartment, but found an old friend who had storage space in the basement of his apartment. Gus — that was how he signed his name in his first letter — appropriated that space as a bedroom, sleeping on a mattress he found at the curb outside his friend's building. In the morning he showered and shaved in the men's room in the lobby. He worked at the first jobs that came along: as a hospital orderly, as a restaurant dishwasher, as a parking lot attendant. They were demeaning jobs, but he didn't mind.

"What do I care about losing face? Nobody around here knows me," his letter read.

Later, he decided to work for himself to give him more time for his studies. He salvaged a red Beetle that had been abandoned on Riverside Drive, got a driver's license, called a few small companies, and he was in business delivering urgent mail and paychecks. He flourished.

"America is amazing," he wrote me. "Here you have so much freedom, you can do anything, be anything you want." I had heard that line many times before, but coming from my husband alone in the New World, it tolled with new resonance.

All those years we were separated I was faithful to him. Not that the occasion didn't present itself. I was working as a staff nurse for an American mining company and made friends with several American men who all looked like Hollywood actors to me. I worked long hours, earned an excellent salary and took care of Butch. My father's machete, stiff, gleaming in his hand, remained for me the symbol of marital fidelity. At the office, I fended off advances from the Robert Redfords and

Paul Newmans of the American community — amorous adventures which at night transmuted into the lusty adventures of my fantasies.

We now live in New York, in a one-bedroom apartment on Morningdale Heights. We are saving for a house in nearby New Jersey. Gus has started working for Merrill Lynch as a financial analyst and is finishing his MBA at Fordham. We want to build a good, decent life for our son and other children that may come. I've found a job as a secretary at the United Nations medical clinic. A good job for a woman from a remote Asian town. But no big deal, really. Hundreds of other girls from my country — pert and pretty — who otherwise would be working the big new hotels along Manila Bay or be illegals in New York, work at the UN.

Before I found a job, Butch and I stayed home most of the time, disoriented, existing in a haze, as we tried to fit into the fixed, busy rhythm of Gus' life. Through the hoarfrost of our window, I watched people swaddled in thick clothes, feet encased in heavy boots as though geared for battle. I didn't have the nerve to go down and join that blustery swirl of humanity. Why are they running, Mom? A worried Butch would ask me.

My son and I periodically craved native cooking. When that happened, we indulged ourselves; I don't believe in depriving ourselves. I would take the bus to Port Authority to buy the ingredients at an ethnic store on Ninth Avenue. Gus refused to eat native food. "You've been cooking that stinking dish again. The whole building knows what we're eating," he would say, sniffing the apartment's lingering odor of garlic, coriander and fermented shrimp. He made me feel backward, especially when I chopped bok choy, scallions, and dried mushrooms with a sharp heavy knife. He had sloughed off his origins and expected me also to adopt to the New World. Butch had no problems; he quickly lost his accent.

I could not bring myself to ask my husband how he

had found sexual outlet during our separation. It's not my way. I took it for granted he had slept with white women. Asian men harbors dreams of making love to a white woman at least once in their lifetime, if only to find out, first hand, if her secret hair is naturally golden as that of her head, her nipples pink, not the nut-brown of Oriental women, to see if Americans are as sexy as they are portrayed in Hollywood films.

Gus told me once how he had been kept awake all night by a couple's lovemaking just above his apartment. The couple have since moved out so I have no way of corroborating it.

"Every single night," he said. "I don't think they ever rest. Americans are really oversexed."

"Overfed and over here ..." I quickly added. It was silly. The words were from a popular joke about Americans in my native country and they automatically came out of my lips. This kind of banter added levity and humor to our marriage.

I did not plan to, but I had an affair. My lover was French, a journalism student at Columbia University. It was so convenient: he lived in the same building, in the south wing for unmarried men; we lived in the wing for married couples. I'd go to Pierre's apartment after dinner, while Gus was still at Fordham and Butch slept. Sometimes I'd come home in the middle of the day to be with Pierre. Those were the times he was supposed to be covering news assignments for his advanced reporting class. Sometimes on my way home on the local subway, I'd stop by at the Journalism Building to see him. He introduced me to his classmates as his girlfriend. "Hi, I'm Perla Cuevas."

When we were together at his place, Pierre double-locked his door but unlatched the fire-escape window. We did drills the first summer we got together on how to climb down the ladder. The steel bars burned my palms. I imagined them like ice in winter.

"I love you, cherie, but fighting a duel is so corny," he

told me the first time we made love. I felt diminished, unimportant. I could do an Emma Bovary.

"The important thing is not to panic, not to attract attention, and everything will be okay," he had instructed me. Drawing up the sheet and the chenille bedspread to my chest, I felt our warm body juices trickle down between my legs.

"I wouldn't worry," I said.

I could not see Gus inflamed by my infidelity for he, too, had a lover. I found that out by accident from Pierre when I proposed, on a dare, going out for dinner as a foursome. (Coming to America, we tried to shake off moral shackles.)

"Maybe he should take Caroline along," Pierre suggested. He had known Gus and Caroline for a while, but either he had elected to be discreet or infidelity does not mean anything to him. I did not go to pieces. I had seen Caroline a couple of times in our lobby although she didn't live in our building. She is a receptionist at Merrill Lynch, a tall, heavy-set woman, somewhat older than I am, with milky white skin, shoulder-length blonde hair, and small pointed white teeth. Plump legs with huge red splotches at the calves. She resembles a Fernando Botero woman. America is so generous, even to its women.

Pierre made me feel desirable, exotic, beautiful, as delicate and ephemeral as a tropical bloom. He had a passion for svelte, brown-skinned, doe-eyed Asian women, with high cheekbones, and was an indefatigable lover. With him I was lascivious, carefree; I could forget the brutality of life in New York. Pierre's dream is to flee it, to go to Southeast Asia and work as a correspondent for the *International Herald*. His brother, who worked for the French embassy in Bangkok, drove a Porsche, owned a pet puma, and had beautiful Thai girl for a housemaid. In France his brother was a nobody.

I met Pierre Latrouneau at an international student's fair sponsored by our apartment's tenants association three months after I arrived in New York. The guests were mostly foreign students and visiting professors who came in native costumes. Gus would not wear the beaded G-string of his tribal ancestors that I had brought with me as a souvenir. He wore a dark three-piece suit, his Merrill Lynch attire.

At the fair, held in our apartment lobby, Gus played the piano for an all-student band. He is a musician. I manned one pf the ethnic booths, wearing my native dress, a long, ecru gown with butterfly sleeves and décolletage. With my long hair in a French twist, I looked like a young Imelda Marcos before greed and power bloated her.

A man, pale-blonde, slightly built, with a sharp, inquisitive look, came over my booth, smiling with anticipation. He fingered the plastic palm leaves that decorated my booth and looked over the display of food, smacking hid thin lips, like a hungry schoolboy.

"My name is Perla Cuevas. Would you like to try the lumpia? It's like an egg roll. Or rice cake? They're both good."

"Yes, please. I would like very much to try the egg roll. It looks délicieux," he replied, rubbing his closed fists together. I brandished wooden tongs, then delicately plucked two lumpias which I placed on a small paper plate.

"Here you go," I said, handing him the plate. "Remember my name now, Perla Cuevas," I shouted through the hubbub. Why did I say that? What would he think of me? I looked at him and saw him staring at me, his brown eyes dilated like a startled animal. As he took a bite of the lumpia, he leaned against the booth, sending the plywood and cardboard hut crashing to the ground. The food and drinks fell in a heap on the floor.

"Oh, pardon, madame. So, so sorry. Mon dieu, how stupid of me ..." Contrite words tumbled out of him but I couldn't care less. I felt violated, demeaned. I was ready to stomp out of the place, fuming like an offended prima donna, but I stopped when I saw him hike up his pants, go on his knees, and with his bare hands calmly collect the scraps of my native country's culinary pride.

The band stopped playing and the ruckus subsided into a conspiratorial drone as the merrymakers gawked squeamishly at the mess.

"What happened, Perla?" Gus was at my side, with a bemused look on his face. He looked at the man on his knees and broke into laughter.

"Pierre, my golly, what are you doing? Don't worry about that. That's nothing; someone will come and sweep it up."

"Nothing? My whole day's work? You'll let that guy get away with it?" I was furious. Pierre rose, shaking off bits of food from his beige corduroy trousers, his face now red with embarrassment.

"I'm sorry. I didn't know that thing was so light."

"By the way, have you met my wife Perla?" Gus asked, helping Pierre to his feet.

I shrugged.

"Well, this is Pierre Latourneau, did I pronounce it right? He lives in the building," Gus said, then turned around to join his band. As he walked away, he scanned the lobby. His eyes rested on a blonde, plump girl munching on a chicken leg at the Nigerian booth. As though on cue, she looked at Gus and smiled.

On our first date Pierre and I went to Brass Rail, across from Columbia University. He placed his arm lightly around my waist as we followed the waiter to a corner table. The place was dark. On each table, small candles flickered in squat, thick red glasses. Instinctively I grasped the one on our table to warm my hands even though it was late spring. We ordered beer and drank a toast to each other. Pierre rose and sat beside me. When he placed his hand on my thigh, I looked around to see if someone would recognize me, but no one was even looking in our direction. I took Pierre's hand and sidled up to him, brushing my breast against his side. I felt — self-assured, sophisticated. We held hands coming out of the restaurant. At the subway station a train waited, but we didn't board it. We were alone on the platform. Pierre leaned me against the tile wall whose coolness seeped through my clothes, and pressed his body against mine. His mouth was like a suction pump on my lips. Two shafts of light pierced the tunnel's darkness. We boarded the IRT local, taking a corner seat where we sat, embracing, legs tightly closed at the thighs.

For three months our passion held sway. In the subway, in the apartment lobby, the laundry room, we kissed and necked shamelessly.

"You're not afraid?" he asked me.

"No." My father would have blood on his head if he had seen me.

Summer, we didn't see each other for three weeks. I sneaked out of the office to go to Pierre's apartment, but no one answered his door. My notes filled his mailbox in the lobby. I asked Bill, our super, if he knew where Pierre was. He smiled at me mockingly, and shrugged his shoulders. Bill liked Gus, who had bribed him with a month's rent to get us our apartment in this building.

Desperate, I asked my husband if he had seen Pierre lately.

"Search me," he quipped, not budging behind the pages of *The Wall Street Journal*. I considered telling him I missed Pierre so he would get suspicious, jealous, and we would have a fight. Gus would proclaim his fidelity and I'd feel better. But I did not think that would provoke him. Maybe, as a commodity, my virtue had tumbled in value to zilch.

"Who's Caroline?" I asked, not looking up from filing my toenail.

"What's gotten into you, you out of your head?" After a pause he laughed, put down the newspaper and came over to embrace me. "Come on, hon, this is America. You got to be broadminded." I shooed him off, jabbing his middle with my nail file.

Monday night, after three unbearble weekends, Pierre called me at home just as Butch and I were getting ready for dinner. Gus was still at Fordham where he had started on a teaching assistantship.

"Allo, Madame Cuevas." I recognized his voice right

away and my heart twirled like a windmill. "This is Pierre and I'm calling overseas from Bali." He had gone on vacation, he explained. Didn't tell me, afraid I would go on a jealous rage and he'd come back to a sulking lover.

"I'm coming back tomorrow morning; could you spend the day with me? Ca va?" I clasped the receiver long after I replaced it, feeling the burning rush of love rise to my cheeks. I staggered into the kitchen and bumped into my son who could not wait for me to set the table. He had dug a fork into the wok of noodles and eaten a forkful hungrily, burning his tongue. He spat it all out into the sink. I rushed to him with a glass of ice water and stroked his head.

After dinner I opened the bottom drawer of my bureau and took out the new black lace bra and panties I would wear the next day under my halter and shorts. I had bought the new underwear at the sale the first week Pierre was gone and I had a fit of depression.

It is August. The New York heat makes me feel I'm back in Manila, where I went to college. In Manila we don't use thermometer to tell the temperature. We know it's hot when dogs — panting, glassy-eyed, foaming at the mouth — take to the shady streets, their tongues hanging out; when people stay off the streets because of the rabid animals and the flies that seek refuge in people's noses and ears.

Pierre's apartment is air-conditioned so we stay all day in his bed, our bodies warm and moist. My eyes scan the room like a searchlight. I like his room — clean, spare, uncluttered, a masculine room, except for my clothes which are strewn on the carpeted floor around the bed, with the sarong Pierre bought me from Indonesia, a piece of cotton cloth with flower and bird prints in orange and crimson. I reach out for the box of tissue on the night table and see a couple of light-brown hairpins (mine are black). I picked them up, reach across Pierre's body, whose back is turned to me, and twirl them before his face.

"Whose are these?" I ask. This coarse, vulgar jealousy surprises and embarrasses me and I flick the hairpins back on the night table.

"Oh, I don't know," he grunts, then turns toward me to see if I am surly or mad with jealousy; to see if two little hairpins will unleash any green demons in my breast so he can mock me, a married woman in another man's bed. On impulse, he makes love to me again. My lust renewed, I return his thrusts recklessly. I do not want to make a scene.

I know this love will run its course and we will go on with our lives. Pierre will graduate and go his Southeast Asian Eden; Gus and I will embark on a new hectic, domestic life in New Jersey. The closing on the house is in two weeks. In the suburbs maybe I will be seduced by the mailman or a neighbor. Caroline and Gus will meet at Ramada Inn or Howard Johnson off the turnpike. We will continue with our secret games. With nothing, not even each other, to fear; no machete cleaving the air in vengeful wrath.

My thoughts are on the wallpaper I'll choose for Butch's room in our new house when the doorbell rings. "Merde," Pierre grumbles, reluctantly sliding off the bed. I pull the bedspread over my head while Pierre goes to see who is calling. I can hear the voice at the door.

"Bill here, got suhmin fo' you. Open the door." When Pierre returns to the bedroom, I am sitting up in bed. His eyes sweep the floor for his clothes which mixed up with mine. He plucks the orange and crimson cloth, the sarong, from the heap like a magician's scarf, tucks it around his waist. We laugh lightly, nervously.

Footsteps die down in the hallway. The elevator door bangs close, then whines away. I wait for Pierre to come back to bed, but he tarries. Someone is at the door. I can hear him: Gus.

"She's here, I know she's in there. Let me in, you son of a bitch, or I'll stick this into your guts." My husband's voice shatters my guts. I jump out of bed, swathed in a printed pima-cotton bedsheet smelling of our sweat. Barefoot, I climb out of the window to the fire escape. At the landing, I wait, my ears wired to Pierre's room. Below people hurry by without looking at me, naked underneath the bedsheet. When I don't hear anything I climb back up to Pierre's room to retrieve my clothes.

Just as I poke my head into the window, someone outside, below, shouts, "Look out, get out, everybody! He's going to kill us!" I look down and see people dashing out of the apartment building as if it's on fire. I go down to the ground and walk around to the main door, nearly getting crushed in the rampage from the lobby.

People dart here and there, panicky; doors swing open, slam shut. I take the stairs and on the second floor, I catch a glimpse of Pierre in the sarong as he blazes past me, heading for the exit. I fling the bedsheet behind the door and see Gus, his dark eyes flashing through a curtain of disheveled hair, a bloody kitchen knife in hand. He is hacking away at my naked lover crouched in a corner, underneath the row of mailboxes. Pierre is holding up his arms, crisscrossed, but Gus keeps hitting them in quick, sharp thrusts.

"The important thing is not to panic, not to attract attention …" Pierre keeps saying.

Police cars whine and stop in front of the apartment building. I bask in the warm, crimson light their flashers beam upon my naked body.

Pierre's wounds are shallow; doctors say he will live. Passion is brief, its perils lasting. I am mounting a defense for my husband, who is charged with attempted murder. I have retained Dr. Amada Solano, a psychiatrist at the Pilgrim State Psychiatric Hospital, an expert on the phenomenon of running amok. She's from the old country. She begins: "Tell me everything about your father."

NADINE R. SARREAL

DAD TOOK a gardening job in Seattle in the summer of 1955 so he and Mom could afford to have me, the first of three children. Mom says I must've gotten womb-boredom and forced my way out three weeks early. So while Mom and I bonded in the hospital, Dad had to attend my baby shower in our place!

Since that summer, I've moved seventeen times: Washington, Montana, North Carolina, Manila, Baguio, Connecticut, Quezon City, back to Connecticut, and now here I am, plop in the middle of Texas. And my folks were teachers, not military people.

Since that summer, I've earned a Statistics degree at the University of the Philippines, gotten married, had two children, and used many computer hours as an insurance programmer-analyst. And still, I don't know what I want to do when I grow up. Well, yes, I do. I want to write —poems and stories and books. Interesting stuff that will touch people who are quite different from me and yet have the same basic human concerns. They'll say, "I've felt like that before." Or "I know just what she means." A good story begets another. I'm working on it. I really am.

TUITION

OH, SUE, I got your letter last night and read it over a cold supper. It was the highlight of my day. Phil and I had just come home from evening class and we were both pretty tired. I was feeling sick, too (my sinuses again). After I put your letter down, Phil kind of cleared his throat a couple of times and said he needed money for his brother's tuition. Lando was going to summer school. I think my face must have clouded over the way it does when I try to hide my reaction to things I find unpleasant. I must have said something cool like, sure, there's some money in our box upstairs. Then I heard myself sigh and before I could bite my tongue, I was saying we never seem to have enough money to get through from one paycheck to the next. How are we going to save enough to have this baby? Who are you these days, my husband or Lando's brother? And what are we going to use for groceries on Saturday?

All of what I was saying was true in a sense, but even as I was saying it, I was praying that God would slice off my tongue with a lightning bolt. I was wishing I could shut my mouth or he'd be so deeply hurt that he would probably be driven to much later taking an awful job just because it paid well and no matter what I said then, he'd stick it out for the money because this night I'd made him believe money meant happiness to me. And I was probably hurting him so much, too, that he'd end up not taking our money but getting what he needed from someone else, maybe borrowing it from another teacher, and then paying it back little by little, out of his weekly pocket money. I knew all these things as I spoke, but spoke anyway, letting my voice carry anger that I didn't even feel anymore.

He clenched his jaws and looked away, probably keeping angry words back. He's never hasty to speak. Then there was silence between us and we haven't talked to each other since last night.

Oh, Sue, I hate myself. This morning, when he was out of the bedroom, I saw he hadn't touched the money in our box, so I took it and put it in my pocket because I did want him to give Lando the tuition. I had to think of some way to hand it to Phil, you know, nonchalantly. I just didn't know how to back up and eat my words, how to put things right in a graceful way. Too, I think, I was afraid he'd say something pained, like never mind, he didn't ever want his family to be a burden to me, or something equally rotten that would cut me right down and then I'd hate him, too.

On the way to work in the car, I kept planning and planning over and over in my head how I'd ease over the money and say one phrase, just the right mix of words, that would tell him I sure was dumb and very sorry. That I didn't mind at all if we paid his brother's summer tuition and that actually I was glad his brother was studying, too. I wanted to say in five or six words that it didn't mean anything more than that — just that we had money someone else needed and that was no big deal. I kept thinking, re-phrasing how I was going to say it. Casually, like, did you get the money for Lando? No, better yet, something a little off-tangent like are you meeting Lando for lunch to give him this money? (As I handed it to him.) No, first I'd pluck him on the sleeve and ask him in my fake Jamaican accent (just as we pulled up to his bus stop) — coot ya gif dis bread to you bruddah, mon? There, that was just light enough, but funny, too, so it would break the tension between us. I'd make it like a joke so he could laugh with me and then we'd be fine again. He'd understand.

He was sitting there beside me, frowning at a lesson plan and pretending to memorize formulas. I could tell, though, he was thinking about things I'd said last night. He's terrible about hiding his worry. He looked so worn I wanted to hold him right there in the middle of Main Street traffic and tell him — Hey, it's fine. Don't worry, old man. Things just hit me wrong last night. Don't believe I'm the hard woman I appear to be. I love you.

But, well, we got to the bus stop. Things happened so fast. I turned to face him squarely, but he was already out of the car, leaning towards the bus. And then before I could even open my mouth, he was gone,

The bus chose that exact moment to come roaring by so that all I caught was a glimpse of his powder blue shirt and then he was on the bus, swallowed up in a swirl of dust. I was stunned. I hadn't said anything, not a word, and he was already in the bus. And there I sat, my heart aching with love and remorse, and the damned money still in my pocket.

And never mind the money, I hadn't even told him everything was okay. That there shouldn't ever have to be a choice between me and Lando. That my tantrum was over.

Somehow, I got to the office. I don't remember how, which I route I took, if traffic was heavy or light. I wasn't tired but my knees were shaking as I walked into the building. Now I'm at my desk, hiding behind a stack of papers and writing you this letter. I've been here a couple of hours, just thinking. The awful, really awful thing, Sue, is that I know he's already forgiven me. I knew that even last night. I'm sure that he's only bothered because he does think he's a burden to me and that, perhaps, he shouldn't be supporting his brother anymore now that he's married.

I wish he resented me instead, or hated me the way I hate myself for saying things I only half-mean, saying stuff just to get the weight off my chest, and then not being able to say the healing things. I wish he wouldn't be so forgiving right away. I wish he'd blame me sometimes for the cruel things I do. The way it is now, I know I've lost him a little, but enough so I'll feel the difference and blame myself. It's funny how hard it is to say what you really want to the people you are closest to.

So, how about you, my friend, how are you?

MARIANNE VILLANUEVA

I WAS born in Manila, and came to the San Francisco Bay Area in 1979 for the Master's Program in East Asian Studies at Stanford University. I've lived in the Bay Area off and on ever since. In 1983 I was given a scholarship to attend the Creative Writing Program at Stanford University, and that changed my life. Before then, I had been told I could write, but I had always regarded such comments as slightly suspect, as being prompted more by kindness rather than genuine admiration. But after the Writing Program, I began to feel that indeed I not only could, but should, write. I began to take my writing seriously, and I began to meet people who encouraged me to persevere at this very difficult vocation.

In the years since I was admitted to the Writing Program, I've been lucky. I got married and had a child, and began work at the Stanford East Asia National Resource Center. I had short stories published in Story Quarterly, Matrix, *and the* Journal of Philippine Studies. *Another short story included in* The Forbidden Stitch, *an Asian American women's anthology complied by the editors at Calyx Books. And this led eventually to Calyx agreeing to publish my own collection of short stories,* Ginseng and Other Tales from Manila.

Looking back over the past couple of years, I can say that balancing everything — the writing and my job and my family — was difficult. But I can also say that this life has given me immense satisfaction.

OVERSEAS

ALMOST EVERYONE in Manila has an uncle or a brother or even a father in Saudi Arabia. Since the government began exporting cheap labor there, there are long lines in front of the Overseas Workers Bureau.

In Sepa's neighborhood only a few men remain — Sepa's father, and Mang Pepe who runs the sari-sari store, and a few other men at whom the others laugh because, even though they want to go, their wives won't let them.

Everyone talks about the big money to be made in Saudi Arabia. Mang Kadyo, who just a year ago had been a jeepney driver like Sepa's father, now drives a bus in Riyadh. His wife, Aling Marta, says he earns more in one month there than he ever made in a year in Manila. Before, Aling Marta was always complaining about Mang Kadyo. She said that he was lazy, that he was not a good provider. Her hands were always red and sore from washing other people's clothes in the big houses in Forbes Park. Now she stays home all day, listening to Sharon Cuneta tapes on a brand new cassette deck.

But a few men in the neighborhood have wives that don't care about the stories of big money coming back from abroad. Such wives only want their men with them, beside them every night. When a man goes to Saudi Arabia, it may be a year, even two, before his return trip home. Some wives simply cannot bear it. There is Aling Mameng, for instance, whose husband is very handsome so one can understand why she can't bear to part with him. But then there is Aling Nena, whose husband looks like a laughing Buddha with a great big belly and spindly legs, and she is as jealous and possessive with him as though he were a Vic Vargas or an Eddie Garcia.

Even Sepa's older brother Rudy left. He had just turned eighteen. Before going to Saudi Arabia, he had sold Blue Seal cigarettes behind the Shell station on Pasay Road. She and Rudy used to sit on the bamboo ladder that led up to their house, telling funny stories and laughing and joking. Rudy bought her little trinkets from money he had left over after he gave their father his share. If Sepa wanted a Coke from the tiyanggi, or money to see a movie, Rudy always gave her some. He was very good to her.

The day he told her, they were sitting on the bamboo ladder, watching the mosquitos skim over the scummy green surface of the canal that ran beneath them. In the rainy season, this canal overflowed its banks and turned the neighborhood into a lagoon. Then Sepa would stay home from school and swim with the other children in the murky water. But now the middle of the dry season; monsoon was a long way off.

She and Rudy sat on the steps and watched the smaller children standing ankle-deep in the water, catching tadpoles. There was a sickly sweet smell of rotting banana peels wafting over the canal from the far end, where piled-up garbage blocked the water's flow.

All the houses, including theirs, stood on stilts, with roofs made out of salvaged sheets of corrugated tin. The ground below was always muddy, even in the dry season, and sucked at the feet at every step. Under the houses lurked skinny bad-tempered cats with patchy fur. Some nights their wailing could be heard all over the neighborhood.

It was the time of the year when it was so hot that the men walked around with their T-shirts up, exposing their beer bellies. And the women washing their clothes at the neighborhood pump could be seen wetting their necks and shoulders, not minding how they looked in their wet blouses. Sepa's loose blouse also clung to her back and shoulders and breasts, damp with perspiration. She lifted the ends of her blouse with both hands and tried to make the cloth flap. When her brother looked she began to laugh.

At twelve, her breasts were just beginning to push up through her blouse. They were small, but the nipples looked enormous. She had been with a man once who told her that they looked like cauliflowers.

Sepa wondered if Rudy knew that she had begun seeing some of the young men and letting them buy her Cokes and treat her to movies. These young men always took her to the balcony and turned out not to be interested in the movies after all. But it was cool there in the dark of the movie house, and with the flickering image on the screen it was the closest Sepa had ever come to seeing the insides of a real disco, and so she didn't mind.

When she saw the look on Rudy's face, Sepa stopped laughing. "What's the matter?" she asked.

Rudy was silent for a few moments. Then he told her. I've been thinking — maybe I'll sign up at the Overseas Workers Bureau." When she didn't answer, he continued, "Make a little money."

Sepa just looked at him. Rudy turned his back to her and began stretching, as though he'd gotten cramped from sitting too long.

Rudy was tall dark and had big eyes. The women in the neighborhood found him handsome. He could have any girl he wanted, but he was faithful to one, the daughter of Mang Tomas. She was only a few years older than Sepa and not even very pretty, but Sepa would see them sometimes, pressed up against each other in the dark alley or beneath stairs. Sometimes she would shout at them, "Hoy!" and they would both turn and look at her and laugh.

So she had not thought her brother would want to go to Saudi Arabia. It would be bad for her, too, to be left alone with her father at home. Sepa didn't have a mother — just someone who'd died of tuberculosis when she was four, and whose picture, encased in a plastic envelope, dangled from the rear view mirror of her father's jeepney. Her father was rarely home, and when he was she could smell him coming from a long way off, because of drink.

227

"Why do you have to go?" Sepa said. "We have enough money."

Her brother only shook his head.

"They want people to work in construction. You don't know anything about that," she continued. "And even if you're lucky enough to get there, you won't like it. You know how Boyet complains every time he comes home."

"I've made up my mind," Rudy said.

Sepa looked around helplessly. The neighborhood was so familiar that she had never stopped to look at it as a place other than home. She knew everyone in the surrounding houses, knew when they quarreled, knew when they made love. Surely that meant something. And no matter how ugly the place — yes, she already knew that the neighborhood was ugly — surely it was far better to be with people one knew, people one had grown up with, rather than people who dressed strangely and spoke a language one could not understand.

She turned to her brother. "I didn't think you would be so selfish. How can you leave me alone with Tatang? All he does is drink, and he never gives me any money."

"I'll send you money," Rudy said. "And you can always go to Mang Pepe or Aling Tancing if you need help. You won't be alone."

"I'll run away," Sepa said. "I will."

Rudy looked annoyed. "Stop talking crazy," he said.

Sepa merely shrugged.

Sepa thought she knew all she cared to know about Saudi Arabia from listening to the men talk at Mang Pepe's sari-sari store. In Saudi Arabia one couldn't have women and couldn't have wine and the Filipinos were penned in at night, just like cattle, in a walled compound. When one arrived, one had to sign a piece of paper that said you agreed to turn over sixty percent of your money to the Overseas Workers Bureau. Once a Filipino was caught stealing and instead of turning him over to the proper officials, the Saudis had cut off his right hand. The OWB officials there did not even bother to protest.

Sepa had the feeling that if her brother left she would

not see him again for a long time.

"Don't leave," she begged, feeling near tears.

"I'll send you money every month," Rudy said.

Later, when Sepa told her father about Rudy's plan, she noticed he seemed pleased.

"Did he really say he was going?" her father said, rubbing his hands together. "That's good."

"He says he wants me to go a proper school, to stop hanging around here with the older women," Sepa said, making a face. She never thought much about her future, about what was going to happen to her. That was why Rudy said she was stupid.

"With the money I send, you'll be able to have new clothes any time you feel like it, and you don't have to be ashamed to be with the other girls at school," Rudy said, guessing at the reason why she had stopped going. "You'll be happier. You won't have to depend on Tatang for things."

That was the last statement made Sepa stop and think. Perhaps Rudy was right. The money *would* be nice. There would be more to eat, for one thing — more than just the daily fare of galunggong and rice. And there might even be some money left over — after Tatang picked over his share, of course — for a small transistor radio, one she could carry around with her on the street. Then she could listen to Sharon and Martin and Pabs all day, without having to wait outside the local Disco-Rex to hear snatches of songs. And she could buy make-up, like the women she saw in bars, who to her were the most beautiful women in the world, and who were always accompanied by pink-cheeked foreign men with plenty of money.

When the time came for Rudy to leave, Sepa was not as sad as she had expected to be.

"Write!" she begged.

"Sure!" Rudy said, smiling and giving her the "thumbs up" sign he had imitated from an American tourist.

He was going on a big ship with many other men. He had described for her many times the route it would take. After leaving Manila, the boat would pass through the Strait of Malacca, cross the Indian Ocean, and head up the Red Sea to Jedda. At Jedda, the men would go different ways. Rudy was going to a city called Dharan.

Dharan. Sepa said the name over and over to herself. She imagined it to be a city in the middle of the desert, a city with sand-colored houses and buildings, where the tabletops might feel like sandpaper and even the food might have a gritty taste, the way it gets when cooked at the beach.

As Rudy prepared to go, Sepa thought he seemed sorry. He kept looking around, as though he were searching for something. There were a few people sitting out on the ladders of their houses: Aling Marta — picking the lice from the head of her eldest daughter; Mang Tomas, newly returned from Saudi Arabia, getting a haircut and a scolding from his wife, Aling Lita. They all stopped what they were doing to watch as Rudy made his way carefully down the ladder, all his belongings in a brand-new nylon bag, bought for the occasion by Sepa.

"Oy, Rudy, are you really leaving us?" Aling Marta said, punctuating the sentence with a loud guffaw.

"Yes, Ale, I'm leaving at last," Rudy said. "Look after Sepa, will you? I don't want her getting into trouble."

Everyone laughed.

"Do you know when you're coming back?" Aling Lita asked.

"Ay, Don't expect to be back in less than two years," Mang Tomas sighed. "They try to get as much out of you as they can, while you're still fresh. Look at what they did to me..."

"Shuss!" Aling Lita said, boxing her husband's ear.

One by one, the neighbors from various houses came to their windows and doors. A few of them waved. The air was full of warmth and good feeling. "Goodbye! Goodbye! May God be with you!" everyone was saying. Everyone was smiling, except for Rudy's girl, the eldest daughter of Mang Tomas. She was crying and blowing her nose into her skirt. In the last few weeks she and Rudy were always together in dark corners.

"Stupida!" her mother chided her. "Everyone has to leave sooner or later. Better that it was before you got pregnant!"

After that, Sepa didn't hear from her brother for a long time. The rainy season came and a few of the houses were blown down during a typhoon. But in a few days, they were up again with the occupants none the worse for wear. The canal overflowed its banks and the water rose halfway up the houses' stilts and for two weeks the girls had to walk with their skirts hitched high up to their thighs to keep their clothes from getting wet. At night the wind howled through the narrow alleyways and the rain lashed the houses. The cats wailed like abandoned babies.

Sepa thought of her brother living in a city of adobe houses the color of the desert. Perhaps he had taken up with a Saudi girl. It made her happier to think so, to think that was the reason he had not written, though she knew it was unlikely — it was against their rules. When she passed the daughter of Mang Tomas on the street, the girl averted her eyes with an angry look. Once she even turned around and spat. Sepa shrugged. It was just one of those things.

Around the time of Typhoon Insiang — the typhoon that nearly knocked the figure of the Virgin from its pedestal in the tower of the Sanctuario de San Antonio, the old lady who sold fried bananas at a corner of the Avenida de Rizal had one of her periods of clairvoyance. She looked up at the grey sky and she noted the shapes of the clouds and she said the men were coming home. That was why, even before the word got around that a few of the men from the neighborhood were going to be returning for a while, the wives had already begun their preparations — dusting and sweeping, putting up new curtains, buying new dresses. Vangie, the girl from El's Beauty Parlor, came several days a week to do perms. Sometimes she brought along a friend who did manicures.

Sepa was at the bus stop to greet the returning men, but her brother was not among those who stepped off the bus that had brought the men from the pier. There was Mang Enteng — and darker and thinner than even she would have thought possible — and a few of the younger men, but no Rudy.

That night Sepa let someone take her to a movie, the first time in nearly a year. They sat in the darkened balcony a long time, and later the man did not want to bring her home, because, he said, he hadn't had enough. Sepa went with him to a motel, and there they lay together in a bed which creaked and hurt Sepa's back. Afterwards, the man had not paid much attention to her. Sepa had hoped he might give her a little money, but he did not. When she returned home, her father was angry. He had waited for her to serve him his supper. He had to make do with leftover rice. He called her a slut and other bad names. Sepa had stared at him impassively. "What's the use?" she was thinking. "It's all the same to me."

It must have been a few nights after that when the trouble between Mang Enteng and Aling Tancing began. People said later that they had seen it coming. Aling Tancing had acted a little crazy when her husband was away. The women whispered that she'd been taking tea from bamboo roots. They said she'd been trying to lose something that was growing inside her, that perhaps was not her husband's. Then, just before her husband came home, someone saw her at the herbolario stand in front of Quiapo Church, buying little bottles filled with suspicious white powder. She said it was medicine to calm her nerves, a powder made from camias leaves. That was how matters were when Mang Enteng came home.

Then, the first few days after his return, no one saw him leave his house. It was very quiet. So quiet that people began to talk about it over at the sari-sari store. Then men began to exchange lewd jokes about what Mang Enteng was probably doing to Aling Tancing. Sepa, hearing this talk as she passed the store, would hurry on without looking up, folding her arms over her breasts and exhaling sharply, as if in anger.

She did not believe the stories about Aling Tancing, who was still young and always gave Sepa a little of the food she sold from a basket she carried on top of her head — fertilized duckling eggs, mostly, but sometimes also fried banana and peanuts. Aling Tancing often looked very sad, but when she saw Sepa she brightened up and fussed over the girl's hair, combing back her bangs or arranging the ribbons Sepa liked to tie around her head. Perhaps it was because she alone of all the women in the neighborhood still did not have any children. Mang Enteng was older than she, and they said he did not have much of his manhood left. Sometimes men would say what they would like to do to Aling Tancing if they had a chance. But all this was just talk. Sepa knew that the men said these things about Aling Tancing out of boredom, out of not knowing what to do with themselves. Aside from such talk, there was really not much happening where they were.

Anyway, the thing happened on a night when there was a full moon. The people say the full moon makes people a little crazy. On this night, everyone was outside because of the heat. And everyone heard the cries coming from Mang Enteng's house, and saw Aling Tancing running our, her nightgown torn from one shoulder, blood dripping from her nose.

"Help! Help! Enteng is trying to kill me!" she called out.

Mang Pepe took pity on her and let her in behind the counter of his store. She clung to him, sobbing. A few moments later, Mang Enteng himself appeared, shirtless, with a butcher's knife in his right hand.

"Where is she?" he shouted.

It looked as though Mang Enteng had become juramentado, and all the men ran away except Mang Pepe.

Mang Pepe was not a very big man. It was on account of his slight build that he had not been accepted for a job at the Overseas Workers Bureau. Yet he spoke calmly to Mang Enteng, as though he did not see the butcher's knife.

"Now, what's all this about, pare?" he asked.

"My wife has been cheating on me!" Mang Enteng cried.

At this, all the neighbors crept a little closer to their windows.

"Now, now, now," was all Mang Pepe could say.

"It's true! I can tell when my wife has been with other men. She doesn't kiss the same!" Turning, he caught sight of Aling Tancing and pointed his knife at her. "You! Who used to be modest! Now what makes you so hot? Learned a few things while I was away, ha?"

He made as if to leap over the counter. Aling Tancing screamed.

"Enteng! Enteng!" Mang Pepe was saying, holding him back. "If she had someone, don't you think the whole neighborhood would have known about it? And don't you think we, your friends, would have let you know? But Tancing is a good woman. She has never even so much as spoken to another man while you were away. Ask Sepa here, they are good friends and spend almost all their time together."

Mang Enteng glared distrustfully around, but Sepa was cowering behind a wall, trembling and shaking her head — no, no, no — as though her head were full of cotton, as though everything happening were just a bad dream. She was shaking and would not come out.

At any rate, Mang Enteng seemed to have been pacified. He lowered the knife and scratched his head. He began to look confused instead of angry.

"But how is it that she is so aggressive now?" he said to Mang Pepe. "Now it is so hard to satisfy her. Before, anything I did was all right with her."

Aling Tancing began to scream at him: "Walang hiya ka! Don't touch me! I am going back to Antique, to my mother's house!"

The people watching from their windows laughed. Then Mang Pepe took Mang Enteng aside and explained to him that it was because Aling Tancing loved and missed him so much while he was away that she had nearly gone crazy from strain and now behaved like a "low-flying woman."

"But — on top? On top?" Mang Enteng was heard to say.

Mang Pepe coughed discreetly. To Sepa, he seemed to have grown taller. She would look behind the counter and she would never be able to think of him in the same way again. "Go home now, Tancing," Mang Pepe said. "I'll walk home with Enteng later. You go on now."

Aling Tancing was ashamed of her condition. She did not look around her at the people. She half-ran down the alley, and it was a week before anyone saw her again.

The first to visit her was Sepa. She brought some sweet rice cakes. And the two women sat on the floor of Aling Tancing's house, eating and having a good laugh at Mang Enteng's expense.

The first letter from Rudy came after the third typhoon of the year. The street was still littered with debris from the storm, but Sepa ran all the way home, the precious letter clutched tightly to her chest. That night, she read it aloud for her father by the light of the kerosene lamp.

The handwriting was bad, practically a scrawl. It said:

"My dearest Tatang and Sepa, forgive me for not writing for such a long time …"

He went on to explain that it had taken him a long time to adjust to conditions there. It had not been at all what he expected. The heat was dry and made him ill, and he spent some time in a hospital. But he was back at work now, shoveling and loading bricks at the construction site for a housing development just outside the city. It was hard work, he wrote, and he had to keep at it all day. Sometimes the heat went up to 110 degrees, and then he felt dizzy and nauseous but knew now what to do to keep from passing out. The other men had taught him how to drink scalding coffee and how to get by on just that all day. Anything else," he wrote, "makes you sick to your stomach."

He wrote that he envied some of the others, like Mang Tomas, whom he'd heard was a driver of heavy equipment in Riyadh. "But they put me here because I'm big and strong," he wrote. And there were worse jobs. A friend of his, a Pampangueño, had been assigned to do roofing work. After two weeks, he'd asked to be sent home. If the heat was 110 degrees on the ground, it was 135 degrees on the roof. "Enough to make one burst blood vessel," he wrote. Hot tar had to be piped to the roof and spread out before they could lay the asbestos rolls, and his friend had burns on his back and arms from where the tar had burned through his clothing. After a week, his hands had turned black and the stink of tar was always under his fingernails.

Other than the work, there was not really much to say about life in Saudi Arabia. One ate and then one slept. "My companions and I talk all the time about going home. And you know? I have a longing to see the color green ..."

The letter made Sepa very sad. She thought she could understand what Rudy must be feeling, out there in that other country with no rain, no greenery, perhaps even no sweet tastes. But her father — her father was angry.

"What! No money!" her father said.

He shook the envelope upside down, then poked around in it with his dirty forefinger. He opened the pages of the letter one by one, and then, when he realized that there really was nothing there, he flung the letter to the floor in disgust.

"Tatang!" Sepa cried, reproachfully.

"I'm going to the store," her father said, and went out.

Carefully, Sepa collected the scattered pages of her brother's letter. When she had them all neatly back in the envelope, she moved to the window. The rain had let up briefly. There was a fresh, clear scent from the trees that not even the stench from the canal could hide. The TV antennas that had sprouted in the neighborhood since the men started going to Saudi Arabia stood erect against the dark night sky.

The next day Sepa decided she was going to see the old

lady, the clairvoyant. She had gone once before, only the old woman had frightened her by probing her stomach with her long, tiny bony fingers. The woman had told her about magic, how the force behind it resided in the will. Now this will was coiled up in her abdomen like a snake. It came not from the head, which was all reason, or from the heart, which was all emotion, but from the belly. It was like hunger.

Sepa closed her eyes and spread her hands over her belly. She thought she could feel something there, like a life force, stretching from her belly becoming bigger and bigger. If she kept her eyes closed she could imagine this force growing so big it could swallow up the whole oceans. She could not tell Rudy about what was inside her now — she knew it had something to do with the fact that her monthly period had stopped. And now her whole body felt tender and bruised, her ankles and her wrists were swelling as if her feet and hands wanted to separate from the rest of her. She had caught Aling Tancing looking at her once or twice, looking at her with an expression of wonder and sadness in her dark eyes. Aling Tancing's own belly was flat as a young girl's. Sepa had wondered at that — wondered why Aling Tancing could not grow anything inside her.

After a few moments, Sepa had to sit down. But she continued to think about Rudy, far away in Saudi Arabia. She thought he might be sleeping now, she imagined him lying on a cot in a room filled with other men. She imagined herself entering the room wandering among the silent, sleeping shapes. She imagined herself stopping by one cot in the far corner. The figure was wrapped in a white blanket. She put her hand down softly on the blanket, and when the face was revealed, her brother smiled up at her.

MANUEL R. OLIMPO

HE THINKS if anyone would remember him in grade school, he would think of the quiet boy one could depend on if in need of sweet phrases to impress a girl or light but swift punches to scare a bully.

In high school, some may recall the gentle one, the wild one, the one who spoke in metaphors and preached virtuous lives to troublesome members of the gang he himself led.

In college, he attributed his restlessness to the "exploitative, dictatorial regime," which sent him to the stockade. Pulled from detention by a relative after three months, he moved from house to another to avoid arrest as he was supposed to report to authorities every week but never did.

As he was gradually being "forgotten" by the military, he tried raising a family, writing, doing odd jobs, teaching, proofreading for a national magazine, writing. He named his daughter "Layana" which means "free already."

From Gen. Trias, Cavite, he emigrated to the United States in August 1985 and has since been "working and writing" for the Philippine News.

He is fascinated by Elinor Wylie's stoic "Eagle of the Rock."

When flocks are folded warm,
And herbs to shelter run,
He sails above the storm,
He stared into the sun.

IMAGES

THE BRIDE threw the bouquet of flowers and the bridesmaids gamely jumped for it, screaming. Lea, the *winner*, was hugged and congratulated.

"Perfect shots," she said, showing Eman the photos of how she enjoyed grabbing the bouquet as though she prized its supposed message: *You're next!* The wedding of her best friend was held last week. Eman, the official photographer, had brought the wedding album which was his gift to the newlyweds. She would take it to her friend.

It was Monday night and they were watching the 49'ers and the Giants game in her place. *The night defense took center stage.*

Montana was able to complete a short pass. The receiver ran for a touchdown, their first score to lead 7-3.

"All right!" they exclaimed and gave each other a high five as they sprang up from the black leather sofa. Lea put the album on the round glass table, its pages showing The Catch of the bridal bouquet.

"I wish you did run like that for a touchdown after you caught the flowers," he said and sat back.

With her eyes fixed on him, he felt her wondering how serious he was. She poured wine into their glasses. She took a sip, crawled to him and rested her head with her shoulder-length hair which he loved fondling. She looked up and tenderly touched his face, her ever effective way of saying that she wouldn't mean to do anything that would hurt him.

"What's the latest from the Philippines?" she asked.

Oh my God, does this woman know him better than

he knows himself to quickly decide that it was something about the Philippines?

"I love you," he said and kissed the tip of her nose. "I want to spend the rest of my life with you."

"But can you promise that you will stay here?"

She had been frank, she was not strong enough to survive the kind of life waiting for him in the Philippines. Besides, she was finishing her M.A. in Business Administration. The opportunities for her in the U.S. where she was born and grew up were unlimited.

He thought, her responses now were based on his image as a *warrior,* a freedom fighter, which he was afraid had worked as his chief vehicle to her heart. It could also be the reason she couldn't totally give herself to him.

Eman remembered the day they first met. He was holding an exhibit in a Manila gallery. The images consistently produced then by his camera depicted the plight of the sacadas, the slum dwellers, the prostitutes, the street parliamentarians. There had been this woman who carried herself with such effortless grace in her blue jeans, white T-shirt, and black boots. She had been quietly examining his photos while he was wrestling with whether he should just drink in the sweetness of her presence or go get his camera and beg this woman to be his model for The Filipina Everybody Would Simply Love.

She had been with another woman her age, twenty-two, slightly taller with her shapely 5'5". They walked towards him. "I don't live around here but I can now feel how your *people* suffer," she had said.

Mesmerized, he had not been able to move his lips.

"Very powerful images that must have come also from a very brave man." She had been suppressing a smile while her companion was giggling apparently because of the way he had been looking at her.

"Thank you," he had finally answered, apologetic and embarrassed at the length of his tongue-tied ordeal.

He had learned that she was vacationing from the U.S. He had discussed his art and his *people* and of the need not only to create art out of the situation but also to directly participate in the struggle to free the masses from poverty and oppression.

She had bought one of his pictures, the girl in college uniform holding a megaphone, in front of a crowd of protesters, articulating with scary intensity her political views. It never occurred to him that he would see that picture again. He thought that he would go back to San Francisco and the photo would not even remind her of the "brave" artist who dared to exhibit creations defying the dictatorship.

But they met again, after four years.

He had become a wedding photographer, to survive in the U.S., after fleeing from sure persecution by the dictatorship in the Philippines. For three years, the images he had been creating were promises of domestic bliss. It was Saturday, a routine Saturday for him who had established a reputation for pleasing whoever hired his camera.

"I'd bet those are very powerful images from a very brave man," he had heard behind his back. They were inside the church. The People Power had just astonished the world.

He had turned around and was instantly sent four years back. Some of those words he hadn't been able to forget, had been bugging him every now and then. He had seen this woman who had never aged a minute — and his lips were paralyzed again.

When he recovered, he had been in her downtown apartment, and she had shown him the picture she bought at his exhibit in a Manila gallery.

He had relentlessly pursued her, with positive signals from her, of course, and he learned to love the photos he had been producing of valiant couples looking at a romantic, peaceful future.

"Let's dance," Lea said. She turned off the TV and went to the radio sitting beside the lampshade close to the window. The 49'ers had won, the score didn't change. The defense of both teams had shown impenetrable fierceness. He thought, can I rock her defenses? Maybe it's not the night.

Julio Iglesias' caressing, haunting voice engulfed the room. *Fools rush in where wise men never go ...*

"We have to wait," she pleaded as she nestled her head on his chest while dancing. "Maybe our love for each other can make us strong enough to face life anywhere as long as we are together."

But right now, he thought, we must be content with what we have. We see each other often, we have each other on holidays and when one's spirits are down.

He felt he must do the quarterbacking. Press on with the offense! "I can fight here."

She pulled him closer and with her eyes shut she said softly, "C'mon, you know it's not that the kind of fight that can quiet you down."

The images of the wedding ceremonies he had photographed ran through his mind. And the children of friends and relatives, oh how he loved to play with them and how his heart cried out for his own. He was 28 and he felt an unbearable emptiness every time she was out of his sight.

"I'm in love." But he also heard a part of him say: *"You can't change what you are, an exile longing to return to his homeland, who regrets ever leaving it and secretly wishing to pick up where he had left off."*

But his anger was real. He almost shouted: "Can't we stop this intellectual crap? Can't we just let out our emotions rule our lives?"

He stared at his picture of the student activist, the one Lea bought and which was hanging on the wall on the left side of the bed. He remembered the other photos and tried to recapture the same sense of triumph and fulfillment whenever he felt he had moved his viewers. No, it's no longer there, he said to himself.

Maybe the image I created for myself is not essentially true. Maybe I'm just a self-absorbed man who tries to wear the features of a compassionate, heroic one. Maybe I adore this image because people that I respect adore me for this, even Lea. I hope this image hasn't become too powerful that I can't break away from it anymore.

He made love to her with a vengeance. At least I can do it with the woman I love, he thought. But it's not enough!

He didn't notice that he had uttered it.

She climbed on top of him and held his face with both hands. "It is enough," she said, on the verge of tears, "at this stage. Please let it be enough."

He rose and gathered his clothes. He had to leave. She had work and classes the next day; she had been complaining that he always kept her awake. He thought, *She has to pursue the American Dream where I may not have any place in.*

In the elevator, after putting on his black leather jacket, his memory transported him to their backyard which was the neighborhood playground. He was ten years old again and his playmates had left as soon as they heard the ballad of the Tuko — the gecko — the community's resident poet that stayed up in their tamarind tree. Tuk-ko! Tuk-ko! It's getting darker and lonelier.

Before he opened his '75 Corolla, he looked up at her fourth floor room. She was at the window, waving at him, trying to signal her own pain. He wished he were less real than a Filipino-American, with an image as different as Richard Gere's character in *Pretty Woman*, who climbs the fire escape up to his ladylove, knowing that he can't live without her and he has flower and power in his hands to make her fairytale wish come true.

He sighed, got inside the car and started the engine. *I can't go right away,* he decided. Tears were obstructing his vision.

NENUTZKA C. VILLAMAR

I WAS born in the Philippines in April 1968, the eldest child in a tight-knit family of five. I graduated from Pepperdine University with a B.A. in Communications in April 1990 and am a graduate student at Cal State Northridge majoring in Creative Writing. I work as an assistant editor for Avcom Publishing in Woodland Hills.

Since my family moved to the United States when I was five years old, my parents have made a conscious effort to find harmony between Philippine and American cultures. I speak only Tagalog to my father and only English to my mother.

I love to read, and I'm often on two or three books at one time. I always seem to fall in love with characters in novels — Rhett Butler when I was younger and, when I was mature enough to know better than to have a crush on a bully like Rhett Howard Roark from The Fountainhead.

I think one of my most distinctive characteristics is my sense of humor. Unfortunately, not everyone understands it. I'm often sarcastic and slightly offbeat, and I'd like my stories to reflect that. I also strongly believe in the power of intuition, and recently I've become better about following my gut feeling. The moon is one of my favorite objects, and I probably do act more eccentric when there is a full moon.

I love the art of fashion, and if I were not a writer, I would probably be doing something in the fashion industry. As it is, I'm notorious for shopping. I am close to my family, I enjoy dining out, watching plays and foreign films, and making collages.

FALLING PEOPLE

THE WIDE LEDGE outside the window of my eighth-floor dorm room is invitingly smooth. Flat and opaque, it seems to call out for somebody to walk along its surface and leave shoe prints on it. On our campus, all the buildings are brick, and this dormitory is the only one with ledges beneath the window. Rumor has it that a student who used to live here hated the look of all brick so she asked her wealthy father to contribute money for ledges. Most residents put plants on or hang flags from their ledges, but I prefer to leave mine empty. I am curious how much weight it can hold. I fight the temptation to lean over and place my weight on it. It's not too difficult a fight, as I'm afraid of heights.

I wonder if, perhaps, my cousin Serena looked out of her window, experienced the same urge to walk along the edge, and submitted to that urge, accidentally slipping and falling. She was never afraid of heights. When we were five years old and my family still lived in the Philippines, Serena and I used to climb the stacks of rice sacks piled up almost to the ceiling of the warehouse on my father's farm just outside of Manila. It was harvest season, and all the adults were in a good mood, which, for us kids, meant being allowed to do things normally forbidden, like climbing the high stacks of rice. I stayed on the lowest level of stacks, while Serena nimbly climbed to the top.

Someone in the room below mine turns the TV on to CNN, and the newscaster's voice invades my thoughts, bringing me back to the present. I look out the window across campus, and I immediately negate my theory about Serena; her fall and death are what compel me to look out the window and contemplate falling. I am certain it was not mere temptation that drove her to climb and then jump off the roof of her dorm.

Besides, no one inside or near the building heard her scream. When Kuya Abe, her brother, called my family the other morning, he immediately said with finality that it had been an accident. My mother observed that the tone of his voice indicated that he refused to consider even the remotest possibility of suicide. Suicide carries a stigma among Filipinos that I cannot understand, having grown up in a culture that is open about it. My parents were stern in warning my brother, my sister and myself that when we arrive in the Philippines for Serena's funeral, we should make no mention of any possibility other than an accident.

I fog the window with a single breath of air and with my fingers sign "Nadine" in that super curvy way in which I used to sign my letters to Serena. We had been writing since I left the Philippines.

Suddenly, I become lonely, realizing that I no longer have a pen pal.

On the grassy lawn beneath my window, some of my dorm mates lie on their bikinis, desperately trying to get a tan so that they can show their friends back home proof that they really do attend a school in Sunny California. They lie so still that from my perspective, they appear dead.

If I were to walk along the ledge and fall down, I would probably land on top of one of them, perhaps softening the impact of my fall and saving my life. Or, I might crush someone. Or, by chance, I could land on one of the grassy spaces, the result of socially acceptable distance that people learn to keep from each other.

I question if what someone once told me is true: Do people falling from a height die before hitting rock bottom?

I imagine what Serena and other falling people must have been thinking when they jumped off a surface into the indifferent air. Perhaps they invented morbid images of their bloody bodies mangled and splattered across the ground. Maybe they envisioned themselves fluttering gently down, like leaves falling off a tree, landing quietly on soft, complacent dirt.

I wonder, if I were falling, would my life, like a motion picture in fast-forward, play in my head?

Scenes: The first day of school during my first year in America. The only phrase I know how to say in English is "What's your name?" My father is on his way out the door, and I cling to his leg begging him in Tagalog not to leave me in this strange place where I can't understand anyone, and no one understands me. During lunchtime a blond little girl stares at me as I eat. She makes a face, and asks, "Is that what Chinese people eat?" I reach for her thigh underneath the table and pinch a small piece of flesh between my defensive fingers. I look at my food, no longer hungry for it, and wonder if only Filipinos eat pan de sal with corned beef.

Junior high Halloween mixer. My parents forbid me to attend the dance. The "In-the-Philippines" lecture follows. "In the Philippines, a girl is too young at twelve to dance with boys," they say, adding, "Finish school first — no boyfriends until then."

One hot summer day. I am about to go outside, but my father sends me back upstairs to my room to change: Dolphin shorts look like panties, he says. "Gusto mong masilipan ka?" Do you want to be peeped? I am afraid to reply. If I open my mouth, I will cry.

At the mall. My mother is in the shop next door. A salesman from the Glass Slipper helps me try on a pair of shoes. He removes the stuffing out of the fashionable ballet flats and slides each shoe onto my foot. His hand lingers on my left heel, moves up my ankle caressingly, then slowly slides across my calf. His red face leers at me. I pull my leg away quickly and accidentally bang it hard on the chair next to me. I feel like a clod, and the ballet slippers instantly feel clumsy and look ridiculous on my feet. I gather my old tennis shoes and rush out barefooted.

My birthday party. Tita Cora telling me she wishes her

daughters were more like me. So nice, so quiet, so obedient, so smart, so pretty, never talks back — perfect.

"You are such a nice girl," she sighs, looking at her daughters but addressing me. Her daughters hate me.

I pull away from the window, finally, and lie down on my bed. Across me, on the dresser, along with pictures of my family, is a small black and white picture of Serena and me holding hands at the airport just before I departed for the States. Our last moment together, not counting the letters since then. I pull out the stack of airmail envelopes from my nightstand. They are tied neatly together with an old piece of gold elastic salvaged from a past holiday season. I pick a letter randomly and read it, hungering to know what moments Serena remembered as she fell.

My eyelids become heavy, and I drift off to sleep in the middle of reading it.

I am running through a musky jungle and fall into a deep, dark pit. Serena is on the moon running around and around in circles. She hears me scream for help and strains her eyes to see what has happened to me. Without slowing down her running pace, she produces a golden rope from her breast pocket and tosses one end down to me.

"Nadine!" she yells. "Grab hold!"

I hang on to the rope and she pulls. Just when I reach the opening of the pit, Serena begins to sob and releases her grip on the rope. I frantically grab a piece of twine lying on the ground and hoist myself up the rest of the way. Serena stumbles backward and falls off the moon, crashing down on top of me.

Serena becomes a log.

I crawl out from underneath her, bleeding from splinters.

I feel a sharp pain in my leg. A splinter, I think to myself. But it is the sound of the telephone ringing and not pain and eventually wakes me from my sleep.

"Anak," my mother says, "we'll leave this Saturday, and

the funeral is on Tuesday. You have to tell your professors."

"I know. I will."

"Are you depressed?"

"No, not really." I lie. "We weren't that close."

She notices my voice crack slightly. "Don't think about it too much — you'll only make yourself depressed," she says.

We don't talk long.

I begin to pack my clothes for the trip, piling mainly tank tops and shorts into my suitcase. I start to pack underwear when all of a sudden, I start laughing, reminded of Serena's last letter.

She described an incident in which she had been walking across campus when the elastic of her underwear broke and her panty fell to the ground. She wrote that she had simply stepped out of her panty, stuffed it into her purse, and continued walking along. She went back to her dorm and started to cry. She wrote that she was perplexed by her reaction to such a silly incident.

I was not perplexed at all.

From the letters we've written since I came to the States, I have never been able to build an image of Serena that could replace the child I knew in the Philippines. A child that cried bitterly when a playmate blurted out maliciously that she had a flat nose. Serena was sensitive, able to be hurt deeply by, say, the slightest hint of parental disapproval. She felt things more than she should have. I imagined her as a paper heart that keeps getting pieces of it torn off bit by bit.

In that same letter, Serena had resigned herself to her favorite fate. Being "struck" again. To Serena, problems she encountered were "strikes," and if she was embarrassed, she was "struck." "Another strike against me," she'd write, or "struck again," as if she was keeping track of the number of strikes, preparing for the consequences of having too many.

I pick up the stack of Serena's letters from my bed. I pore over each letter, frantically searching for clues. Did Serena know she wasn't singled out like she thought? I want to know if she understood that in everyone's life movie, there are scenes of being struck.

I want to know why my cousin put her life on a ledge and left it to fate to decide where she would land. Her letters leave me clueless as I have been since losing her.

My family is coming to pick me up on the way to the airport. I am anxious about how they will treat me. I am afraid my father will say what he always says when something upsets me. Ganyan ang buhay — That's life. He says it with so much sincerity — packing into that one simple phrase: love, concern, and helplessness at being unable to protect me — that I will want to cry. I prepare to hold back my emotions.

Outside there are even more people lying out because it is Saturday, and it is especially bright and sunny, and no one has classes. In the dorm below, someone listens to an announcer mouth superlatives about the thrill of victory and the agony of defeat on Wide World of Sports. I open the window and, without giving myself time to think of my fear, sit on my window sill, my legs hanging out and my feet resting on the ledge. Other than that, there is nothing to keep me from falling should I happen to lean out too far.

I am perfectly balanced, yet I cannot help but wonder how it would feel to fall. Would I have time to think? Maybe falling people's minds simply skip the life movie and instantly fade to black.

I decide that what I've been told is not true: Falling people do not die until the very moment they hit rock bottom.

If I were falling, I know what I would be thinking: Somebody, please catch me.

LUIS CABALQUINTO

LUIS CABALQUINTO, born in Magarao, Camarines Sur, Philippines divides his writing time between his Bikol hometown and New York City where he is currently based.

During his formative years, he studied at the Ateneo de Naga, MLQ University, University of the Philippines, Cornell University, The New School for Social Research, and New York University. He has been community development officer, teacher, journalist, editor, photographer, computer data processor, and a passionate grower of orchids.

His poems have appeared in anthologies published in the United States, Philippines, France, Australia, and Hong Kong.

He is the recipient of a Fulbright-Hays grant from the U.S. State Department, the Dylan Thomas Poetry Award from The New School for Social Research, an Academy of American Poets poetry prize from New York University, as well as a Fellowship in Poetry from the New York Foundation for the Arts.

The Dog-Eater and Other Poems, *his first book-length poetry collection, was published in 1989 by Kalikasan Press, Manila. A second book of poetry,* The Ibalon Collection, *was released in 1991. Among his current writing projects is a first novel tentatively called* Dancing with the Guests.

PHAELONOPSIS

ONE MORNING in the spring an expatriate Filipino kissed his faithful wife goodbye, embraced his young son, and shook the hand of his boss. He walked over to the park and attached his body to an oak tree.

A crowd soon began to gather about the tree, asking questions. The expatriate's wife and son came pleaded for him to come home. His boss said a big promotion was waiting for him, with increased benefits.

There is nothing that can make me come back, the Filipino told them. I'm tired of lying, of pursuing a life that is not in line with my true nature. I'll stay with this tree until I get to the roots of myself.

But your real nature is to remain with us, they said to him. We need you to affirm with us that the lives we lead are meaningful, that our concerns are important, headed in the right direction.

But the Filipino was stubborn: he clung closer to the oak tree. When they moved to take him away he went higher up the trunk. By the time the firemen arrived, he had already reached the crown.

Maybe we should cut the tree down, the City Mayor suggested. But the Friends of Trees Society objected and the Parks Commission agreed with them. The Mayor, aware that it was an election year, changed his mind.

The man stuck to the oak tree through the next three seasons, nourished, not by ordinary food, but by the oak sap and the fresh wind, sunshine and rain that moved bountifully around him.

After the first year something else began to happen to the man. He slowly lost his human form and coloration. He started growing like an epiphytic plant from a South Pacific rain forest.

After the second year he was a full-grown orchid, showy with glossy green leathery leaves, a stout short stem and long aerial roots that curled like small worms the color of cobalt and silver.

After the third year flower spikes were seen to be pushing out. And in six months hundreds of sprays of white blooms were open. It was a breath-taking sight: nothing like it had been seen before.

Botanists came from near and far to study the phenomenon. Some acclaimed the plant a new species. Others disagreed, calling it a unique genus. Learned articles on the dispute were soon in print.

Tourists by the hundreds arrived from all over the world — to see the renowned plant and take souvenir photos. Others, thinking the plant miraculous, bought fragments of its leaves.

Years went by and the expatriate Filipino never returned to his human form. Each spring, when the blooms reappeared, some claimed to see a curious configuration: in the center of each flower a mouth smiled.

ACKNOWLEDGMENTS

In all cases, unless otherwise noted, permission to reprint previously published work has been granted by the individual authors. We are grateful to the magazines, publishers, and individuals listed below for their support.

CECILIA MANGUERRA BRAINARD: "Doc's Crucifixion" from *When the Rainbow Goddess Wept* University of Michigan Press, Copyright (c) 1991 by Cecilia M. Brainard. "Doc's Crucifixion" appeared in a different form in *West/Word Journal*, 1989, and *Katipunan*, 1991;

CARLOS BULOSAN: "The Romance of Magno Rubio" from *Amerasia Journal*, 1979; reprinted by permission of the University of Washington Libraries; Carlos Bulosan Papers; Part of Carlos Bulosan's biography is excerpted from P.C. Morantte's article "Mister Bulosan Comes to Washington," *Bataan Magazine*, 1944;

VIRGINIA R. CERENIO: "The Dreams Of Manong Frankie" from *Making Waves: An Anthology of Writings by and about Asian American Women*, Beacon Press, 1989;

JUAN C. DIONISIO: "A Summer in an Alaskan Salmon Cannery" from *Philippine Magazine*, 1934; reprinted in *Philippine Writing*, Archipelago Publishing Co., Manila 1953; reprinted in *Asian-American Authors*, Houghton Miffin Co.; reprinted in *The Well of Time*, National Dissemination and Assessment Center, California State University, Los Angeles, 1976.

ALBERTO S. FLORENTINO: "Sabrina" was presented in TV drama form on *Balintataw*.

N.V.M. GOMZALEZ: "A Warm Hand" from *Mindoro and Beyond: Twenty-one Stories*, University of the Philippines Press,

1979; emended edition as *Mindoro and Beyond*, 1989, by New Day Publishers.

ERLINDA VILLAMOR KRAVETZ: "Song of the Mountain" from *The Americas Review*, 1989;

PAULINO LIM, JR.: "Michelle and the Jesuit" from *Requiem for a Rebel Priest.* Copyright (c) 1991 by Paulino Lim, Jr.;

MANUEL R. OLIMPO: "Images" appeared in *Philippine News Magazine*, 1991;

OSCAR PEÑARANDA: "The Visitor" appeared as "Musings" in *Liwanag*, 1975;

BEINVENIDO N. SANTOS: "Scent of Apples" from *Scent of Apples*, by Beinvenido N. Santos;

MICHELLE CRUZ SKINNER: "Faith Healer" from *Balikbayan: A Filipino Homecoming, Bess Press,* 1988. This story was part of the PEN Syndicated Fiction Project in 1988;

LINDA TY-CASPER: "A Swarm of Sun" from *Mr & Ms,* 1980;

MARRIANNE VILLANUEVA: "Overseas" from *Ginseng and Other Tales from Manila*, CALYX Press, 1990;

MANUEL A. VIRAY: "Lapse" from Shawl from *Kashmir,* New Day Publishers, 1992. This story appeared in *Solidarity;*

ABOUT THE EDITOR

Cecilia Manguerra Brainard is the author and editor of over twenty books including her novels, *The Newspaper Widow*, *Magdalena*, and, *When the Rainbow Goddess Wept*. Among the books she edited are *Growing Up Filipino: Stories for Young Adults* and the follow up book *Growing Up Filipino II*.

Her work has been translated into Finnish and Turkish; and many of her stories and articles have been widely anthologized.

Cecilia has received a California Arts Council Fellowship in Fiction, a Brody Arts Fund Award, a Special Recognition Award for her work dealing with Asian American youths, several travel grants from the USIS; as well as a Certificate of Recognition from the California State Senate, 21st District. She has been awarded by the Filipino and Filipino American communities she has served, including an Outstanding Individual Award from Cebu, and a Filipinas Magazine Award for Arts, among others.

She has lectured and performed in worldwide literary arts organizations and universities, including UCLA, USC, University of Connecticut, University of the Philippines, PEN, Beyond Baroque, Shakespeare & Company in Paris, and many others

She has also served as an officer in writers' groups such as PEN USA West, PAAWWW (Pacific Asian American American Women Writers West), Midnight Special Cultural Center, the Arts & Letters and the Cal State University, LA.

She has a website at ceciliabrainard.com and a blog at cbrainard.blogspot.com

Published books by PALH (Philippine American Literary House)

Acapulco at Sunset and Other Stories by Cecilia Manguerra Brainard

Benedicta Takes Wing and Other Stories by Veronica Montes

Fiction by Filipinos in America, ed. Cecilia Manguerra Brainard

Growing Up Filipino: Stories for Young Adults edited by Cecilia Manguerra Brainard

Growing Up Filipino II: More Stories for Young Adults edited by Cecilia Manguerra Brainard

Please, San Antonio! & Melisande in Paris (novellas) by Eve La Salle Caram and Cecilia Manguerra Brainard

A River, One-Woman Deep: Stories by Linda Ty-Casper

Woman with Horns and Other Stories by Cecilia Manguerra Brainard

Kindle Titles by PALH (Philippine American Literary House)

Fiction

Acapulco at Sunset and Other Stories by Cecilia Manguerra Brainard

Awaiting Trespass (novel) by Linda Ty-Casper

Benedicta Takes Wing and Other Stories by Veronica Montes

Contemporary Fiction by Filipinos in America edited by Cecilia Manguerra Brainard

Fiction by Filipinos in America edited by Cecilia Manguerra Brainard

Growing Up Filipino: Stories for Young Adults edited by Cecilia Manguerra Brainard

Growing Up Filipino II: More Stories for Young Adults edited by Cecilia Manguerra Brainard

Magdalena (novel) by Cecilia Manguerra Brainard

The Newspaper Widow (novel) by Cecilia Manguerra Brainard

Out of Cebu: Essays and Personal Prose by Cecilia Manguerra Brainard

Please, San Antonio! & Melisande in Paris (novellas) by Eve La Salle Caram and Cecilia Manguerra Brainard

A River, One-Woman Deep: Stories by Linda Ty-Casper

A Small Party in a Garden (novel) by Linda Ty-Casper

Vigan and Other Stories by Cecilia Manguerra Brainard

When the Rainbow Goddess Wept (novel) by Cecilia Manguerra Brainard

Wings of Stone (novel) by Linda Ty-Casper

Woman with Horns and Other Stories by Cecilia Manguerra Brainard

Nonfiction

Cecilia's Diary: 1962-1969 by Cecilia Manguerra Brainard

Fundamentals of Creative Writing by Cecilia Manguerra Brainard

Magnificat: Mama Mary's Pilgrim Sites edited by Cecilia Manguerra Brainard

www.ingramcontent.com/pod-product-compliance
Lightning Source LLC
Chambersburg PA
CBHW022006010726
47494CB00003B/918